EAGLE IN FLIGHT: THE LIFE OF ATHANASIUS, THE APOSTLE OF THE TRINITY

EAGLE IN FLIGHT: THE LIFE OF ATHANASIUS, THE APOSTLE OF THE TRINITY

Allienne R. Becker, Ph.D.

Writers Club Press
San Jose New York Lincoln Shanghai

Eagle in Flight: The Life of Athanasius, the Apostle of the Trinity

Writers Club Press
an imprint of iUniverse, Inc.

For information address:
iUniverse, Inc.
5220 S. 16th St., Suite 200
Lincoln, NE 68512
www.iuniverse.com

ISBN: 0-595-21393-6

Printed in the United States of America

To Dr. Isidore H. Becker, Ph.D, my husband, my proofreader, and my best friend

Contents

"*...Those who put their hope in the Lord will renew their strength. They will fly on wings like eagles...*"

—Isaiah 40:31

Foreword

"Eagle in Flight" is the true story of the life and times of Saint Athanasius of Alexandria. The author has merely employed the literary form of the novel to make the narrative more vivid. This is also the story of the Church of Christ as it suffered through a period of intense confusion and chaos. The basic doctrines of our faith that had been believed from the time of the apostles were under attack. That which is most vital and essential to our Christian faith, belief in the divinity of Christ and in the Trinity, was questioned and denied. One by one, Athanasius saw his fellow bishops subscribe to the false teachings that were current until the whole Church groaned to find itself practically lost in the darkness of error, when Pope Liberius signed his name under duress to the false creeds. Today the Church appears to be plagued with a little of the same madness. Constantly we hear of strange innovations that are in diametric opposition to the teachings of the Church, as people pick and choose which doctrines and practices they will follow.

In reading the story of Athanasius, we see how an epidemic of error can grow and spread to such an extent that one might fear the universal Church would become lost in error. Standing firm on the promise of Christ that the gates of hell shall never prevail against the Church, Athanasius remained almost the sole defender of truth. Valiantly he fought, almost single-handed, to preserve the true orthodox faith. Only a divinely instituted and sustained Church could survive such a situation. We know that no matter how much the Church might be assaulted from enemies without and within, Christ will never abandon the Bride for whom he lay down his life. In the fight for truth, in the words of St. Teresa of Avila, "God and one make a majority." Athanasius and God were such a majority.

CHAPTER 1

❦

Our sufferings have been dreadful, even beyond endurance. Still my enemies do not shrink from their calumnies, their base wickedness, and their plots against my life. Displaying an insatiable love of contention, they howl for my blood with an incredible passion for intrigue. Like serpents crawling out of their holes, they have spewed forth the poison of their impiety. Heaven is astonished and earth shudders at the evil they have unleashed across the length and breadth of the empire. From Cordoba to Nicomedia, from Alexandria to Lutetia, they have sown the seeds of their pollution. The very first time I saw Arius, I knew there would be trouble. I was convinced that Achillas of blessed memory should never have elevated him to the priesthood. Bishop Peter, the holy martyr, had been correct in his judgment when, after having made Arius a deacon, he forthwith deposed him. Regrettably after the martyrdom of Bishop Peter, Arius succeeded in obtaining ordination to the priesthood from Achillas.

Certain rumors concerning Arius had reached the archiepiscopal residence in Alexandria where I was charged with the duty of being personal secretary to the then reigning bishop, Alexander, my saintly predecessor in the office which now I hold. I was sent to investigate Arius, to listen to him preach to his parish in the fashionable Baucalis suburb of our city. When he mounted the pulpit, I beheld a proud man, arrogant in his every gesture. As I listened to his honeyed words and observed his subtle use of flattery, I understood at once his influence over the minds of men.

He had a melancholy look and with his downcast eyes and his handsome thin, ascetic appearance he managed to convert seven hundred consecrated virgins to his false teachings. As is usually the case with heresiarchs, he was irresistible to women. The day I visited Arius' parish, I watched and studied the faces of the women who were in the congregation as they clasped every word he spoke to their hearts. I made notes on the main points of his teaching so that I could present a full report to His Piety, Archbishop Alexander of Alexandria. The utter impiety of his statements was appalling. He spoke blasphemy when he told the flock that Christ was a creature, that He was not very God of very God.

What Diocletian had been unable to achieve with his bloody persecution of the Church, Arius was accomplishing. The imperial sword had been unable to kill Christ in the souls of the people of God and now Arius, an ordained priest of Jesus Christ, was putting Christ to death in the souls of the people in Baucalis!

What a glorious witness the church of Egypt made when Diocletian determined to eradicate Christ from the face of the earth. I was about five years of age when Diocletian and Maximian set themselves up as living gods in a last desperate attempt to save the empire that was threatened with dissolution from the Persians, the Alemans, and the Burgundians without, and by a multitude of contenders to the imperial throne within. Robed in heavy brocades with their wrists and ankles studded with precious gems, they presented themselves to the people as deities and demanded that whoever spoke to them would first perform the rites of adoration and of proschynesis, in which one was required to prostrate oneself upon the earth and to kiss the hem of the emperor's robe, addressing the Augustus as "dominus et deus," lord and god. In ancient times, Caligula had insisted that people bow down and worship him. He was insane. Diocletian, on the contrary, was of very sound mind. Because he was determined to build a strong state, his war with the Catholic Church was inevitable. On February 7, 303, the order was issued for the destruction of all Christian churches, the burning of all copies of the Holy Gospels, the dissolution of all Christian congregations, and the confiscation of all our properties. All Christians were excluded from public office. The death penalty was to be imposed on all Christians who assembled for worship.

When Diocletian and Maximian abdicated two years later in favor of Galerius as Augustus of the East and Constantius Chlorus as Augustus in the West, the suffering of the Christians in our Egyptian Church reached the breaking point. In the West only a few churches were burned, but in the East an edict was issues that all subjects were to be forced to sacrifice to the pagan gods. Although I was but eight years of age at the time, I can still remember the sound of the soldiers' voices, as they went through the streets of Alexandria proclaiming this edict.

The persecution that ensued was so barbaric that even the pagans were indignant and commonly gave shelter to fleeing Christians. Our people were scourged until their bones lay bare from the flogging. Then salt and vinegar were poured into their open wounds. In some cases, Christians had their living flesh cut from their bones, bit by bit, and fed to dogs. Some were bound to crosses and fed to starving animals that were turned loose to gorge on them, for the sole reason that they professed faith in Christ. Eyes were gouged out, legs were hamstrung, molten lead was poured down people's throats, and sharp reeds were driven under their fingernails. Neighbor settled grudge against neighbor by having him convicted of the crime of being Christian. Catholics were hunted down like animals. My parents, God grant them peace and eternal refreshment, having wealth at their disposal made haste to leave Alexandria and to flee with me to safety in the desert. Never had such persecution befallen any church as that which our Egyptian church bravely endured. Christian women actually committed suicide rather than be taken into arrest, their sole thought being to escape the dishonor which would be their's if they refused to sacrifice to the gods. Happy indeed was the Christian woman who had no more to suffer than to be bound naked to the stake! Persecution in Egypt had become a means for many of the government officials and magistrates to satisfy their lusts and cupidity. Our women were subjected to the greatest possible humiliation and degradation.

Truly, a great wailing arose all over Egypt. As long as I live, I shall remember our flight from Alexandria. The homes of our neighbors were on fire with black curling smoke, hanging heavy in the steamy, humid night. Our friends were being carried off to the city jails. Anyone who tried to resist arrest was killed on the spot. That night was the first time in my life that I ever saw anyone die. I saw an old woman run through by the sword of a soldier who became impatient with her slowness in obeying his commands. I watched the thirsty sand drink in her blood. My mother put her hands over my eyes to shelter them, to spare them the sight. Gently she drew my face into hers and said, "Listen, my son, every Christian must live the life of Christ. That is what we are doing tonight." She took my hand in hers and squeezed my fingers.

"Yes," my father continued, "tonight we must fly from the Roman soldiers just the way that Mary, Joseph and Jesus did the night the rulers of the people sought for Jesus to kill Him."

My father looked at me for a moment and then added with great faith, "God will take care of us."

I looked up at him. He stood tall, straight, and strong. His face was serene. I smiled and replied, "God *will* take care of us just like he took care of Jesus, Mary and Joseph."

My mother gave me an affectionate pat on the cheek as we climbed up on our camels and hurried away into the shadows of the night.

When we reached the desert along the Nile, shimmering like ivory in the moonlight, it was a little cooler. A breeze began to rustle in the fronds of the palms that line the riverbank like children standing on tiptoe and leaning over to catch a glimpse of their reflection in the mirroring waters. For the child that I was, racing through the night to escape the police was like an exciting game. We stopped briefly to water the camels and drank sparingly of the water we brought with us. My father told me that we were going to join a colony of monks who lived in the desert around Mount Pispir.

"We will be safe there. The soldiers have never ventured into the heart of the desert to disturb the monks. Life will be simple for us," he continued, as the camels lapped noisily of the Nile waters. "We will have no luxuries," he said glancing at my mother who was accustomed to the things his wealth would buy for her. "We shall live a life of true virtue the way the holy monks do."

Mother and father smiled lovingly at each other. Inspired by confidence in their love for each other and for me, I burst into a delighted laugh, splashed my feet in the Nile, exclaiming with glee, "No more school for me! No more books! No more tutors!"

"Not so fast, young fellow," my father interrupted, tugging at a lock of my red air. "You will learn to read and to write in the desert. I, myself, will see to that. And you will learn about God from the holy father Anthony who comes to preach to the monks."

This was the first time in my life that I heard of my holy Father Anthony. My natural curiosity was piqued and as we rode on through the night following the meanderings of the Nile, my father answered my eager questions about the holy man of the Thebais.

"He is a great saint," my mother assured me. Her hair, red like mine, was shining in the moonlight like burnished copper.

My father told me that Father Anthony, the son of a very wealthy family of Coma, was born near Heraclea. When his parents died and he received his inheritance, he was only twenty. Burning with the desire to imitate the holy apostles, he gave away all his wealth, except what was necessary to care for his sister, deciding to give himself completely to God. Leaving the world, he went to live a life of prayer and virtue with the ascetics who lived in huts just outside his village. Then, wanting to draw closer to God, he gave up the company of all men and went to live in an abandoned tomb, at some distance from the village. Finally, not content with that, he struck out alone into the desert to seek greater solitude for prayer, wandering into an old tumbledown fort that had been deserted for so long that it was filled with serpents and all kinds of creeping things.

The reptiles fled and the holy hermit descended into the fort with a six months supply of bread, sealing off the entrance behind him. Now after twenty years of fasting, praying, and disciplining himself, he emerged and was living at Mount Pispir, surrounded by a Christian community that he consented to guide in the ways of the Spirit. From what I heard, I expected to see a withered old man, emaciated and pale from fasting, with an austere and dour face. I was mistaken. After we had been dwelling with the community in the desert but a short time, the holy Father Anthony responded to the appeal of the monks to come to visit us and share with us the fruits of his solitude.

Even as a child, I perceived that he was different from other men. When I was older, I learned what that difference was. He was filled with the Spirit of God. Neither fat nor thin, his body reflected the strength of the spirit that was contained in the soul that graced it. There was, furthermore, something in his personality that was magnetic. You immediately felt yourself drawn to him. Although he was no taller than other monks, he seemed to tower over them. I believe it was the serenity of his manner and the great purity of his soul that attracted people to him. If I had to choose one word that best described him, I would say that he was joyful. He was effervescent with bubbling, overflowing, contagious joy that spread to all those that ·chanced to encounter him. I was tongue-tied when he first spoke to me. With mirthful eyes he greeted me, when he spotted me standing in the shade of my camel, as I waited for my parents to take me home to our cell. It was only a few minutes after the holy hermit had preached to us all.

"What are you going to be when you grow up?" he asked me.

I stammered a few seconds and then blurted out the first thing that came into my mind.

"A bishop! I shall be a bishop," I said seriously.

Holy Father Anthony reached over and patted me on the top of my head and told me quite simply, "Yes. You will be a bishop."

Dumfounded, I exclaimed, "I will?"

He looked away from me for a few seconds. His glance rested on the distant horizon. Turning to me again he asked, "What is your name, my son?"

"Athanasius."

"Athanasius, you *will* be a bishop." His eyes, serious as they probed mine, seemed to be looking into the future. I had the feeling that he was looking right through me and seeing things I could not see.

"God has great plans for you," he said very softly. I stared at the ground not knowing what to say, all the while studying his calloused feet that were shod in heavy leather sandals. The nail on the big toe of his right foot was split. I squirmed uncomfortably under his gaze and was ready to run from him. As I made to go, he stopped me, his hand restraining my shoulder.

"Come to see me, my son. When the monks come to bring me bread at my cell in the inner mountain, come with them. There are little things for which I could use a boy like you. You could pour water on my hands, for example. And," he paused smiling warmly, "there are many things I could teach you. If you are going to be a bishop, you will have to learn about prayer, the discernment of spirits, the virtues." He paused again, looked me straight in the eye and asked me point blank, "Will you come?"

His personality was irresistible. Grinning at him and picturing myself already with a large golden miter on my head and a silver crosier in my boyish hand, I promised him, "I will."

I learned reading, writing, courtesy, and the common virtues from my parents. The ways of sanctity, I learned from my holy Father Anthony.

The first time I went to his cell in the inner mountain, I was shy, even timid. After a few visits I began to anticipate and eagerly await the day when I could again go to minister to my Father in God. He taught me great and wondrous things the five years we remained in the desert.

In 309, word reached our community that the bishops Pelaus and Nilus had been burned to death at Phunon. It was my Father Anthony that broke this news to me, telling me that when the persecution ceased the Church would have great need of boys, such as I, to transmit the faith to future generations.

He could not read, nor write. He was utterly unlettered by the standards of the world, but he was filled with a supernatural prudence that surpassed the learning of all my other teachers. Once when I asked him why he had never learned to read he told me, "If you have a sound mind, you have no need of letters. If you don't have a sound mind, studying the wisdom of the schools will do you more harm than good."

Following the logic of the holy hermit, I tried to persuade my parents that I had no need to learn Greek, when the Egyptian language served him so admirably. They were not to be dissuaded. My learning advanced under their careful guidance, but the things I learned in books were as brass compared to the true golden knowledge I imbibed from my holy Father Anthony. He knew God. He had lived with him alone for over thirty years and in his soul he knew him. Many times when I was with him he left off speaking to me and became wholly absorbed in God. When he returned to himself I would beg him, "Tell me about God, Father."

He would begin by quoting the scriptures to me, for although he could not read he had committed long passages of them to his memory that took the place of books for him. Then he would begin to speak of his own personal knowledge of God.

"The greatest thing you can know, my son, is that God is a Trinity. We believe in One God in Three Persons."

He closed his eyes and pressed his fingers to his temples on this particular occasion that I now recall.

"How can it be?" I puzzled. My twelve-year-old mind was awakening to the wonders of thought and I was eager to learn.

"It defies reason. God is a mystery that can be penetrated only by prayer," he explained as he offered me a portion of his hard stale bread.

Declining the bread, not for the reason that it was unpalatable, which it truly was, but because if I ate it, he would fast and go hungry when his allotted ration ran out, I pleaded, "Tell me about it, Father."

"If you pray fervently and exercise yourself in virtue and discipline yourself, someday, I promise you, you will behold the vision of God in your soul at prayer. Then you will know the Three Persons of God." His face was radiant with a certain indescribable light when he spoke of the Trinity.

"Jesus is God?" I asked.

"Very God of Very God, the only begotten Son of the Heavenly Father. Pray, pray very much," he instructed me, "and you will come to know Jesus. You will come to know him as one friend knows another. Then He, Himself, will teach you to know the Heavenly Father. Together they will breathe forth into your soul the Holy Spirit and you will come to know Him as the Third Person in God. But remember this, whenever you see One of the Persons of the Trinity, if you look closely, you will always see in that Person the other Two for they are inseparable. There is only one God."

I listened attentively and realized that what my father in God was telling me was the fruit of his years of living closely united to the Three in One.

"Listen, Athanasius," he said taking me by the chin so that he could look right into my eyes, "I know whereof I speak. There are Three equal Persons in God—the Father, the Son and the Holy Spirit. This is the chief cornerstone of our Catholic Faith. If you were to remove this cornerstone the entire structure would collapse in ruin. God became man that man might be deified—lifted up to dwell in the embrace of the Trinity."

One day when I went to the inner mountain to listen to the wisdom of my holy Father Anthony, I found him kneeling in prayer. In a trance and totally oblivious to my presence, he was pressing to his heart a crudely-fashioned cross that he had made by tying two sticks of wood together. I knelt down beside him hoping that a ray of his heavenly vision would fall on my soul. God seemed so near to me as I knelt there sharing the prayer of my father. At length he turned to me and said, "I am going away, my son."

Pensively he tugged at his beard that was as white as the sun bleached desert sands. I waited for him to explain himself.

"Many are dying for the faith, I must go to Alexandria," he whispered.

"But my Father, they might kill you!" I protested.

He smiled when I said this. Later I realized that he longed to give witness to Christ with his blood.

"I have had a vision, Athanasius. Our saintly Bishop Peter is going to be a martyr soon. I must go to him."

He left that very day. From time to time we received news of his activities in Alexandria, as he went fearlessly about ministering to the Christians there. Boldly he accompanied the martyrs to their deaths, exhorting them to hold fast to the faith. Undauntedly, he stood publicly in full view as the governor passed by. Courageously, he visited the Christians who had been maimed and blinded in one eye and sent to work as slaves in the mines. Meanwhile at Pispir, the entire community of us—we numbered about six thousand—monks for the most part, gave ourselves up to perpetual prayer, day and night, that the martyrs might be strengthened in their trials and that we, too, would have the fortitude to imitate their example, if we were called to do so. All of us prayed especially for our holy father Anthony and that he would be returned to us for the welfare of our souls, for we all missed his guidance.

News came that in one day forty Christians were decapitated at Zoara. On November 25, 311 our own beloved Bishop Peter was seized suddenly without any accusations being made against him. Without any trial he was decapitated. Then only did our father in God return to us. Eagerly I sought him out in his cell in the inner mountain, as soon as I heard that he had returned. Very thin from fasting, he was wearing a fur garment with the fur side, next to his skin, even though the heat was intense. Because of the grievous sufferings of the church, he had increased his austerities. Very solemnly he greeted me.

"Have you been praying for the suffering church of Egypt?"

"Yes, Father," I assured him, as I took my place on the floor at his feet. He was seated on a rock that served as the only piece of furniture in his cell.

"Without the prayers, the discipline, the mortifications of the holy monks here at Pispir who give themselves completely to God, the church would be unable to give such a glorious witness for Christ. The monk, by his life of prayer, obtains strength and grace for others. Bishop Peter was well aware of the work we are doing here in the desert. His last words to me were an appeal for more prayers, more sacrifices for the flock from which he was being snatched away. Always remember, my son, that the strength of the church is in prayer, especially in the prayer of those who leave all to follow Christ."

Rising to his feet, he signified that he had no more to say to me. I knelt for his blessing and then returned to the community.

I grew to love living with the monks in the desert. I especially enjoyed listening to the stories of the men who had suffered for their faith in Christ. Confessors of the faith have a way of imparting their faith to you. It was common to see men who had the tendons of one leg cut, limping from their cells, to go to the altar to receive the Body and Blood, Soul and Divinity of Christ

Our community continued to grow. The visit of our holy father to Alexandria prompted many more to come to join us. Every week there were new faces around the altar. Finally one of the new arrivals brought us news that the Augustus of the East, Galerius, lay dying. Now convinced that his death was a punishment for the brutal persecutions he inflicted on the Church, he issued an edict recognizing Christianity as a lawful religion. He even went so far as to implore our prayers on his behalf in return for his clemency.

It was hard to believe. We could return to our homes. I would have been very happy to remain in the desert, but my mother was overjoyed at the prospect of returning to Alexandria.

"We are going home, Athanasius! Home!" She ruffled my hair with her hand affectionately and added, "You will learn the ways of civilization. You will go to a real school and become an educated man."

I was sad at the thought of leaving the desert that I had grown to love. But most of all, I was saddened, because returning to Alexandria would mean saying farewell to my father in God.

It was my fourteenth year when we returned to the city of my birth. My parents, who managed to preserve their wealth, found a home for us near the sea. Here I found the same peace to pray and meditate on the beach that I had known in the desert. I was no longer a child, but I was still not yet a man. Happy, carefree days I spent playing like a dolphin with the other children my age in the quiet waters of the sea.

As children are wont to do, one day our conversation turned to discussing the most fascinating of all topics for boys—what each of us would become when we were older.

"Priscus," I asked a pagan boy who was about twelve, "what will you be?"

I shall be a sailor," the boy replied splashing water in my face, "and I shall sail far away to Rome."

"And I shall be a merchant," my friend Jovian volunteered. "I will get very rich."

"What will you be, Athanasius?"

I stood on the beach very tall and very straight and replied slowly, deliberately, "I shall be a bishop."

"You mean like Bishop Alexander who lives in that house up there?" asked Jovian pointing to the nearby archiepiscopal residence that overlooked the sea.

"Yes. Just like him," I said, remembering the holy bishop whom I had seen twice in church since we returned from the desert.

Jovian swam over to where I was standing in the surf.

"Will you baptize people in the sea here like he does?"

"Naturally," I replied. "Bishops always baptize people."

Priscus who had been kicking his feet causing a big spray of water to splash all over me yelled, "You can baptize me."

"Me, too!" cried Jovian pulling my feet out from under me so that I fell into the gently breaking waters of the sea. "Come on, baptize us right now!" At heart, I was already a fisherman of souls. Seriously, I inquired, "Will you promise to be good Christians…your whole lives long?"

"We will, Bishop Athanasius!" Both boys sang out in chorus.

So I played the bishop and baptized my friends. We were just emerging from the water when we noticed that a priest was making his way from the archiepiscopal residence towards us. Stretching out and sunning ourselves on the sand, we pretended not to notice him until he stood over Priscus and asked, "Your friend just baptized you, did he not?"

"No," protested Piscus. "You are wrong," he lied.

Jovian made similar denials. I rose to my feet and told him quite honestly, "I, Athanasius, baptized them both."

The priest quickly informed me that Archbishop Alexander had been watching us from his residence and that His Piety wished to talk to me. Upon hearing this, my young friends deserted me. I did not consider that I had done anything wrong, but realized then that perhaps the archbishop might have other ideas about the matter.

I was ushered into a room where Archbishop Alexander was waiting for me. Not knowing how to comport myself in the presence of an archbishop, I knelt at his feet the way I learned from the monks to kneel at the feet of my holy father and begged his blessing. After blessing me, and after I had kissed his hands, he motioned for me to continue kneeling. He towered over me. The distance between us was immeasurable.

"It is the prerogative of the bishop to baptize people," he began solemnly.

I squirmed under his gaze.

"Do you not know," he inquired, "that only bishops baptize the catechumens?"

"Yes, Your Piety, I do know." I stared at the floor for what seemed like an hour.

Tapping his foot firmly on the carpet in front of me he asked bluntly, "Why did you baptize those boys?"

Raising my eyes until they met his, I replied filled with confidence, "Because I am going to be a bishop when I grow up and I need to get practice in these matters."

Very much taken back by my response, he did his best to conceal his surprise.

"You are perhaps planning to replace me?" he asked with a touch of irony that I recognized as a reproof for my boldness.

Lowering my eyes, I remained silent.

Impatiently waiting for me to answer, he kept tapping his foot. "Well, speak up, Athanasius," he commanded.

My eyes met his. "God grant you many years, Your Piety," I said with a smile.

He started to smile back at me but instantly checked himself. "So you are going to be a bishop? How do you know?"

"Because the holy Father of the Thebais told me that I will, and everyone knows that he can predict the future."

"Ah!" exclaimed the archbishop, "so you know Father Anthony?"

I nodded. Archbishop Alexander took a chair and kept me on my knees that were beginning to cramp from resting so long on the hard floor. Having learned from the monks to exercise control over my body, I disregarded the discomfort and continued kneeling as the archbishop sat in silence trying to decide what to do with me. I studied him carefully. He was every inch an archbishop and a very holy one at that. Resembling the monks I had known in the desert, he had the look of an ascetic.

"I want you to come live here with me," he finally said, as he stroked his thin gray beard. "I will talk to your parents about it tomorrow. Run along home now."

Waving his hand, the Archbishop of Alexandria dismissed me.

It was decided that as soon as my elementary studies were completed, which was only a matter of days, that I should go to live in the archiepiscopal residence and be thoroughly educated in ecclesiastical matters.

Almost immediately upon my arrival in the archbishop's household, my education began. His Piety wanted me to study both Hebrew and Greek, for as my saintly predecessor explained to me, one can understand and appreciate the Holy Scriptures well only if one is skilled in exegesis, and the best way to acquire that knowledge is by reading the holy writings in the languages in which they were written. Many men, including Arius, have fallen into error because of poor exegesis of the Holy Scripture. The law and the prophets yielded to me the wisdom of God. I read the gospels and the epistles in Greek under the guidance of men who received their training in the famous catechetical school of Alexandria that traced its origin back to the evangelist St. Mark. I received the best Greek education that His Piety could provide. Logic, rhetoric, oratory, geometry, I pursued most eagerly. I am in debt to Plato, Aristotle, Demosthenes, and Euclid for the development of the powers of my mind.

Time went by. My parents were very happy when I became a deacon of the church of God. Archbishop Alexander then made me his personal secretary. I was twenty years old and very much at home in the archiepiscopal household. I enjoyed the confidence of my archbishop and was even requested to advise him at times. He encouraged me to put my thoughts into writing. As a result, my first book was born. It was a vindication of the Christian religion against the objections of the pagans. I wrote the book about the time that the trouble began, although it took a while for it to come to a head and fester. I am referring to Arius. He was the cause of all the fury that was about to center itself around me. He was not, however, the originator of the lie he was beginning to utter, and which in time would shake even the foundations of Rome.

Arius was ambitious and it was well known that he hoped to be chosen archbishop of Alexandria and gain control of the entire Egyptian church as archbishop and primate of all Egypt and the Libyas. Our present archbishop Alexander was chosen to succeed Achillas. It was also known that Arius was studious and possessed a brilliant mind, but he had fallen under the influence of teachers of false doctrine in a school in Antioch.

In the middle of the last century, Antioch had the misfortune of having Paul of Samasota for its bishop. He came to a shameful end, being both deposed and excommunicated because of his immorality, financial dishonesty, and for his false doctrines. Unfrocked and cut off from the household of faith, he went to live in the palace of Princess Zenobia, a Jewess at Palmyra with whom, quite naturally, Paul of Samasota was more at home than he was in the Catholic Church, because he held a mean and abject view of Christ, considering him to be no more than a mere man.

A certain Lucian, also of Samasota, took up the teachings of Paul of Samasota and, later when he became a priest in Antioch and opened a school, he began teaching with certain modifications his false doctrines that denied the divinity of Christ. Attending this school before coming to Alexandria, Arius became impregnated with false ideas concerning the person of Christ and the Trinity.

As for Lucian, he repudiated his heresy before he died a holy martyr's death in the persecution of 312. Unfortunately, he was not able with his repudiation to erase the errors he had imprinted on the minds of men such as Arius.

In addition to his duties as pastor of the Baucalis church, Arius, also entrusted with the office of professor of scriptural exegesis, was beginning to cause quite a stir in Alexandria.

In clerical circles fiery discussions were raging over the truth or error of Arius' teaching. From my close contact with His Piety, I could see that Archbishop Alexander was deeply concerned about the matter. Late one night he called me into his study where he was seated behind his desk on which flickered an oil lamp that gave off a golden glow wrapping him in an aureole of light. His face was drawn and showed signs of the inward struggle he was experiencing. Motioning for me to sit opposite him, he came right to the point.

"What do you think of Christ?" he asked. His eyes searched my soul as he waited for me to answer.

"Christ is God. When I was but a child I learned from my holy Father Anthony that the cornerstone of our Catholic faith is belief in the Trinity. We believe in One God in Three equal Persons—Father, Son and Holy Spirit."

His Piety nodded slowly. "And what does Arius tell my sheep in Baucalis?

"That He has not always existed. That Christ is a creature."

Archbishop Alexander shook his head sadly. Passing his hand over his eyes and brushing his forehead, he wiped his brow as if to erase from his mind such thoughts as these.

Apologetically I told him, "It is all in the report I made and gave you of my visit to his parish where I heard him preach these lies."

"Perhaps, my son, we have misunderstood Arius. I want to be fair. True, he was a pupil of Lucian, but surely he knows that Lucian, himself, condemned and repudiated these teachings before he died. I, myself, am an Origenist, but that does not mean that I would follow Origen's every lead."

"Nor would I, Your Piety," I replied with a smile, for I knew that my archbishop was referring at that moment to the fact that Origen castrated himself with his own hand." Archbishop Alexander sighed deeply.

"Origen was a genius, but somewhere his mind went off on a tangent. At times his exegesis was deplorable. His was a far greater intellect than that of Arius. His contributions to the church are great in certain of his writings. I don't need to remind you, Athanasiuis, that he was head of the catechetical school here in Alexandria when it was at its zenith. Yet, he was deposed and unfrocked by our Egyptian bishops and Rome sanctioned the action."

The old Archbishop's thoughts trailed off into silence. I listened to the waves lapping on the sand as the tide was coming in on the beach outside the window. Somewhere in the night a cat was mewing. I watched as His Piety folded his hands on the desk and leaned his head back on his chair and sat gazing into the lamplight. I knew that he was silently communing with God, for the room was permeated with the spirit of his prayer. He was a saint, a true bishop of the church of God.

After our many years of close association with one another, we felt perfectly at ease in each other's company. How long we sat there in silent prayer, I cannot honestly say. It is hard to reckon time when one is united to God. Finally my bishop broke the silence.

"Write Arius a letter telling him to present himself to his Archbishop here in my study the first of next week."

No one else was present at the meeting of Archbishop Alexander and Arius, save me in my capacity as personal secretary to His Piety. Arriving promptly at the appointed hour, Arius was impeccably groomed in the cloak and tunic that was his customary attire. When I saw him at close range, I realized that he was older than I first believed him to be—in fact, he showed many signs of aging. Sometimes, however, one can be deceived about such things. I, myself, have been stoop-shouldered since I was twenty.

Stiffly Arius knelt at the feet of His Piety and kissed his hands. Casting his black eyes with a penetrating stare at me, he mumbled a greeting. Wishing to conduct the meeting with an air of informality, Archbishop Alexander received Arius warmly and offered him a chair by the window that gave a sweeping view of the sea. The day being hot, Arius welcomed the cool beverage the bishop had served to him.

Like a crocodile on the scent of its prey, His Piety sniffed out the opinions of Arius. When he succeeded in getting him in deep water, he sprang at him, asking him with a lightening like thrust, "Is Jesus Christ a creature?"

Without flicking an eyelash, Arius replied, "God made him out of nothing."

His Piety squinted his eyes, leaned forward in his chair, and said calmly but with great force, "You are in error, Arius."

Cocking his head slightly and with color rising in his cheeks, Arius burst out, "And you are in error! I have listened to you preach and I find your preaching strongly seasoned with Sabellianism, which is most likely a carry over from your famous Alexandrine, Origen."

Arrogantly, Arius surveyed the Archbishop of all Egypt and the Libyas, who of all the bishops in the world ranked second only to the Pope of Rome. I was appalled by the effrontery of his manner.

With great humility Archbishop Alexander replied quickly, "I am responsible before God for the church in Egypt, for the purity of her faith and morals." Drumming his fingers emphatically on the desk, he concluded, "You will tell your parishioners that you were in error. You will teach them that there are Three equal Persons in God. You will tell them that the Son is begotten of the Father, not created, and that He has always existed and always will. I am certain you understand my orders."

By way of dismissing Arius, Archbishop Alexander waved his hand and picking up a book from the desk began reading it. Arius was not to be put aside so easily. Clearing his throat and rising to his feet, he glared down his long straight nose at the bishop with a sneer. "There are many in Egypt who share my theological views." Tossing a handful of documents on the desk, Arius became very aggressive.

"Here are the signed statements of five priests and six deacons of Alexandria and the signed statements of two bishops of Libya to the effect that the doctrine I, Arius, teach is the correct one. In time I can gather many more such signed statements—statements of those in high ranking circles."

His Piety continued his reading, as if he had heard nothing after the point in the conversation when he terminated the interview. I rose from my chair at my archbishop's elbow, walked across the room to the door, opened it, and firmly, but politely directed Arius to leave. "The interview is terminated."

With fire in his eyes, Arius blazed from the audience. Immediately His Piety ordered me to write a letter to Arius and to the signers of the statements he left on the desk, warning them all that, unless they conformed to teaching the true Catholic faith as handed down to us from the Apostles, they could be assured that the necessary disciplinary action would be taken against them to remove them from their assignments. All the clergy of Alexandria were requested to sign the letter. Little did I dream then that in a short time, I would be suspected of murdering Arius. I wasn't even in Constantinople when he died so horribly.

Summer heat descended on Alexandria. Everyone was not as fortunate as we to live by the sea. In a city of a million inhabitants, life went on, day after day, despite the high humid temperatures. The glassmakers blew their glass. The weavers wove their linen and paper was manufactured in as large a quantities as in the cooler months. In the great harbor of the city, along nine miles of wharves, ships were busy carrying away the goods that had been manufactured. When you strolled along the main avenue of Alexandria that was lined with three miles of colonnades, arcades, and expensive shops, you noticed that there were fewer tourists than in winter, but even so there was a scattering of wealthy Romans who came to see the antiquities. The forum was as busy as ever. The parks and gardens were crowded with children. There were even lines of people filing by the body of Alexander the Great, the city's founder. His body had been preserved in honey and placed in a glass case in a lovely mausoleum so that anyone who wished could view him.

The Roman prefect who lived in the palaces of the Ptolemies went about government business as usual. The prosperous Alexandrians who loved to boat there at night by gondola flooded the amusement park in the suburb at Canopus. The intense heat seemed to give rise to more friction among the different racial groups of the city that has its share of almost every group of people living around the Mediterranean. The sea outside our windows was like a steaming Roman bath. The early morning hours gave no respite, but on the contrary seemed to be the hottest part of the day, for the sun was always up and busy, while the breeze still lay sleeping.

On my morning walks along the beach, the sea—calm like a pond—reflected the sun's light so brilliantly that one could not look at the horizon without squinting. Only the gulls, the little sandpipers, and men who love solitude were on the beach in the early morning. I enjoy the company of the gulls as they hover overhead and sometimes come and perch a few feet from me in hopes that I have brought them some bits of bread. Almost motionlessly they hover in the air with their broad strong wings, extended pure white against the cerulean blue sky. These creatures so peaceful—so gentle—so radiantly pure in their plumage—always raise my heart, my mind and soul to the Holy Spirit who chooses to represent Himself to us under the form of a white dove. Our own spirits are like the little sandpipers that twitter nervously to and fro as fast as their stem-like legs will carry them over the sand in endless pursuit of periwinkles. We settled down to what would appear to be a routine, uneventful summer. It soon became very apparent, however, that the censure that had been administered to Arius and his friends was insufficient.

Word soon came to His Piety that Arius was once more preaching his errors in Baucalis. When we heard that, the summer suddenly seemed a lot hotter. The atmosphere of Alexandria got still hotter when one of the priests of the Mareotis came to the archiepiscopal residence with a letter he received. It was the first of a long series of letters that were to plague us. I scanned the contents carefully while the priest who brought it to us waited for Archbishop Alexander to comment on it.

The letter was in support of Arius and his teaching. The one who wrote the letter informed us that he was a fellow student with Arius in the school that they both attended in Antioch; in the letter he assured the priest of the Mareotis, to whom it was addressed, that His Piety had been wrong in condemning Arius' teachings. Glancing at the signature at the bottom of the letter, I saw that it was signed "Eusebius, Bishop of Nicomedia."

After reading the letter, His Piety, for the benefit of the priest of the Mareotis who desired for him to comment on it, merely took the letter and tore it into a dozen pieces and threw it away. One after another, our priests and bishops of Alexandria, the Mareotis, and the rest of Egypt and the Libyas informed us that they too received such a letter. In them, Eusebius announced to everyone that he was throwing his entire support behind Arius. His Piety and I both knew who and what Eusebius was.

When Constantine grasped the imperial throne and entered Rome in triumph, he attributed his victory over his enemies to his having invoked Christ. Although he professed himself to be a Christian, he made no attempt to enter the Church by the waters of baptism, whereby we are all born again of God. One of the first acts of our new Emperor was to give his sister Constantia in marriage to Licinius who within a few months was to defeat Maximinus and enter Nicomedia as the Augustus of the East. It was the inauguration of a new era. Licinius and Constantine decreed that everyone in the empire should be permitted to worship as his conscience decreed. Soon we saw coins in circulation that bore the monogram of Christ. Knowing that Constantine was an astute politician, we eyed all these events with suspicion and many reservations.

The Church had become too powerful for the state to exterminate us. Our worst persecutor Galerius, realized the futility of trying to stamp us out. The main reason for the persecution was to strengthen and unify the Empire. The contrary effect had been accomplished. We noted that when Constantine entered Rome, bearing the banner of Christ, he restored certain of the pagan temples. He also authorized the establishment of a priesthood for propagating the cult of *gens Flavia*, his family, and retained for himself the office of the pagan *pontifex maximus* and the title of "divine." Foremost in his mind was the necessity to unify the empire.

Because Constantine's sister Constantia was in fact Christian and Eusebius wormed his way into her confidence, Eusebius, the Bishop of Nicomedia, took it upon himself to interfere in the internal affairs of the Egyptian church. Eusebius had but one thing in mind when he wrote those letters supporting Arius and that one thing was the furthering of his own ambition. He had no care for truth or the canons of the Church. Had he not proved what he was when he became dissatisfied with being bishop in his lawful city of Berytus and, in defiance of Church law, he transferred himself to the imperial city and made himself Bishop of Nicomedia? In a similar fashion, he worked his way into the confidence of the Augusta, becoming her spiritual father. Holiness for him consisted not in humility and self-denial, but in riches and in wealthy and influential bishoprics. Being a relative of the Flavians was no excuse for such actions.

The spiritual father of the Augusta notwithstanding, His Piety Archbishop Alexander knew where duty lay. I wrote the letter summoning all our bishops, priests, and deacons to a Synod to be held for the purpose of unfrocking Arius and all who chose to go with him. Sad to say, things were not to turn out the way we had hoped they would. The matter with Arius was not as easy to settle as we had anticipated. We had much to suffer.

When the Synod convened in the cathedral church of Alexandria with almost one hundred bishops present, it was an impressive sight to see so many confessors of the faith assembled. While some of them bore the scars of Diocletian's persecution on their bodies, all of them bore such scars on their souls. Still fresh in the minds of these bishops who led their flocks through those dreadful days were the sufferings the Church endured so bravely.

I believe that even at the time the Synod convened, His Piety was preparing me to become his successor. Perhaps he felt that he had but a short time left, before he would have to turn the miter and crosier over to the hands of another, for of recent months the strain of the difficulties we were experiencing with Arius was beginning to be reflected in his aging body. As the days went by he began to rely on me considerably, especially for all the help I could give him.

When I accompanied His Piety to the Synod at which I was to preside, it was a very hot morning. As I sat in the chancel, I had an excellent opportunity to study Arius and the two bishops and the handful of priests and deacons who had taken his side in the dispute. In fact, Arius was sitting just across the chancel railing from me. From time to time, with serene audacity, he would cast frowning black glances in my direction.

At the appointed hour His Piety Alexander, Metropolitan Archbishop of all the assembled bishops, nodded to me to commence the proceedings. After a prayer for divine guidance, I launched into the business at hand. Since they all knew why they had been summoned, despite the unbearable summer heat, to leave their sees and come to participate in a synod, there was no need to relate the reason for assembling. Already, in small groups among themselves, they had discussed the teachings of Arius. Only two of the bishops, Secundus and Theonis, both from Libya where Arius was born, supported him. All the rest, staunch supporters of their Archbishop, were waiting for him to address them.

Briefly I touched upon the events that had brought us to the Synod. I related how his Piety had tried to settle the matter privately, but unable to come to a satisfactory understanding with Arius, found it necessary to convene the entire Egyptian and Libyan Church with the intention of pointing out to Arius the error of his ways and giving him a fair hearing and an opportunity to subscribe to the true teachings of the Catholic faith.

When His Piety rose to his feet and made his way slowly to a lectern that was placed slightly to the right of the center of the sanctuary, a great hush fell over the cathedral. Before beginning his address to the bishops, he knelt before the altar and bowed his head in silent prayer. Arising and turning to face the synod he began to speak.

"My brothers in Christ, it grieves me to assemble you here today to report to you that in the midst of our glorious church has appeared a rank and detestable heresy. Never has anyone in the three hundred years that the Catholic Church has been in the world fabricated a heresy so fundamentally and diametrically opposed to all we hold sacred. The heresy of Arius attacks and vitiates what is most fundamental in our faith—the divinity of our Lord and Savior Jesus Christ."

The archbishop paused with an expression of sorrow on his face. Deliberately he looked from one to another of the faces of the bishops that were seated before him. Allowing his glance to fall on Arius and looking straight at him, he continued. "Unless the one who is propagating this false doctrine recants his errors, I have no choice but to remove him from his parish and depose him." Then glancing from Secundus to Theonas, the only two of our bishops who supported Arius, His Piety added: "And all who choose to follow him will suffer the same fate."

Arius sat with eyes downcast, his face betraying no emotion.

"I had hoped," Archbishop Alexander continued, "I had hoped that this affair would terminate quietly in time of its own accord. I reprimanded Arius privately—but to no avail. A short time later, I was again grieved to hear that he was once more preaching in Baucalis that Christ is not true God—but rather, that he is a creature. It is the desire of your archbishop that Arius be given a fair hearing so that none may ever say he was unjustly treated. I want you to be informed of all the actions taken in the matter." Turning to me, His Piety directed, "Summon Arius to come forward and give his defense."

Before his Piety seated himself and before I could give the order for Arius to address the synod, Arius, having heard His Piety call for him, had already bounded to his feet and made his way to the center aisle of the church where he stood just outside the chancel rail. Calmly he surveyed the assembly of holy bishops.

Although Arius was about sixty, he moved and talked always with so much vigor that he gave the impression of being a much younger man. Dramatically, he waited for a few moments before speaking. Casting his eyes towards heaven, he looked like a saint, for he was thin and wiry, as if he spent much time fasting.

"Although I was fifty years old when I was ordained to the holy priesthood," Arius began, "I have been a student and a scholar all my life. I am a learned man," he proclaimed boldly for all to hear. "I studied with the famous Lucian in Antioch. You are all aware of how he gave his life for the faith. The doctrines I teach are the true and orthodox ones that are held by educated men everywhere." Emphasizing the word "educated," he shot a glance at Secundus who supported him and whom he intended to flatter by this statement. "Archbishop Alexander has, I am certain, misunderstood my teaching."

With honeyed words Arius gave a brilliant defense. I listened with great distaste as I heard him take passages of scripture out of context and cleverly and shamelessly twist them to make them suit his purposes. He had the audacity to tell the synod that Christ has not always existed, even though in the scripture it states plainly, "In the beginning was the Word!"

Many of those assembled put their hands over their ears and protested when Arius told them that Christ is not true God. In conclusion, Arius spoke even more boldly and arrogantly.

"I am ready to answer any questions. I will gladly explain to all of you the true doctrine concerning Christ."

Halfway back in the crowded church, just left of the center aisle, a very old bishop stood, begging to be recognized.

"Yes!" responded Arius with utter self-confidence. "State your question," he added with a smug smile.

"Why were you deposed by our blessed Archbishop Peter who was martyred for the faith?"

It was one of the bishops from Lower Egypt who spoke. The smile froze on Arius' face. Stammering he retorted: "That has absolutely nothing to do with the issue at hand."

The old bishop from Lower Egypt pressed his advantage "I think it has everything to do with the issue at hand. If you do not wish to tell the venerable bishops why you were deposed, I will. You were deposed because you turned against your lawful superior, the holy Bishop Peter, who had raised you to the deaconate. You took up the cause of Meletius, that infamous enemy of the Church, who is still plaguing us. You deliberately chose to take up with Meletius, whom we deposed in a general council because of his manifold crimes—including that of sacrificing to the pagan gods during the persecution. You have had a contentious spirit ever since you came here."

Arius raised his hand and begged for a chance to speak. With false humility and downcast eyes, he began his defense. "You are correct. I erred. I was but a new deacon. I atoned for my mistake. Achillas reinstated me and ordained me a priest."

The bishop from Lower Egypt sprang to the attack.

"You were a new deacon, yes, but you were fifty years old. If you could make such an error when you were fifty, might you not be making a worse one now that you are sixty?"

Arius' face reddened. I could see that he was fighting for self-control as he tapped his foot nervously on the floor while his opponent continued.

"I have been a priest for fifty years and a bishop for thirty. You have been a priest for only ten years and in that length of time you have not yet mastered the fundamentals of the virtues of humility and obedience. How is it that you, being ordained only ten years ago, presume to tell us and our father in God, His Piety Archbishop Alexander, what the true Catholic faith is?"

Stretching out his arm its full length and wagging his gnarled finger at Arius, the bishop roared at him. "Rather you should kneel at the feet of your archbishop and beg him to instruct you!"

As I surveyed the faces of the bishops before me, I could see that they were highly animated. A murmur of agreement spread through the church. Arius, unable to comment on what had been said, ran his hand through his thin gray hair, mopped his forehead and looking into the hostile faces that peered up at him asked, "Are there any further questions?"

One of the younger bishops rose from his seat near the front. In a strong and clear voice he demanded, "Is Jesus Christ a creature?"

"Yes," replied Arius boldly with positive assurance. "God made him out of nothing."

A wave of shock ran through the synod. Then dead silence gave way to a tumultuous protest at the brazen impiety that Arius had dared utter right before the altar of God. The young bishop turned his back on Arius and addressing the synod said, "What further need do we have of listening to such blasphemy? You have heard his answer."

When Secundus signified that he wished to speak, you could have heard the sands of an hourglass measuring time, so silent did the great church become.

"There must be some mistake—some misunderstanding—for I have examined the views of Arius and find him completely in accord with the teaching that I received in Antioch."

With the permission of His Piety, I addressed Secundus. "You believe that Jesus Christ is a creature?"

"I do, and so does my fellow bishop Theonas and all these priests and deacons who are seated here with us."

"That is true?" I asked pointing at the group that huddled around Secundus. They all nodded affirmatively. Arius smiled proudly, and bowed his head curtly at me. Boldly I strode over to him and loud enough for even the bishops in the back rows of the church to hear me clearly, I demanded, "You say that Jesus Christ is a creature. If that is true then you must admit that he is capable of changing. Creatures change, we all know that."

"Yes," agreed Arius. "Christ is capable of changing."

"Can he change as the devil changed?" I snapped.

"Yes!!"

I shot a glance at Secundus who was rising to his feet, all the while nodding his agreement with Arius. Turning to the Synod with outstretched arms I exclaimed: "Your excellencies, you have heard him say that Christ is capable of sinning! What say you? Can God sin?"

"No!!" shouts of protest rang out from every corner of the great church.

"Let them be anathema!" I cried.

"Anathema!!" The cry came from the throats of all the bishops, save Secundus and Theonas.

Solemnly we anathematized them all, unfrocking Arius, and removing him from his parish. Unfortunately, we were unable to crush his arrogant spirit that was filled with the seeds of pollution that he was soon to spew over the entire East.

Glaring angrily at me, Arius shook his fist and muttered audible threats against me. All his pent up hatred, he seemed to direct at me personally. Not waiting for the holy Synod to adjourn, Arius strode from the cathedral with his followers at his heels.

His Piety was deeply grieved by the necessity of deposing Arius and the bishops, priests, and deacons who chose to follow him. Sitting behind his desk with the memoranda I had drawn up giving all the details of the deposition of Arius, His Piety looked at me gravely. "I fear, Athanasius, that we have not written the last pages of this deplorable history. I had hoped that Arius would change his mind before he actually took leave of his parish, but as you know he left Alexandria. I hear he bought passage on a ship sailing to Palestine."

I could see that the deposition of Arius had caused His Piety much suffering. His face, usually joyful, was now haggard. His almost transparent skin was very pale, and the bluish veins of his neck protruded. God grant him a long life, I prayed, for I knew he intended to select me as his successor. I trembled at the thought of the solemn responsibility that the episcopal consecration and the archbishopric would impose on my soul.

"What do you think Arius will do?"

I drew my chair closer to His Piety who was in the habit of speaking softly in tones that showed his great humility of spirit.

"I wonder?" He shrugged. "The priest Collustus is agitating among the clergy for me to send letters all over the East warning the bishops everywhere of Arius. I keep hoping that it will not be necessary and that the affair will die down now. I hate the thought of calling the entire Church at large to witness to the shame of his deposition."

Speaking of letters reminded me of the reason I had come on that occasion into His Piety's study. "Here," I said extending a letter to him. "This just arrived. The messenger is waiting."

Curiously I watched as he slipped his finger under the wax seal and opening the letter began to read. His face grew red. The vein in his temple began to pulsate very rapidly as he perused the contents. Tossing the letter on the desk, he sighed deeply and explained. "It is from Eusebius, Bishop of Nicomedia!"

I waited for him to tell me what the letter contained. Instead he merely slammed his right fist into the palm of his other hand, rose to his feet and began pacing the floor, back and forth, from the window to the door.

"Here, read it yourself. He is not satisfied with promoting himself from Berytus to Nicomedia! Now he wishes to run the church of Egypt!"

I scanned the contents of the letter rapidly. The bishop of Nicomedia had written in support of Arius, begging His Piety to reconsider, to reinstate Arius, and to receive the heresiarch into communion. Eusebius went so far as to vouchsafe for the doctrines of Arius saying that he, himself, was a fellow Lucianist. He concluded by stating that all the bishops of the East were behind him in supporting Arius. Thoughtfully, I replaced the letter on the desk.

"What shall I tell the messenger who brought this letter?"

Archbishop Alexander had become very calm. Pensively he stood at the window gazing out toward the distant horizon over the sea. In times of crisis he always seemed to find strength contemplating the sea—even as I do.

"Show him in," he whispered.

The young deacon boldly stalked into the study of His Piety. Without extending to him the proper reverence that is due an archbishop of the church of God, the deacon blurted without preamble: "There is more to the message than is contained in the letter. I have been instructed to *warn* you," he emphasized the word warn, "that unless you comply at once with the orders of Bishop Eusebius of Nicomedia, he shall be forced to take measures against you."

Curtly the messenger nodded his head and waited for His Piety to answer. I was aghast at what I had heard! Nicomedia had no right to interfere in the affairs of Alexandria! And as for threatening to take action—such precedent was unheard of in the annals of Church history. Serenely, His Piety regarded the young deacon. In a voice that was utterly devoid of any emotion he spoke quietly and with determination. "My orders come from God, not from the Bishop of Nicomedia."

Without another word His Piety took the letter from Eusebius and tore it in half a dozen pieces and tossed them in the trash receptacle beside his desk. Without being asked, I ushered the messenger from Nicomedia brusquely out of the study. His Piety was justly indignant at the intrusion of the ambitious Eusebius in our affairs. We soon learned that many Eastern bishops courted the favor of the Bishop of Nicomedia due to his influence over Constantia, the emperor's sister, because letters began pouring into our see, first to His Piety and then to our bishops and other clergy, from bishops who had decided to support the Nicomedian in his defense of Arius. Judging from the letters that came to Egypt, the bishops all over the East had received the impression from Eusebius that we had dealt unjustly with Arius.

With an ashen face His Piety said to me: "Eusebius, with his detestable ambition and his lust for power, is intriguing against me."

"It is hard to believe." I shrugged my shoulders. "It is hard to believe that Eusebius could be more interested in advancing himself than in promoting the true faith of Christ." The only bishops I had known until this time were holy men, self-effacing men who wholeheartedly embraced a life of perfection. How could any Christian be so base as to lay hold of the office of a bishop as a means of personal aggrandizement?

His Piety, who could read my soul, said gently, "Do not be scandalized, my son. Our Lord has told us that there will be false prophets who inwardly are ravenous wolves. We can recognize them by their fruits." Laying his hand on my shoulder he continued, "There are robbers in the fold, that is true—but the sheep shall recognize the voice of the Good Shepherd."

The time arrived when Bishop Alexander decided that we had to take up the pen in defense of truth. Day after day, he dictated the letters that I wrote to the bishops all over the empire, explaining to them the course of events that had made it necessary for us in Alexandria to depose Arius. Boldly we wrote against Eusebius, referring to him as being the head of the Arian apostates. We advised the bishops of the church at large to ignore letters coming from the man who had deserted his bishopric at Berytus to assume authority at the city where the Augustus Licinius had his imperial residence.

These letters, which we felt in conscience bound to write, served but to make matters worse. They infuriated Eusebius. As a consequence, more letters began to flood our office. Sadly we learned the Bishop of Caesarea had endorsed the Arian cause. All the letters were not in favor of Arius. We also received letters strongly applauding our stand in deposing Arius and holding fast against Eusebius' interference. I was to have more to complain of than writer's cramp in the months that lay ahead! Apparently the influence Eusebius exercised over Constantia did not extend to her husband, Emperor Licinus, for he found many ways to persecute the churches, especially after his quarrels with Constantine broke into open warfare and Constantine took Greece, Macedonia, and Illyria from him. To retaliate against Constantine, he thought to wound him by making the Christians of the East suffer.

It came as no surprise to any one when on the eve of a battle with Constantine, Licinius resorted to pagan sacrifices and oracles. Then, just when Licinius was about to inaugurate a widespread persecution of the Church, Constantine fought him on the sea near Adrianople, sank his three hundred galleys, and brought him to a miserable defeat. The news reached Alexandria quickly that Constantine was now the sole Augustus of the Empire. We also heard that Constantia raced to Constantine, her brother, and pleaded for her husband's life. We began to have fresh insights into Constantine's character when we learned that he allowed Licinius to go into exile in Thessalonia, only to have him strangled six months later. We learned still more of Constantine a short time later when we—His Piety and I—came under his scrutiny.

One day as I was employed in the tremendous task of answering our correspondence which was voluminous, I was surprised by the arrival at the archiepiscopal residence of a foreign bishop, who in very faltering Greek asked me for an audience with His Piety Alexander. Perceiving that he was a westerner, I greeted him in Latin, much to his relief. You can imagine my amazement when I learned that we were entertaining Bishop Hosius of Cordova in Spain. His reputation of being a great confessor of the faith during the persecutions was well known throughout Egypt. I was to become better acquainted with Hosius as the years went by. I can honestly say that my admiration for him was born the first instant I met him. His Piety Alexander welcomed Hosius most warmly.

"It is a great honor to have you with us. Pray tell us what it is that brings you to Alexandria. I am certain you did not come here just to view the antiquities of the Ptolmies." Alexander extended his hand and clasped the hand of the venerable Hosius who responded with openhearted warmth to His Piety.

Although he was past seventy, Hosius was tall and straight of stature. With great dignity, he took the chair by the window opposite me. I could see a large scar—a livid purple streak—on his face reaching from the bridge of his nose, running underneath his eye and extending to the tip of his ear. He knew what it was to suffer for Christ.

"The honor is all mine, Your Piety," responded Hosius with a seraphic smile. "You are correct. I did not journey halfway across the Empire just to see the pyramids or to get a glimpse of your famous Nile. I am here," he explained, inclining his head affably as he spoke, to bring you greetings from Victor Constantine Maximus Augustus!"

Bishop Alexander's eyes narrowed to slits at the mention of the Emperor.

"Constantine sent you?" he asked without showing his surprise. He acted as if it were an everyday occurrence to receive envoys from the Emperor.

"Yes, with this letter." Hosius extended a letter which I could see bore the imperial insignia.

His Piety took the letter and handed it to me.

"My personal secretary, Athanasius, here, has eyes that are sharper at reading fine script than mine." Turning to me he said, "If you please, Athanasius, let us hear what Augustus has to say to a poor old bishop of Jesus Christ."

A bit nervously, I opened the letter and began to read. The Emperor accused His Piety of stirring up vain contentions over mere words. The emperor went on to say, furthermore, that the subject of controversy between His Piety and Arius was one of insignificance. My voice trembled when I read the lines that directed that His Piety should purify his soul and receive Arius to his bosom. Avoiding looking at His Piety, I laid the letter on the desk before him. For the first time in all the years that I had known him, His Piety was at a loss for words. It was incredible! Constantine wanted us to forget the entire affair and to continue as if nothing were wrong. Pointing to the letter, His Piety leaned forward in his chair and turned the conversation away from himself by asking Hosius, "What do you think of this?"

Hosius began to chuckle. His brown eyes were greatly animated as he replied. "I think my old friend Constantine is a very poor theologian."

Alexander heaved a sigh of relief. "You understand what we are up against?"

"Perfectly," agreed Hosius, raising his hand, by force of years of habit, in a gesture of blessing. "But, you, for your part, must try to understand Constantine. I have known him for years. He trusts me. I understand what motivates him." Hosius tugged pensively at his beard and continued speaking. "You must realize that Constantine places his entire hopes for a unified, peaceful empire on the Church of Christ. He places unity before all else. Now that he is the sole Augustus, it was his plan that the unity of the Catholic Church would unite the empire. Suddenly he finds that the Church is torn apart by the quarrel between you and Arius…"

His Piety raised his hand to interrupt. "The quarrel is not between Arius and me. It is between Arius and Christ." he insisted politely but firmly.

"I am well aware of that. I know what is at stake. I am here on orders from Constantine to deliver his message. Now, that I have done that, let me assure you that I embrace your cause—not only I, but Silvester as well."

At the mention of Pope Silvester, His Piety's face lit up. Eagerly he inquired, "Have you seen his Holiness?"

"Yes. More than that. We have discussed your difficulties. He sends word that you are in the right and that we will support you, no matter who might be persuaded to assail you."

"He received my letter?"

"Yes. He studied it carefully and says that your doctrine concerning the Godhead is the true one handed down in Rome from the Holy Apostles who taught that there are Three equal Persons in God—Father, Son, and Holy Spirit."

His Piety rubbed his baldhead with his hand, as was his habit when perplexed, then asked: "How will Constantine fit into this fight for truth against error?" What does he know of the faith? He is as yet unbaptized."

Tapping his finger for emphasis on the windowsill beside him, Hosius continued gravely. "His Holiness Silvester and I have pondered this question at great length. Constantine has decided that unless I can restore unity between you and Arius during my stay in Alexandria, he will summon you and Arius to appear before him and he will decide what is right."

"But that is ridiculous! He is no theologian! It was bad enough when the emperors persecuted the church without having them rule on matters of doctrine!" The vein on His Piety Alexander's temple was distended, betraying his agitation.

"Precisely! Now, Alexander, you are beginning to get a true picture of the situation in which you have become embroiled. You can understand why I so willingly responded to Constantine's request that I come to you and explain the situation."

As I silently listened to the venerable Hosius explain the affair in which we had unwittingly become involved, I was filled with reverence. The words of the Holy Gospel came into mind. "Render unto Caesar the things that are Caesar's." It was better when the affairs of the Church and the Empire were separate. I marveled at the vivacity of Hosius and at the alacrity of his mind in penetrating men and events. I later learned that his ability of assessing people and events at their true value was one of his greatest assets. Furthermore, he possessed the virtue of prudence in an heroic degree.

His Piety's face was creased with deep lines of concern. "What do you suggest we do? We cannot turn the keys of the kingdom over to the emperor."

Confidently Hosius smiled and explained his thoughts on the matter. "We have a plan. Silvester and I have discussed it at length. It has to work. While I am here in the city of Alexandria, I shall have a meeting of your clergy, including any in the city who still favor Arius. We shall air the matter to please Constantine. Then I shall leave Alexandria and go to the Emperor. He is still in Nicomedia now. I will tell him that Arius is clearly in error."

"Do you think that will solve our difficulties?"

"No, truthfully, I don't. Not only must Arius be censured, but also this heresy must be rooted out before it spreads any further."

His Piety and I both agreed.

"I am going to propose to Constantine when I go to him in Nicomedia that he assemble all the bishops of the entire Church—the world over—and that we have a council that will decide the Arian affair—once and forever."

"An ecumenical council?" I blurted out in my amazement. So far I had contributed nothing to the conversation. Hosius looked at me, as if I were a child who had intruded into adult affairs. Then he softened and smiling asked me, "What do you think of it, young fellow?"

The thought of an ecumenical council at which the bishops of the whole Church would convene with one mind, the mind of Christ, and settle this dispute was exciting and so very logical.

"I cast my vote for it," I told Hosius eagerly.

"Yes," replied Alexander with the reserve that comes with age. "But we must be sure our bishops understand about Eusebius and his ambition. He will try to seize control of the council."

Having broken into the conversation once, it was easier a second time. "We must prepare at once for such a council," I said eagerly. I knew that I would have many letters to write, before we were ready to face the Arians in council.

Before Bishop Hosius left Alexandria, we met with our clergy, as he had suggested. He made it very clear to all present that he condemned Arius, while at the same time, proclaiming his belief in the Holy Trinity. Some of the Arian followers, furious by these proceedings, caused a riot. It was a small riot, but a few statues of the emperor were smashed. This was but a preview of events yet to come.

The only thing we accomplished by this assembly was to further the confusion that the priest Colluthus caused when he separated from the Church, set himself up as a bishop, and began ordaining clergy of his own, because he became enraged with His Piety, whom he felt had not dealt severely enough with Arius.

Not long after Hosius sailed for Nicodemia, we were pleased to learn that he had been successful in dealing with the emperor. An ecumenical council would in fact become a reality. The idea of bringing all the bishops of the world together in unity appealed to Constantine, because it would serve to unify the Empire. Bythnia in the city of Nicaea, which is not far from Nicomedia, was to host the council in the coming May, leaving us all winter and spring to prepare for it.

Constantine spent the winter laying the foundations of the city that he said would be the New Rome. We spent the winter corresponding with bishops everywhere making the most of the time we had to inform everyone of the truth. I was taken by surprise and overwhelmed when His Piety informed me that, in as much as the Arian affair had been born in our city, it would be incumbent on us to address the council and present our side of the matter. It was a stunning blow when I heard what he had in mind.

"I am old and tired. My voice is not strong. Therefore, you, Athanasius, my son, you will address the council in my stead as the official spokesman for Egypt and the Libyas.

"But, Your Piety…," I began to plead my inexperience. He silenced me with a wave of his hand.

"Are you insinuating that I—your archbishop—do not know what is the right course of action to follow?"

I dropped to my knees. "Forgive me, Piety. With the help of God, I shall do as you wish."

Laughing, he motioned me to my feet. "I am certain my red-headed deacon will have flaming words for the council fathers when they convene in May. I have heard you preach on the Holy Trinity. It is a subject which always give rise to the most sublime in you. I want the council to hear you speak of the Three Persons of God."

Prayerfully I approached the task of preparing the address. Feeling my inadequacy, I asked for a few days leave. There was some place I wanted to go.

Spring was just blossoming in the fertile fields along the Nile as I set out for Thebes. It had been a long time since I had seen my Father Anthony. I was afraid that perhaps he would have forgotten me. Now I needed his prayers. I needed him, even as Bishop Peter had needed him when he gave his witness to Christ in his blood. I had no reason to fear. My father in Christ greeted me as if it were only yesterday since I was last in his cell in the inner mountain. Ten years faded away. I found myself sitting on the ground at his feet, while he sat on his rock that served as a chair. He had not changed. He had the same firm step, the same quick, penetrating, blue eyes. His tall straight back had not become the least bit bowed by the age he bore.

"What can I do for you?" he asked, peering into my soul. His joyful face told me that he was truly glad that I had come. "How can I, an old monk, help a young deacon who will soon be his archbishop?"

"No! No, Father—surely not soon!" The thought of succeeding Alexander as the highest-ranking bishop in the church after Pope Silvester terrified me.

The time is drawing near when I will kneel at your feet, Athanasius, and ask for your blessing."

The thought of addressing the council weighed heavily on my soul. The thought of assuming the weight of the See of Egypt and the Libyas was more than I dared contemplate.

"Perhaps I should become a monk, Father?" I said looking for an escape. I dropped to my knees before him. "Let me come here and live a life of prayer—alone with God the way you do. I want to leave the world."

With a glance, he penetrated the nethermost recesses of my soul. "You wish to do God's will, do you not, Athanasius?"

I merely nodded. He had grown holier, closer to God, in the years that had passed. He could read my heart like a sundial.

"God has great plans for you. I told you that when you were a child. I repeat it now. You will be the Archbishop of Egypt and all the Libyas."

I was crushed to the earth under the weight of such a sentence.

"What must I do, Father?"

"Pray! Pray! Pray without ceasing."

I bowed my head. "You will help me?"

"With constant prayer. You will never be alone. My prayer and the prayers of six thousand monks will go with you everywhere."

"Even to Nicaea?" I knew that with the prayers of my holy father I would be sustained in any situation.

"Ah! So! I have heard of the council that will convene in Nicaea. Someone must speak out for truth before the entire Church. Someone must defend the doctrine of the Holy Trinity so that even Eusebius will sign his name to the doctrine!"

I was happy to see that even though my father lived a hermit's life, he was well informed on the affairs of the Church. Again I bowed my head. He continued reading my heart.

"You will speak well. I will be with you in prayer. The Holy Spirit will speak through you."

I stayed with the monks at Pispir for seven days of spiritual retreat. During this time I abandoned my will completely to God's that he might do with me as he pleases. I feel that, at this time, I died to myself so that when I sailed for Nicaea I would able to make the words of Blessed Paul the Apostle my own. "Although I live, it is no longer I, but Christ who lives in me."

CHAPTER 2

❖

*W*e were disappointed to learn that His Holiness Pope Silvester, Bishop of Rome, and successor of the Apostle Peter, would be unable to be present at our council in Nicaea. Already in advanced age, he had taken ill and his failing health prevented him from making the long and tedious journey. In his stead, we were informed, he was sending two of his priests, Vicentius and Vito to represent him.

Our Egyptian church was to be well represented in the council. In addition to His Piety Alexander and myself, as his secretary and spokesman, Paphnutius, the Bishop of Upper Thebes and the heroic Potammon were both planning to sail shortly after we left. Both of these holy men had their right eyes gouged out and their left legs hamstrung during the persecution in 312, when they had been sent as slaves to work in the mines. Although the Council was not set to convene until May 20, His Piety decided that we should sail early in May, so as to be certain that nothing would prevent our arriving at Nicaea in time.

The day we set sail, I suffered quite a shock. When we were on the dock getting ready to board our ship, I heard the sailors on the docks of Alexandria singing a strange new song. I thought at first that my hearing was defective. When I listened more closely, to be certain that I had heard correctly, there was no doubt about it. Their words were perfectly plain. His Piety cocked his head to one side and listened too as the sailors sang, "God speaks many words which then are we to call Son and Word, the only begotten of the Father?"

Aghast we listened to the entire verse. In dissolute and loose meters we heard Arius' heresy sung as a ballad in the mouths of seamen. Addressing the Savior, they asked defiantly, "Why do you being a man make yourself a god? We later found out that Arius had composed this blasphemous song and called it "Thalia." It was an atrocious piece of writing, in the style of the great Egyptian writer Sotades. In addition to being blasphemous, it was effeminate and ridiculous. With the use of sweet words and anapestic cadences, he thought he could deceive the children of God by making "Thalia" the very symbol of his irreligion. As time went by, his song was bandied about even by drunkards over their cups. This irreligious mockery by Arius was even taken up by the pagans who saw in it something of a fad to be exploited in farces on the theatrical stage. So that he would have a harvest of companions in death, Arius, departing from the household of faith, busied himself sowing his deadly poison and scattering error with the evil one.

Our sailing vessel was a sea-worthy ship bearing a load of barley and linen to Rome. We were to put in at the Piraeus, where we were to board another vessel that would take us to Bythnia. Since the sea was relatively calm and the wind was to our back, we glided quickly over the ink-like waters.

As we drew near Athens, I became restless. I thought of Blessed Paul, the apostle, and of how he set out to preach Christ to the Athenians. In meditating upon his life, I found courage. Before the learned and aged philosophers of Greece, he preached the divinity of Christ in the Areopagus. Against almost impossible odds, he struggled to win the entire world for Christ. I knew the secret of his courage. In his own words he had said, "I am able to do anything when Christ gives me the strength." In his own words he also said, "Imitate me, as I imitate Christ." This I have always tried to do. I find the Apostle Paul a source of great inspiration for my life.

When we arrived at Nicaea, we found the city crowded with churchmen. Constantine had arranged to pay for the transportation and lodging of any bishop who wished to come for the Council. The bishops responded wholeheartedly to the opportunity. It was extremely moving to see bishops from every country arriving daily in the council city. There were Parthians, Medes, and Elamites. Staying in our own inn, not far from the imperial palace where the council was to be held, there were Syrians, Celicians, Phoenicians, Arabs, and Palestinians, among others. In the street in front of our hotel, I saw a Persian bishop talking to a bishop from Gaul. During the week before the Council convened, we met Mesopotamians, Scythians, and a Galatian. Strolling side by side in the streets of the city, we saw clergy from Pontus, Pamphylia, Cappadocia, and Phrygia. The Council was going to be really ecumenical.

Since the Arian affair arose in our Egyptian Church, and since His Piety as Archbishop of Egypt and the Lybias was therefore the center of attention in the dispute, bishops who wanted to hear from us what happened constantly sought us after. Before it was over, I was to meet some very great saints of God.

One afternoon, a bishop came to our rooms and with a soft voice and great humility introduced himself as a "Shepherd from Cyprus." I did not know who he was, but His Piety recognizing him immediately, rose to his feet, and extending his arms, warmly greeted him as Bishop Spyridon.

Although he was tall and gaunt, he had a very friendly, almost boyish, grin, "It is wonderful to be in Nicaea," he exclaimed, "but I hope my sheep don't miss me too much and go hungry."

"The people of God will manage without us for a few weeks. The Holy Spirit will see to that," responded His Piety.

"I am not talking about my people, I am talking about my sheep. You see I really am a shepherd. I am just a simple shepherd. I always try to find time to feed the animals myself even though my episcopal duties take priority on my time."

God often uses simple uneducated men to confound the wise. At once I liked this shepherd-bishop who spoke simply and plainly and from the heart.

"What is your opinion of the Arian affair?" his Piety asked without delay.

"I am for you. All the way," Spyridon replied enthusiastically. "It doesn't take great learning to see that Arius is in heresy. I am afraid that he is deceiving some men of great learning. I hear that Eusebius of Nicomedia is already in Nicaea and stirring up trouble for you."

"We expected as much," his Piety nodded and smiled. "We have heard that groups of bishops have been entertaining Arius privately in their rooms and that he has been trying to persuade them to take his position."

"Theognis, the Bishop of Nicaea called on me," related Spyridon with evident displeasure, "and asked me to support Arius, I told him and Maris of Chalcedon, who was with him, just what I thought of Arius and his blasphemous 'Thalia.' I was surprised to learn from them that Eusebius Pamphilius of Caesarea, who will give the opening address at the Council, is a supporter of Arius. It is unbelievable that a man with his learning could be deceived by this heresy."

I noticed that Spyridon did in fact look like a shepherd. He had the rugged complexion of a man who had spent much time exposed to the elements. As we sat there and talked, I recalled his reputation as a miracle worker and a healer. His own health was certainly robust and radiant.

"Have you talked to many other bishops?" his Piety asked with interest, peering intently at the Bishop of Cyprus, as he sat perched rigidly on the hard bench beside the window.

"Yes, I saw Paul of Neo-Caesarea. Poor fellow! Licinius burnt the tendons in his wrists and scarred his hands with red-hot irons. I don't see how he is even able to offer up the Holy Sacrifice anymore. But, he is here, and backs Your Piety. You should see his hands! He says that now he bears the scars of Christ which he tells everyone is a very great grace. Macarius of Jerusalem is here also and is on our side."

For hours we continued discussing the Arian affair with Spyridon. I said "we," actually, His Piety did most of the talking, while I listened. After Spyridon left, I felt that I had been in the presence of a man who was a giant in the ways of God.

When the Council convened with three hundred and eighteen bishops present, it was a triumphant hour for the Church. How things had changed since the days of Diocletian and his persecutions! Having been invited to Nicaea by Constantine, he paid for our food and lodging. Since the imperial palace was the only place large enough to house such a vast assembly, we held the council there.

The hall of the imperial palace was lined with chairs that May 20, as we filed in and took our places. His Piety and I had very good seats near the throne that had been set up for Constantine on a dais at one end of the hall. The emperor announced that he intended to be present at the council and take part in the proceedings. It was truly strange to see the imperial throne of shimmering gold in the midst of a Church council. Excitement was in the very air as we waited for Caesar to arrive. For three hundred years Caesar had been the enemy of Christ. The Church was familiar with dealing with Caesars who persecuted her, but this new Caesar, Constantine Augustus, was something of an enigma. Constantine, or to give his full name, Flavius Valerius Constantinus was born in Naissus about fifty years before the council. A member of the same family from which Claudius sprang, he was a Flavian on his father's side, but he was very sensitive because his father never married his mother, Helena, a barmaid from Bythnia. Later when his father married Theodora, he put Constantine's mother, his legal concubine, aside. It was then she sought salvation and converted to the Catholic faith. Many said that she was instrumental in leading the emperor to Christ.

Having received a very meager education in the court of Nicomedia, where he had grown under the surveillance of Diocletian, Constantine was practically illiterate. His talents lay in military affairs and in his ability as an administrator and organizer. I held my breath when the moment came for Constantine to arrive. His robes were so splendid that Nero would have looked like a pauper beside him. A man in the prime of life—in his early fifties, I would say—he had a neck like a bull, which is a characteristic of the Flavians. On his head, which I would describe as majestic, he was wearing a thick blond wig in an attempt to hide the fact that he was practically bald. When the Emperor entered, all the clergy rose to their feet, as, with great dignity, Constantine made his way to the throne. Out of respect for the bishops, he waited to sit down until they invited him to do so. After observing a few moments of silence, he gave the signal for the council to convene. From my chair at the right hand of His Piety, I could get a close look at Constantine. His eyes reminded me of those of a lion, as he regally surveyed the council fathers.

Because of his great erudition, Eusebius Pamphilias, Bishop of Caesarea, was chosen to make the opening address. He was librarian for Pamphilius who was martyred in 310 and who had the largest Christian library in the world, having acquired the library of Origen that he had added to his own. Logically it would follow that Eusebius would be an Origenist. Why he decided to embrace the cause of Arius, I cannot comprehend.

Because of his fulsome praise of the emperor, there was no doubt that Eusebius Pamphilius was courting the favor of Constantine with his address. I have an idea that it was when Constantine heard this oration that he decided to hire Eusebius Pamphilius to write his biography that the Bishop of Caesarea was to write at a later date.

Obviously pleased with the praises of the opening speech, Constantine took the floor to address the bishops. He thanked them for giving him the privilege of being permitted to sit in on their council. Actually, he did not provide us with a choice in this matter. With grave and sincere words, he pleaded with them to be of one mind. I listened with great interest as Constantine said, "Of all evils the greatest is dissension in the Church of God." The emperor was evidently sincere as he spoke of the distress he experienced from the quarrel that was disrupting the unity of the Church. Vigorously he asked for a speedy return to harmony.

Since we did not know all the bishops by sight, we did not realize, at first, that the bishop who was seated directly across from us was our archenemy—Eusebius of Nicomedia. We found out who he was, during the morning recess, when we spied him with Arius in the corridor outside the Council hall.

Since he was not a bishop, Arius was not seated in the council, but rather waited outside the council hall until the recess, when he engaged Eusebius of Nicomedia in conversation. I could not hear their words, but there was much head shaking, nodding, and agreeing, and I felt—conniving.

When Constantine finished speaking, I noticed that Eusebius of Nicomedia was glaring at me. I realized that he had already learned who I was. I regarded him coldly. I think all his personal animosity for me dates from this council when we were seated face to face and fought on opposite sides.

As a final gesture, Constantine took all the formal complaints that were given to him, both by the Arians and by us, and ordered them burned before our sight. He said that he intended to approach the issues at hand with an open mind. I watched the carefully prepared defense that I had so painstakingly compiled, as it flickered and flamed in the metal brazier at the foot of Constantine's throne.

With an air of utter confidence, Eusebius was smirking at me. Many years older than I, he had great experience on which to draw and his theological training had been thorough. His face, his whole body, had an emaciated appearance and his skin was like wax. His eyes were deeply sunk into his head and his cheeks deeply hollowed, all of which made it possible for one to see the bony structure of his skull quite plainly. I turned my glance from him and observed our old friend Hosius of Cordova, as he was assuming the duty of presiding over the Council. Since Pope Silvester was unable to be present, Hosius was chosen as Council Moderator. Ordinarily the Archbishop of Alexandria would have been the logical bishop to preside over the council in the absence of his Holiness, but in view of His Piety's personal involvement in the Arian affair, Hosius was chosen. This came as no surprise to me, for I had suggested this to every bishop I had met since our arrival in Nicaea.

Hosius did not even need to call for silence. When the council fathers saw him standing before them, hands upraised, and with the great livid, purple scar from his eye to the tip of his ear, they grew silent out of the respect they felt for this great confessor of the faith. With enormous vitality, rare in an old man, Hosius began the task of getting the council underway. Three days were set aside for the discussion of the Arian question in committees. Once the committees were set up—one with His Piety at its head, one with Eusebius of Nicomedia, and also various others, we adjourned to begin the real work of the day.

Followed by Paphnutius and Potammon and the rest of our Egyptian bishops who came to Nicaea, his Piety and I made our way out into the corridor that led to the committee rooms. We noticed that Arius was waiting there for Eusebius of Nicomedia. When he spotted him coming from the Council Hall, he hurried to meet him. Together arm in arm they talked feverishly as they entered their committee room.

Lingering in the corridor outside our committee room, I could see who the bishops were that were going in with Arius. There were about twenty of them in all. As expected, our two Libyan bishops, whom we deposed, briskly entered Arius' meeting. The bishop of Nicaea I knew already to be an ardent Arian, for he had been also one of Lucian's pupils, as was Maris of Chalcedon, who was one of the first to enter the Arian committee chambers. About twelve others joined them, some of whom I did not expect to see in the Arian fold. I spotted Menophantus of Ephesus, Gregory of Berytus, Theodotus of Laodicea, Paulinus of Tyre, Aetius of Lydda, and some others I could not identify. I later learned they were Patrophilus of Scythopolis, Narcissus of Neronias and Athanasius of Anazarba.

As I stood at the door of our Committee room, I greeted our supporters as they filed in. Most of them I did not know. When about thirty had arrived, I took my place at his Piety's side. After a prayer to the Holy Spirit, Archbishop Alexander asked us to be seated at the long marble-top table that almost completely filled the room. His Piety then began to study the faces of the bishops who were seated around the table. He rubbed his baldhead with his hand. I knew this gesture to mean that he was puzzled. I realized that he did not know all the bishops who had joined us. Stroking his thin gray beard, he began to speak.

"I am sure that you all do not know each other, therefore let us begin by stating our names. I am Alexander of Alexandria."

I stated my name and Paphnutius, Potammon, and the rest of our Egyptian bishops, who were seated together, did likewise. Next to Hosius, who was at the end of the table directly opposite His Piety, a voice called out. "I am Macarius of Palestine." He was a rugged weather-beaten, old man. Next we heard, "Eustathius of Antioch." He had the look of a fighter. I was glad he had taken up our cause instead of that of the enemy. "Marcellus of Ancyra," the bishop at his right announced. Hellanicus of Tripolis and Asclepas of Gaza were the next two to introduce themselves. They bore a few scars on their bodies.

Once the introductions were completed and by prearrangement with His Piety, Hosius began making the first statement to the committee.

"Most of the bishops assembled in the council are not aware of the danger in which the Church has been placed by the Arian heresy. A large majority of our bishops have no great amount of theological training. Most of them are quite incapable of drafting precise theological statements concerning their belief. The Arians have only about seventeen on their side, but these seventeen are all well-trained theologians, who are determined to force their ideas on the whole Catholic Church. We have about thirty of us who realize the importance of defining our faith in the Holy Trinity in precise terms that allow no Arian interpretation. Until now the simple creed devised by the apostles has sufficed. No Christian, much less a priest or bishop, has ever questioned the divinity of our Lord. We must prepare a creed which defines His divinity in no uncertain terms so that future generations will be transmitted what has been handed down to us from the Apostles."

After giving the assembled bishops writing materials, Hosius requested that each one draft a creed that was more explicit than the Apostles Creed on the doctrine of the Trinity. We read each other's creeds, correcting and revising as we went along, so that when the three days of recess were over and the council reconvened, we had prepared a statement of belief that we felt exactly expressed the faith once delivered to the apostles.

During the three days of the committee meetings, Arius visited various groups of bishops and was questioned by them so that everyone was prepared for the debates that followed.

When the council reconvened, Eustathius of Antioch was the first to speak. Boldly he condemned Arianism as an unprecedented novelty. With his snowy, white hair and his long, flowing beard, he reminded me of one of the biblical patriarchs as he spoke.

"I am from Antioch where we were first called Christians—Antioch—the church of Paul and Barnabas and of Peter. I tell you never—never—has the divinity of Christ Jesus been questioned in Antioch! Christ is God—very God of very God, light of light, begotten not made!"

When Eustathius bowed and returned to his place, a tremendous roar of applause broke out in the council in response to his passionate statement of faith.

Next Hosius recognized Theognis, Bishop of Nicaea. He was short and fat and his voice cracked when he spoke. "I am a pupil of the great martyr Lucian—I am a fellow student of Arius. I ask you, honored bishops, how is it conceivable that any son could coexist with his father? It is not logical. Surely there was a time when Christ did not exist since he is a son. Surely there was a time when the Father was not a Father. That *is* logical. Christ is a creature—an instrument created as an intermediary between God and all else. God is transcendent. No one can know Him—not even Christ!"

To the Lucianist, there was no heart of love in God—there were no Everlasting Arms. To the Lucianist, there was no incarnation, no assurance that we are redeemed with all our sins forgiven. Before the Bishop of Nicaea finished speaking, the council fathers began to stamp their feet in protest.

Macarius of Palestine rose and asked leave to speak. "I have a question to put to the Bishop of Nicaea. "Do you worship Christ?" He glared across the hall at the Bishop of Nicaea.

"Of course, if we did not worship him, we would not be Christians."

"If you worship the Christ you believe in, you are not Christian. You say that Christ is a creature—and yet you worship him? Only pagans worship creatures. You are a pagan, Theognis!"

Macarius was shouting now. Violently he shook his fist at Theognis and yelled so that his voice rang through the council hall. "You are a pagan!"

I noticed that Eusebius of Nicomedia was showing signs of agitation. Losing his customary calmness, he began pounding his fist on the table before him, and then, jumping to his feet and without asking Hosius to recognize him, began addressing the council. Many of the fathers began stamping their feet in protest of his Arian doctrines. With difficulty Eusebius tried to talk over the noise. Hosius called for silence, but to no avail. The protest of the council fathers became deafening, when Eusebius told them that God had created

Christ out of nothing for our sakes and that Christ only participates in the nature of God as a creature.

"No! No!" resounded from all sides of the council hall. One of the bishops even reached over and snatched from Eusebius' hands the document he was reading to them and tore it to shreds while the council fathers cheered him on.

Like chameleons the Arians began to change color. They were beaten. One by one they began to say that they accepted our teaching. At the same time they signaled to one another, signifying that they accepted what we said, but with an Arian interpretation.

At this moment, His Piety told me that the hour had come when I must address the council and give the death thrust to Arianism. Prayerfully, I rose to my feet and, sustained by the prayers of my holy Father Anthony and six thousand monks, I took a deep breath and, inclining first to Constantine and then to the council fathers, I launched into the most important sermon I ever preached. Many of the bishops were surprised to see a young deacon with a hooked nose and a red beard take the floor for the see of Alexandria. God often uses the simple to confound the wise.

"Jesus…Jesus in the language of the Jews means Savior. Is the Christ of Arius a Savior? Can a man, albeit a prophet or a holy man, save you and me from our sins? You know the answer to that. If Christ is not Light of Light, True God of True God, begotten of the Father before all ages—you are dead in your sins. If Christ is not the image of the Father—the very radiance of his Light, then there is no salvation—then there is no name under heaven whereby we can be saved. In the theology of Arius, we see a man, Christ, who by his own efforts became a god. Bishops of the Church of the Living God, I ask you to consider. Here is the old paganism served up in a new guise. The Arians worship a Christ who is not true God. They worship a creature! They have turned Christianity into a new paganism. I grant you that such a concept of Christ would appeal to the pagan world in which we live. A pagan could easily be converted to a religion in which a man becomes a god, for they have worshiped creatures since time began. The Catholic Church does not give *latria* to creatures. We worship only the living God who became man!"

Loud cheering from the bishops made it impossible for me to continue for about five minutes. When they became silent again, I proceeded.

"If Jesus is not begotten of the Heavenly Father and of the same substance as the Father, there is no redemption. The entire economy of redemption that plays such an important part in the theology of Blessed Paul the Apostle is based on the fact that God became man. In the words of the Apostle John, 'the word became flesh and remained with us and we saw his glory, the glory of the only begotten of the father, full of grace and truth.' It is plain that those who support Arius have never beheld his glory. They do not know Christ! They have not experienced the joy of his salvation! They cannot bear witness to Christ crying out 'Blessed is the lord God of Israel for he has visited and retrieved his people and he has established a tremendous redemption for us in the house of his servant David.'

"Let us condemn the Arian doctrine, but let us have compassion on those who have erred. It is possible to be a follower of Jesus and not to know personally the joy of his salvation. Saint Peter betrayed Him. The words of Peter might easily be put in the mouths of Arius and his followers who deny the divinity of Christ. 'I don't know the man,' Peter said. I think Peter would have been more correct if he had said, 'I know not the God.' Saint Peter knew Christ as a man and denied him. After the crucifixion effected our redemption, Peter experienced the salvation of Jesus and then knew him no more as a man but as God. Then it became impossible for Peter ever to deny him again.

"Council fathers, do you know the Savior? To a soul that knows the everlasting arms of the Savior and the mercy of his Heart there can be but one response to the dastardly teaching of Arius and his followers. Anathema!"

"Anathema! Anathema!" the council fathers began to yell. "Let them be anathema!"

The ovation that followed my address lasted a full fifteen minutes. Then, calling for order, Hosius presented the creed we had drafted leaving out the key word "consubstantial" so that Constantine might have the privilege of inserting it himself. With great consternation written on his face, Eusebius listened as Constantine suggested that we incorporate in the creed the phrase that Christ is consubstantial with the Father.

Forgetting himself, Eusebius jumped to his feet and challenged the Emperor. "It is unscriptural! Nowhere in the scriptures is the word consubstantial. Let it be changed to read that Christ is of like or similar substance, but not of the same substance."

With this remark, Eusebius only managed to bring the wrath of Constantine down upon his head, as the emperor's face grew red with confusion and anger. Even though Eusebius submitted and signed the creed with the phrase that Christ is consubstantial to the Father, Constantine insisted that he vacate his bishopric at Nicomedia. With the exception of the deposed Libyan bishops who were sent into exile, every bishop at the council signed this creed. Arius and his followers were excommunicated and Arius was prohibited from entering Alexandria. Theognis of Nicaea was also removed from his see.

Before the council adjourned we took up two other issues. We decided that in regard to the time of celebrating the feast of the resurrection, our Alexandrine see was to be entrusted with the duty of announcing the correct date to the principal churches throughout the world, so that all would keep the feast at the same time. We also settled the Meletian affair. Perhaps you will recall that Bishop Peter deposed Meletius as a bishop, because Meletius sacrificed to idols during the persecution. Instead of trying to reinstate himself with the Church, he ordained his own clergy and continued in schism. At this time, we restored him to unity with the Catholic Church. Later on the followers of Meletius were to turn on me, join ranks with my enemies and cause me untold anxiety.

I might add that Eusebius did not sign the deposition of Arius. He did, however, put his name to the condemnation of his opinions and of his "Thalia." I knew that I had not heard the last of Eusebius of Nicomedia!

Constantine was jubilant with the success of the council and the unity that was achieved in the Church of God and in the empire. To celebrate our oneness and the twentieth anniversary of his ascension to the throne, he invited us to an extravagant and opulent banquet in the Imperial Hall, before we all returned to our churches. Brimming over with emotion and with Chios wine, Constantine insisted that he was a bishop outside the Church just as we are bishops inside the Church. This statement caused me to shudder—the very implications of it!

Confident that all divisions of heresy, schism, and dissension had been healed, Constantine loaded us all down with presents and sent us home. In my soul, I knew that Eusebius of Nicomedia was not to be defeated so easily. A short time later, he turned the fullness of his fury on me. He had only just begun to fight!

The first of the month of Mesori, found us back in Alexandria. Potammon was still blushing every time someone mentioned that Constantine had kissed his empty eye socket in a moment of religious enthusiasm. Almost for the first time since I could remember, our Egyptian Church was at peace. Meletius brought a list of his clergy to His Piety and promised that he would ordain no more. It seemed that we had nothing more to fear from Arius and his followers, but that was far from true. Very far from true indeed.

About six months or a year after Nicaea, I first met Mark. He stopped at the archiepiscopal residence one afternoon on routine business. He was just twenty and had been recently ordained a deacon. I liked him at once. Having just returned from a trip with his family to Rome, he was bursting with enthusiasm for the Eternal

City, where he prayed at the tombs of the apostles and visited the Circus Maximus, where so many were martyred for their faith in Christ. When he spoke of the holy martyrs, his eyes shone with emotion and then they darkened again when he spoke of Constantine.

"You know, of course, about Constantine?" He folded his hands in his lap as he sat opposite me in the study I call my office.

"I got a good look at him at Nicaea. He appeared to be devout for an unbaptized person." I had no intention of saying more.

"Then you don't know—"

"Know what?" My curiosity was aroused,

"He murdered his son."

I said nothing, but waited for the details.

"Everyone liked Crispus. In Rome they loved the dashing young Caesar. Well, when Constantine came to Rome a short time back, he was not very well received. Without warning and without apparently any reason, he seized Crispus, threw him into prison in the fortress at Pola. Almost immediately, he had Crispus killed."

Mark waited for me to register surprise. I did not give him that satisfaction. Instead I said, "Constantine told us at Nicaea that he thought of himself as a bishop outside the Church."

Mark ran his hand through his thick black hair and continued as if he had not heard me. "Then Constantine ordered his sister Constantia's son, Licinianus, killed also. How that woman continues to get along with Constantine now since he has killed both her husband and her son is more that anyone can understand."

"They say his mother is a Christian? What effect did all this have on her?" I glanced out the window and studied the clouds on the horizon over the sea, and sighed inwardly that Constantine was on our side and not that of our enemies. Of course, I knew that he was capable of changing sides at any moment like a chameleon changes colors when it moves from the sand to the grass.

"His mother, Helena, came rushing to Rome. She screamed at Constantine so loud that they say they could hear her on all seven hills of the city of Rome." Mark's honest brown eyes sought out mine.

"What good did it do—his mother preaching at him?" I wondered just what kind of man Constantine really was.

"None! Absolutely none! The next thing he did was to murder his wife! Poor Fausta! The soldiers thrust their swords into her one day when she was stepping into her hot bath. They held her under the steaming waters until they were blood red."

"God have mercy on his soul!" I could no longer conceal my horror. Has the man no conscience?"

"Perhaps he has. He took all Fausta's money and turned it over to his mother. She is using it to make a pilgrimage to the Holy Land where she hopes to excavate and discover the tomb of Christ. You know that when the city of Aelia was built over the ruins of the Jewish Jerusalem that the pagans built a temple to Venus Aphrodite over the sight of the crucifixion?"

The thought of a temple to sensual love built over the tomb of our Savior was abhorrent and nefarious. "Helena plans to destroy the temple of Aphrodite?" I knew that the priestesses of Aphrodite were nothing but prostitutes.

"Yes, and she plans to build a fitting Christian church on Calvary that will also include the Holy Sepulcher. Since the pagans marked the sight of Calvary with that temple, she should have no trouble finding it. She took with her the finest archaeologists of the empire. Already the excavations are well under way."

This *was* news, exciting news to contemplate what she might discover. "Perhaps she will even discover the cross and nails!"

"Exactly. That is what everyone in Rome is praying for. But I heard something before I left Rome that does not sound too good. I heard that Constantia is pleading with Constantine to give Eusebius back to her at Nicomedia. Reproaching him for taking away her husband and her son, she is begging for him to restore her spiritual father to her."

Mark was studying my face as he spoke to determine the effect his words were having upon me.

"That could mean trouble." I spoke almost in a whisper.

It did mean trouble, plenty of trouble, but we were still to enjoy a period of calm before the storm broke with cyclonic winds. I spent as much time as I could in those days in the great library of Alexandria. It is almost in the shadow of Cleopatra's needles situated as it is between the pagan temples of Poseidon and Serapis. One day, when after spending the entire afternoon in the library pouring over some ancient papyri, I returned home to the archiepiscopal residence where I was immediately alarmed, for I observed that His Piety's physician was in the house.

Dropping my reading material on the table by the door, I bounded to the bedroom of my archbishop. The physician was bending over His Piety and chafing his wrists. I noticed that his fingertips were bluish and his face, as it lay against the white pillow, was ashen. He had suffered some kind of attack, the physician informed me. After he gave him a stimulant, His Piety rallied slightly, but under no circumstances was he to leave his bed.

I knew he was failing ever since I wrote his Easter letter for him, but I was struck dumb by the realization that he might die at any moment. Dropping down on my knees at the side of his bed, I took one of his hands in mine. How cold his hand was! It was as if death were draining him of the warmth of life. Inch by inch the coldness of the tomb was already beginning to make itself felt. When I kissed his fingers, he opened his eyes. At first, I was afraid that perhaps he did not recognize me. He stared at me a moment, as if through a fog and then smiled faintly.

"Athanasius—my son..."

"Yes, Your Piety—I am here." My voice quivered.

"Feed my sheep."

Having murmured these words, he fell into a state of unconsciousness. During the night, which I spent at his side, he would awaken, from time to time, and ask me a question about the churches of Alexandria or else murmur again, "Feed my sheep." When I reassured him that all was well with the churches, he drifted off again.

Seeming a bit stronger the next morning, he took a little lamb broth and then began to talk about God.

"I am going home, my son…in a few days…but, my son, do not be sad. I long to dissolve and be with Christ." He smiled joyously at me. "I have only one wish—I want to see my suffragan bishops before I depart this life." He made an effort to sit up. Gently I had him lie back on his pillows.

"The physician says you are to have no visitors."

Shooting me a glance filled with fire, he retorted with some of his old vitality. "As long as I live—as long as I have breath—I will give the orders around here!"

"Yes, Piety." I couldn't help but admire him. "I will summon the bishops at once."

Word spread fast that His Piety Alexander, Archbishop of Egypt and all the Libyas lay dying. Almost immediately, the bishops began to arrive to make their way through the silent house to the curtained room where the second-ranking bishop of Christendom lay waiting for his departure from this life and entry into the next. One by one, they tiptoed over to his bed and dropped to their knees.

My heart was torn with grief when Potammon came and dragged himself over to the bed and with great effort managed to kneel reverently. When he picked up His Piety's hands and kissed them, His Piety tried to smile and then slowly lifted his hand and with his fingers he gently caressed the empty eye socket of Potammon and whispered to him, "Pray for me, old fellow."

Potammon nodded sadly. Then His Piety whispered something to him that I could not hear.

Gravely one by one, the bishops all filed past, knelt, and kissed his hands. He had a word of blessing for each of them. I noticed that he was also whispering something to each. I drew closer to hear what it was. My heart turned to stone when I learned what he had told all the suffragan bishops: "Athanasius is my successor." This time he said it plainly with the knowledge that I was in earshot. My eyes met his for a second. I shook my head and turned to run from the room.

"Athanasius!" he cried with all the strength that remained him. You think you can escape—but you cannot!"

I had to get away—as far away as I possibly could. The thought of assuming the duties of the See of Alexandria was overpowering. Taking the first boat I could get, I made my way up the Nile. I needed to take council with my Father Anthony.

So engrossed was I in my thoughts that I did not notice the beauty of the river, nor of the fertile fields that lined it, nor did I pay attention to the fellow occupants of the boat. Hastily I went ashore, almost forgetting to pay my passage. I rented the first camel I came upon and did not stop until I knelt at the feet of the holy monk.

"I have been expecting you," he said severely with a frown. "Why are you running away?" He motioned me to sit down on the well-worn rock that served as his chair. I obeyed. He proceeded to seat himself on the floor at my feet.

"I am too young!" I blurted out.

"You think you know better about these things than God? Do you think you can improve on His Providence?" His words carried a sting that did not fail to reach me. I shook my head and buried my face in my hands. "I am not good enough! I am not worthy! I am not capable of being an archbishop! I'm weak and feeble—I'm not good enough."

"Silence! Listen—all of that is false humility. All these self-accusations of your unworthiness are—I tell you—nothing but false humility."

Drawing my hands down from my face, and without batting an eyelash, he peered into my soul. I bowed my head and asked almost in a whisper, "Father, tell me, what is true humility?"

His clear blue eyes smiled at me. "True humility consists in becoming like a little child. Our Lord has told us that unless we become as little children we shall not enter into the kingdom of heaven. When you become as a little child, Athanasius, you turn with complete confidence to God, trusting him to provide for all your needs the way a little child looks to his father to supply all his wants. Perfectly humility consists in firmly believing that you can do all things through Christ who gives you the strength. Saint Paul found this to be true. Not only is humility perfect when we can truly affirm that we can do all things through Christ, but our faith is also perfect—because we hereby affirm our perfect trust in God to supply all our needs according to his riches in glory."

I gazed at him in wonderment. Smiling a broad happy smile at me, he continued speaking.

"The belief that you can do all things through Christ also shows that your hope is perfect. And, my son, the more we hope for, the more God gives us. If you can say with Saint Paul 'I can do all things through Christ,' I will know also that your love is perfect, for when we love heroically we want to do heroic things. God will make you a saint, Athanasius, if you only say yes to him. I told you when you were a child that you would be a bishop—now I tell you, my son—that you will also be a saint!"

I was speechless. As if I were already a bishop, my Father Anthony took my hands in his and knelt at my feet.

"You must hurry, Your Piety, they need you in Alexandria." He almost pushed me out the door of his cell.

When I returned to Alexandria there was a large crowd of bishops, priests, and deacons milling through the archiepiscopal residence. As I entered the courtyard, Potammon spotted me and hobbled towards me and addressed me reverently.

"Your Piety, you have been chosen to succeed Alexander."

I bowed my head in submission to the will of God.

"We have arranged for your consecration to take place as soon as you are ready."

"Whatever you wish, whatever God wishes, "I told him simply. "You make the arrangements." Taking my hand, he clasped it warmly. Turning and walking solemnly into the archiepiscopal residence, I dismissed the crowd politely but firmly.

The next morning we buried Alexander. To take my mind off the burden of the episcopacy, which I was soon to assume, I occupied myself with the pyramid of correspondence that had accumulated during the past few days.

His Piety died on April 17. On June 6, I was made a bishop of the Church of God. How alone I felt that night after the ceremonies were over and all the people were gone and I was left alone in the house where I had lived as Alexander's secretary those many years. I missed His Piety. I missed his cheerful, "Good Night," as he blew out the lamp in his study and made his way to his room passing my door. No one, I discovered, is more alone that a bishop in his study. The skin on my hands was sore from having been kissed by so many of the people of God.

I decided that night that I would ask Mark, the young deacon who had told me of his visit to Rome with so much enthusiasm, to be my personal secretary. He would come and share the large empty house with me. I became a priest and a bishop all in one day. The burden of the office of a bishop was tremendous, but I found more than sufficient compensation in now being able to go to the altar of God and offer the Holy Sacrifice. The Body and Blood of Christ sustained me—lifted me up and gave me joy.

Not long after my elevation to the fullness of the priesthood, the first forebodings of trouble surfaced. My secretary informed me that Eusebius and Theognis had both sent letters to Constantine recanting their heresy. As a result they were reinstated in their sees. With Eusebius back at Nicomedia almost anything could happen!

I suppose the first thing every bishop wishes to do after his consecration is to make a visitation of all the churches in his cure. I began to make my visitations in the autumn of 329. My secretary, Mark and two priests, Alphis and Macarius, accompanied me on the journey South, which was to carry us as far as the Ethiopian border. We stopped in the Thebais to see Father Anthony and his growing colony of monks. Although the old hermit was almost eighty, he still brimmed with vitality. Coming out to meet me as we drew near, he knelt before me with the simplicity of a child and begged my blessing. We stayed only briefly at Pispir for we had many parishes to visit and also, as I learned from the holy hermit, a new colony of monks which had sprung up at Tabenne on the Nile in Upper Thebais.

Realizing the great value to a bishop that holy monks at prayer are, I went at once to Tabenne, where I was delighted to find eight separate monasteries flourishing. As we drew nearer the foundations there, a great multitude of monks, having learned that we were coming to visit them, came out to meet us. They took us to their spiritual father Pachomius, who was responsible for more that eight thousand monks. I had no difficulty in believing that Pachomius had been a soldier in Constantine's army, for he had regimented his followers into monasteries where they lived a communal life as opposed to the hermitic life that Anthony lived. They lived a regular life of prayer alternating with work, for ingeniously Pachomius had hit upon the idea of writing a rule for them to live by. The rule was moderate in order that it would be easily kept by anyone who wished to give himself to a life of prayer. Strong spirits, however, were encouraged to adopt greater austerities. When Pachomius told me that for fifteen years he had never lain down to sleep, but rather spent all his nights leaning against a wall or half seated on a stone bench, I reprimanded him. I feel that monks should exercise discretion and a holy moderation in their penances. I discovered that part of my duty, as a bishop, would be to incline the monks to prudence in regards to their mortifications. Before I left Tabenne, I ordained Pachomius to the priesthood thus making his community self-sustaining.

One of the main purposes of our visitations was to strengthen the ties between the Meletians and the See of Alexandria. Most of the Meletians gave us a hearty reception. Now that they had returned from schism and heresy, Meletius, having lived up to the Nicene agreement, was residing without followers at Lycopis and had ordained no more schismatic priests. Although he was allowed to retain the title of bishop, he was denied all the prerogatives that went with the title.

We stopped at the Mareotis on our return journey to Alexandria. The Meletians had never been able to penetrate the parishes around the Mareotic Lake. Therefore we were perturbed when the priest of the township told us that in the tiny village of Irene, a certain Ischyras, who was not one of our priests, was conducting church services in his village. Furthermore I knew his name was not on the list of the Meletians that had been submitted to His Piety when he reinstated them to communion with the Catholic Church.

I sent Macarius and Alpis to the hamlet of Irene to rout out this Ischyras who made himself a priest. After giving them orders to bring him to me, Mark and I continued on our way to Alexandria.

A few days later Macarius came to the archiepiscopal residence to report. Ischyras was not with him.

"Well, where is the man Ischyras?

Macarius bowed, shrugged his shoulders.

"The man is sick."

"A likely story."

"He could not leave his bed. When we arrived, he was in bed behind the door. His father would not let us talk to him."

Macarius turned his head so that the sun streaming in the window would not be in his eyes. Impatiently I pressed him. "Did Ischyras get my message that he desist from holding services of Christian worship for the faithful of Irene?"

"Yes, Your Piety. Actually, however, the church of Ischyras was only a cottage in which an orphaned child was living. No one would attend his services anyway except his seven relatives." Macarius dismissed the entire episode as if it were not worth considering.

"Nevertheless, I will have no self-ordained priests in this see." Folding my hands on the desk in front of me, I pursued the matter. "You warned him?"

"I spoke to his father. His father is a good Catholic and has promised to straighten him out." Macarius was about my age although he already had a few gray hairs.

"You will kindly keep watch over the situation and report to me at once—at once, if anything further develops."

My orders were clear. Little did I imagine that Eusebius would find a way of turning this episode into a trap for me. Soon I would find myself caught like a beetle in a chameleon's mouth.

Eusebius wasted no time once he returned to Nicomedia and to the favor of the imperial family. Together with Theognis, he began plotting to overthrow the decisions of the Council of Nicaea and seize control of the entire Catholic Church!

Eustathius was the first to feel the bitter revenge of Eusebius. Soon all the bishops who had fought for the Catholic faith at Nicaea would begin to feel the enmity of Eusebius. The other Eusebius—Eusebius Pamphilus took the lead in a dispute with Eustathius. He did not scruple to accuse Eustathius of the heresy of the Sabellians, who believe that the Father and the Son are one person. As if by prearrangement, the rest of the Arian bishops called Eustathius to account for his views before a synod in Antioch. Once they got him there, they promptly accused him of immorality and heresy and deposed him! They charged that saintly man, who reminded me of a biblical patriarch, with the crime of defiling the priesthood by unholy actions We knew it was not true. The Arians are lawless men—enemies of Christ who will stop at nothing to further their own interests. Before Emperor Constantine, they charged Eustathius with insulting Helena, his mother. Since he was openly known to be very sensitive about his origins, this hit Constantine in a very sore spot. Naturally Constantine supported the deposition of Eustathius. When Eustathius was out of the way, they gave his bishopric to one of their fellow Arians. In this manner, the See of Antioch fell into the grasp of the Arians.

Such was the state of affairs when Macarius returned again to my study with further news for me. He was very nervous, I noticed, as he entered my presence and sauntered briskly across the stone floor and stood before me bursting to speak. I urged him to be out with it.

"Yes, Your Reverence?"

"I am afraid I have bad news for, Your Piety." He cleared his throat and tugged at his tunic, and looked quite morose. "Meletius has died."

"God grant him perpetual refreshment and light. All of us must go in time." I couldn't understand why Macarius had burst into my study to tell me this.

Violently he shook his head. "There is more to it than that. Before he died he violated the Nicene agreement and ordained John Arcaph to take his place as head of the Meletians."

"Not a revival of the Meletian schism!" My predecessor in the See of Alexandria had been greatly harassed by the Meletians.

"Worse," he cried wringing his hands. "They have been negotiating with the Arians—you know the original supporters of Arius here in Egypt."

That was bad news. Now that he had informed me of the worst, Macarius seemed relieved. Becoming calmer, he crossed to the chair at the window. Waiting for me to be seated first, he took the chair at my left.

"I suppose Eusebius of Nicomedia had a hand in all this?"

"There are rumors that he made the Meletians exaggerated promises if they will back him."

Begging me to excuse the intrusion, Mark, my secretary entered the room abruptly. A messenger, he told me cryptically, had arrived and refused to deliver his message to anyone except the archbishop personally.

"Show him in."

The "messenger" who entered my study was none other than Arius! Brazenly and with a smirk, he strode briskly towards me. The Council of Nicaea excommunicated him and forbade him to return to Alexandria, yet here he was, the same defiant man he had always been. He had not changed one bit. Defiantly, Arius disregarded the decision of over three hundred bishops and returned to Egypt and even had the impudence to gain entrance to my presence!

"Cast the wicked man from your midst," the Blessed Paul wrote. I intended to follow his advice. With mock humility, Arius bowed before me. I refused to extend my hand to him. With a face of stone—like the great sphinx–and without speaking a word, I eyed him coldly as he handed me a letter and stood with downcast eyes, as I took it. At once I recognized the seal of the Bishop of Nicomedia. To be certain that I understood the message clearly, I read it twice.

Eusebius wrote that Constantine and the bishop of Nicomedia had recalled Arius from his exile and "requested" that I restore Arius at once to communion with the Catholic Church. As I finished the letter and laid it on the windowsill, Arius arrogantly seated himself in a chair without having been invited to do so. I did not hesitate to tell him just what I thought.

You have been excommunicated and deposed by an ecumenical council of the Catholic Church. Constantine has no authority to revoke that sentence. As far as the Church is concerned you are an unrepentant heretic and cast from her midst." I paused, surveyed him coldly and said, "I must ask you to leave this residence immediately." Rising to my feet, I pointed to the door. Arius made no move to leave.

"I think not. I don't plan to go anywhere—but there is a distinct possibility that you might be going somewhere." He was threatening me. With a calculated look, he regarded me coldly and then made his demands.

"I want my parish in the Baucalis returned to me." His eyes were like knife points.

"You will leave this residence at once!" Taking a step towards him, I commanded him to leave with great force.

"I have a message for Your—," he hesitated a moment and then said distastefully "Piety. Eusebius of Nicomedia says that either you restore me to my parish immediately or he will have you removed as the Archbishop of Alexandria, Egypt, and all the Lybias!"

His face turning red, Arius clenched his fists, trembling in an uncontrollable burst of passion.

Calmly I walked to the door and called to my secretary. "Would you please show our messenger out? He is really quite finished."

Arius jumped to his feet and raged towards the door, shouting over his shoulder at me. "We shall see who is finished in Alexandria!"

I looked over at Macarius who had been observing the entire proceedings. "We are in for trouble," I remarked as I filed away the letter for future reference.

"What can they do? They have no jurisdiction over Alexandria," remarked Macarius naïvely.

"Constantine is not aware of Canon law on this point! They have succeeded in deposing Eustathius and also Eutropius of Adrianople. They got one of the women of the royal family–Basilina–to help them take Eutropius' church from him and drive him from his city, and replace him with an Arian."

"Surely not the Bishop of Adrianople. He was a good man."

"His only crime was that he opposed Eusebius."

"But Your Piety, no one can depose you. The entire Church of Egypt is loyal to you." Color rose to Macarius' cheeks.

"Except the Meletians and the Arians." I smiled. "We shall watch and pray."

"You can rely on me. Come what may!"

I bided my time waiting for Eusebius to attack. He had threatened me. I knew that he meant to do everything that lay in his power to destroy me. One dark, rainy morning, he struck his first blow. Two officers of the palace arrived at the archiepiscopal residence with a letter from Constantine. I read the letter twice to be certain that I had understood it correctly. The emperor threatened to send someone to depose me and remove me from my see if I excluded anyone from communion with the Church!

Although I knew that he murdered his son, his nephew and his wife, I was not afraid of him. Following the inspirations of God, I wrote him, telling him that the Catholic Church holds no communion with the enemies of Christ. In no uncertain terms, I further informed him that I could not admit the detestable Arian heresy into the bosom of the Church. Immediately, I dispatched Alypius and Macarius with this letter to Constantine at Nicomedia.

Committing the entire matter to God, I waited. A second letter came from the emperor. The plot against me was starting to take form. Constantine told me that Ision, Eudaemon, and Callinicus—all clergy of my archbishopric—accused me of imposing a tax on linen ecclesiastical vestments. The letter demanded that I sail at once to Nicomedia where I would be required to answer to this and other charges that had been made against me.

I knew who Ision, Eudaemon, and Callinicus were. Ision of Heliopolis and the other two who were from Pharbetus were all Meletians. John Arcaph and Eusebius of Nicomedia were making a desperate effort to have me driven from my church and office.

Catching the first ship that sailed for Constantinople, Mark and I left Egypt once again. With fair skies, we skipped across the open sea, glided into the torturous Bosphorus, made our way through the Sea of Marmora and docked at the Golden Horn. Although I did not linger to see the sights in Constantine's New Rome, I observed the magnificent church Sancta Sophia which was still under construction, as I hurried by en route to Psammathia in the suburbs of Nicomedia where the imperial palace was located. Before I did anything else, I sought out Macarius and Alypius who confirmed my worst suspicions. Constantine blamed me for all the troubles that were plaguing the Church, having become convinced, that if he deposed me, he would have the peace he so greatly desired.

Armed only with prayer and with confidence in God, I presented myself at the gates of the imperial palace. One of the guards took me to a room that was small, cramped, and had only one tiny window, up so high, that when night came I suffered for want of ventilation. I was ordered to remain in that room until I was sent for. The only piece of furniture was a bed—a very lumpy, uncomfortable one at that. Kneeling on the stone floor, I prayed most of the night. My thoughts turned frequently to Blessed Paul who had been tried before Nero—not to mention Festus, Agrippa, and all the rest. Recalling the words of our Lord when he told his disciples that they would face persecution, I treasured in my heart his promise that we are blessed when men persecute us and despitefully use us for his sake.

When a soldier brought me a tray of breakfast the next morning, I declined it. He then ushered me to the throne room where I found Eusebius of Nicomedia standing beside the Augustus. Making the customary obeisance before the emperor who was seated on his throne, elevated on a dais in the center of the room, I waited for Constantine to address me.

Dressed in heavy purple brocade, Eusebius was wearing a solid gold cross that was studded with diamonds on his breast. Toying with the cross, which I guessed to be a gift from the emperor, he sneered at me contemptuously. Because I am shorter than most men, Eusebius made the most of his height to look down at me. Smiling, he turned and whispered something in Constantine's ear. Casting a side glance at Eusebius and nodding, Constantine arranged his voluminous robes pompously and, pointing a finger at me, began to speak.

"Athanasius of Alexandria? Is that not correct?"

"I am Athanasius of Alexandria—Archbishop of all Egypt and the Libyas" I stared boldly and fearlessly into his wide-set eyes.

"What defense do you make against the charges leveled at you?" He presumed that I knew why I had been summoned.

"Truth is my only defense!" I hurled this remark into the face of Eusebius. Constantine shook his fist at me. "Why do you persist in harassing me with your troublesome quarrels?"

"I have not broken the peace that was made at Nicaea. I have strived to uphold the decrees that were adopted with the approval of Your Imperial Person." I was not to be browbeaten. Looking intently at Constantine, I saw him for than first time as a soul that needed to be saved, as a sinner confounded with his crimes, with the stain of murder on his, as yet, unbaptized soul. Since Nicaea, his evil deeds had changed him into a suspicious, broken, and nervous man. He had obviously lost weight.

"I am no theologian," he whined, "I only want peace. I must have peace. Why did you put a tax on linen vestments?"

"My legates, Macarius and Alpis, have repeatedly assured you that no tax was levied. Whoever started that lie is the one you can condemn for disturbing your peace. As for me—I wish you the peace of Christ—the peace that passes all understanding."

I told him honestly with full knowledge that the only way he could find peace was by obtaining forgiveness of his sins. As his forehead furrowed with wrinkles, he considered what I said for a few moments and then began to relax, until Eusebius whispered something into his ear that made him grow rigid and suspicious again. The muscles of his face grew taut. He screamed at me. "You conspired against me! You are an enemy of the state!"

I begged the Holy Spirit for help. I knew that Constantine's suspicions had killed those dearest to him. Before I could answer, he rose to his feet and in a rage yelled at me. "You conspired against me. You sent a purse of gold to my enemy Philumenus!"

Obviously enjoying his revenge, Eusebius leered at me smugly and watched as I tried to squirm my way out of the situation into which he had thrown me.

"No!" I protested. "Truth is my defense. I know no Philumenus! I have not given a gold purse to anyone. Where are they who accuse me? Let them bring forth proof?"

Constantine motioned to two soldiers that were guarding the door. When they opened the door, in came Ision–one of the Meletians. I should have expected as much of them. Upon seeing me, the Meletian's face reddened. Demanding that Ision stand beside me before his throne, Constantine, began to question him. "You say you saw Athanasius give a purse of gold to my enemy?"

"Yes." This lie caused the Meletian to shift uncomfortably from one foot to the other.

"Where did this take place?"

"In the Mareotis"

"What was the name of the person who received the purse?" Constantine stamped both feet impatiently.

"Sozomenus."

I saw Eusebius wince at this answer from Ision, who was then led away. Eudaemon was next brought forth to stand beside me. I knew him well, for in my visitations I had spent the night in his house. As he sized up Eudaemon, Constantine's eyes flashed like those of a lion stalking its prey.

"You saw Athanasius give my enemy a purse at Heliopolis, did you not?"

"Correct, Your Exalted Worthiness—yes—it was at Heliopolis."

Eusebius was no longer smiling.

"Take him away," commanded Constantine.

After leading Eudaemon from the room, the soldiers returned with Callinicus of Pelusium, a man I knew and who was obviously very embarrassed at meeting me here face to face.

"You saw Athanasius give my enemy Sozomenus a purse of gold in Alexandria, did you not?" asked Constantine pouncing on his prey.

"Yes, I did," lied Callinicus.

Constantine nodded. After the soldiers took the witness away, Constantine addressed Eusebius.

"My dear bishop, someone must have given you a false story. In your innocence you were deceived—but I am not so easily fooled."

I was the one who was smiling now and Eusebius was chewing his tongue, as Constantine rose from his throne and walked down to me. Laying his hand on my shoulder, he said with great sincerity, "Most venerable bishop, you are a true man of God. Go! You are fully cleared."

I shot a glance at Eusebius, turned silently, and left the palace.

I was not to return to Alexandria right away. That very day I fell ill with an exceedingly grievous and protracted illness. When I finally became well enough to travel again, my secretary Mark informed me that the severe storms of winter had closed the seas to all shipping.

I sent my Easter letter that year from Nicomedia. Finally, with the lintels of my heart sealed with the blood of Christ, I arrived in Alexandria in the middle of Lent in 332. I was not to have much peace. Another blow was struck at me—a blow designed to be fatal and unfailing. Very soon Constantine sent for me again. This time the charges were far more serious. I was accused of smashing a chalice of a priest at the very altar of God. This was the first charge. It was a minor compared to the second charge. I was accused of murder! Murder! I was informed that I was to stand trial for the murder of a priest—a man by the name of Arsenius! My enemies were no longer satisfied with having me deposed they wanted me dead! They wanted to glut themselves on my blood!

I was summoned by Constantine to appear at a council at Caesarea! Caesarea! I was not about to go to Caesarea! That was the see of a known Arian–Eusebius Pamphilus. I wouldn't have escaped from Caesarea with an ounce of blood or dignity. I refused to go. Summoning my loyal staff, I sent them to gather all the evidence they could find, as I began to prepare my defense. I knew I couldn't stall Constantine for very long.

CHAPTER 3

❁

The emperor's mother Helena met with great success on her expedition to Palestine. After clearing the site of the Holy Sepulcher of the pagan temple that stood there, she tore up the paving and the mound of earth that hid the holy place for the past two and a half centuries. Helena then uncovered a tomb, three crosses of wood, and another separate piece of wood that bore the inscription in Hebrew, Greek and Latin, "Jesus of Nazareth King of the Jews." Not knowing which of the crosses was the cross of Christ, Macarius, the Bishop of Palestine, had all three crosses applied to people who were seriously ill. One cross was found to work miracles of healing.

With great joy, Helena sent Constantine the nails that pierced the sacred body of the Savior and a large relic of the cross. The remainder of the cross, she had enclosed in a silver casket that was destined to repose in the Jerusalem church, the Great Martyrium, that she was constructing on the site of Calvary and the Holy Sepulcher. Constantine took the relic of the cross his mother sent him and enclosed it in a statue of himself that now stands on a large column of porphyry in the forum of Constantinople. What he did with the holy nails—I hate to think of that! He took the nails of the crucifixion and had them made into a bridle bit for his horse and a war helmet for himself!

While all this was going on, my enemies were busy sowing their lies about me among the members of the Church of God in Egypt. It was common knowledge that I was charged with the murder of Arsenius. Furthermore, the story was told everywhere that I sent Macarius, one of our faithful priests, into the church of Ischyras, who was in reality not a priest, and at the altar, during the Sacrifice, desecrated his chalice and overturned the altar. We knew that his "church" was a mere cottage and that his congregation was composed of only seven of his own relatives. It is true that we sent Macarius to summon Ishcyras for an audience, but there was no violence committed. Another version that was circulating of the same story said that it was not Macarius, but I, myself, who had smashed the chalice and assaulted Ichyras, the self-appointed priest.

Dispatching Macarius to the hamlet of Irene. I gave him orders to bring Ischyras to me immediately. No matter how sick he might claim to be, he would not put me off again as Macarius was previously by his protestations of illness. I could easily prove that Ischyras was not a priest and put an end to the charges that I assaulted him. It would be more difficult to defend myself against the charge of murdering Arsenius.

Determined to get a signed statement from him clearing Macarius and me and to find out who propagated the lies about me, Macarius searched the Mareotis in vain. Ischyrus was nowhere to be found. Furthermore, no one had seen him or knew his whereabouts. However, everyone was repeating the dastardly lies about the smashed chalice and the overturned altar. Within a short time, the calumny spread throughout our entire church in Egypt, the Libyas, and Pentapolis.

The second charge that Constantine leveled against me was far more serious. It was difficult for me to believe that my enemies would stoop to accusing me of murder. I had not even see Arsenius, whom I was accused of killing, for five or six years. We heard a rumor that the said Arsenius was living with a community of

Meletian monks in the Thebais. If he was anywhere in my archdiocese, I was determined to ferret him out and end once and for all the abhorrent lie that I murdered him. I sent Mark to find Arsenius.

Having talked to some monks who confessed that Arsenius was indeed living with them, Mark returned quickly from the Thebais. I thereupon sent Mark back there with two other deacons with orders to bring Arsenius to me. Unfortunately, we were too late. Arsenius had been spirited up the Nile. There was no telling where he was. We did, however, manage to capture the pair who took him away—a priest named Pinnes and a monk by the name of Helias. When we brought these two men to the civil authorities at Alexandria, they both confessed that Arsenius was still alive.

I wrote the facts to Constantine. I was extremely thankful to receive a letter from him condemning the Meletians and commanding them to desist from further disturbing the peace, and threatening them with taking civil action against them.

I considered the matter to be quite closed. I could not have been more wrong. It turned out that the real instigators of the trouble were not the Meletians. Eusebius and Arius were in back of it all! Unwilling to drop the matter, Eusebius, began to whisper in Constantine's ear that perhaps I might be guilty after all, since we could not produce Arsenius. He insisted that perhaps it would be a good idea to investigate the matter fully.

To make matters worse, some of my enemies, were circulating a story that they had seen the withered hand of Arsenius that, they claimed, I cut from his murdered body and which I used for purposes of magic! They continually challenged me to produce Arsenius alive—which, of course, we could not do, for they had spirited him away.

Infuriated with all the contention that kept breaking out in Egypt, Constantine ordered me to appear before Count Dionsyius and a council of bishops that was to assemble at Tyre to investigate the charges made against me. The Emperor advised me that if I did not go willingly to Tyre, he would have me taken by force.

Although I knew the situation was critical, I did not realize just how volcanic it was, until soldiers seized Macarius, as he was leaving his church one morning, and placed him in chains.

I made plans to go to Tyre, setting sail July 11, 335 in company with a large number of our Egyptian clergy who wished to assist in my defense. I was honored that those highly respected men of God, Paphnutius and Potammon, freely volunteered to go with me to Tyre, since it would be possible for them to stop at Tyre en route to Jerusalem where they wanted to be present at the consecration of the Great Martyrium, the magnificent church Helena constructed on the site of the crucifixion to mark the thirteenth anniversary of Constantine's reign. The Emperor ordered a synod of bishops to be present at the consecration.

As soon as I arrived at Tyre, I saw at once that the Arians outnumbered us two to one. His Holiness Pope Silvester, the Roman Pontiff, had not even been invited to attend! We waited in Tyre until Count Dionysius summoned us to appear. Paphnutius was on my right and Potammon on my left as we entered the council. Behind us followed Mark and a mysterious figure that was cloaked from head to foot. Providence had been good to us. We had managed finally to catch up with Arsenius. For some unknown reason he decided to come to Tyre where one member of our party spotted him. Although he refused to admit his identity, a friend, Paul, Bishop of Tyre, identified him. We were now taking him incognito into the council. At a crucial time in the trial, I would produce Arsenius and confound my enemies right in the council court for all to see.

As I began to take my seat with my suffragan bishops, a soldier wearing full military regalia came over to me. Roughly, he grabbed my arm and addressed me sharply. "Come with me. You are to stand before the chair of the Count."

Because of his lack of respect for the clergy, I knew the man was not a Christian. He led me to a spot before the chair of Dionysius that was on an elevated dais above the assembled bishops who were still filing into the basilica. Following after me, Mark took a place beside me as my secretary, while I stood like a common criminal, waiting for the Count to arrive and begin my trial.

With his sword rattling at his side, the soldier walked away only to return with Macarius, whom I had not seen since he was arrested and taken prisoner in Alexandria. With chains on his wrists, Macarius greeted me bravely.

One by one the Arians were entering the courtroom. Maris of Chalcedon and Theognis of Nicaea walked passed me, pretending not to see me. Eusebius on the contrary spotted me, smiled at me ironically—a wry twisted smile—and, with a supercilious lift of his eyebrow, sauntered to a chair in the front row where he could observe and direct my trial.

Next to Eusebius, I saw a richly dressed young bishop. Although he had the face and mannerisms of an Egyptian, try as hard as I could, I couldn't recognize him. I knew all the bishops of Egypt and he was not one of them. John Arcaph was seated next to this young bishop, so I was certain that he had to be a new Meletian bishop. Arcaph was rubbing his hands together like a hungry man sitting down to a feast. Both he and the unknown bishop smiled obsequiously every time Eusebius of Nicomedia made some remark to them.

Tapping me on the arm with his manacled hands to get my attention, Macarius whispered in my ear the name of the unidentified young bishop. "The new bishop is Ischyras. They made him a bishop as a reward for his toils. I hear they are going to build a cathedral in his hamlet of Irene!"

I shook my head in disbelief. Ischyras was not even a validly ordained priest! Just then six soldiers threw open the doors of the platform permitting the Count of Tyre to enter and seat himself. The count, a man of about forty, virile and commanding in appearance, began the trial with military precision. Accompanied by a bodyguard of soldiers who surrounded him, Eusebius Pamphilus, the Bishop of Caesarea, took his place on the platform as the bishop chosen to preside for the Church. As if he needed protection from Paphnutius, Potammon, and me! Smoothing the few remaining strands of his once black hair over his baldhead, Eusebius Pamphilus, cleared his throat and began speaking.

"Honored bishops and other clergy, we are here to decide upon the guilt or innocence of Athanasius of Alexandria. He is charged with using physical violence against the clergy of Egypt and of carrying that violence to the point of committing the crime of murder in the case of Arsenius, a Meletian bishop."

Bitterly the bishop of Caesarea surveyed me as he made this remark. When he learned that I protested to Constantine that I would not get a fair trial if he were to preside at it, he became my personal enemy. Arrogantly he addressed the assembly, "I shall now select from our numbers able men to act as judges in this case."

Eusebius proceeded to select as judges my most bitter enemies—Theognis of Nicaea, Maris of Chalcedon, Macedonius, and Theodorus. The enormity of it! I was to be accused and judged by my enemies! "I object to the judges," I called up to the count. "They are my personal enemies."

I was resolutely determined to fight for right and justice. Frowning at me, the count shrugged his shoulders and refused to make any changes in the men selected. I was as good as deposed already.

The first witness against me was called to testify, John Arcaph, the head of the Meletians, who had been consecrated in schism in defiance of the Council of Nicaea by Meletius on his deathbed. With his shifty eyes avoiding mine, he took his place before the judges, squirming nervously as the count addressed him.

"Is this Athanasius whom you accuse of maltreating your clergy?"

"It is," answered the schismatic taking his cues from Eusebius of Nicomedia, who was leaning forward in his chair in the front row so as not to miss a word.

Eusebius Pamphilus took up the questioning. "What exactly did the accused do?"

John Arcaph avoided looking at me as he answered. "He has beaten my clergy…many of them." He shook his fist at me. "He murdered Bishop Arsenius!"

A roar of mumbled conversation broke out in the courtroom.

"You have evidence?" asked the count who I was sure was an Arian.

"That I have. I can prove it with this!"

Dramatically he drew a small black box from his pocket and waved it in the air before the judges. "Here is my proof! Wrenching the lid from the box, he exclaimed, "The hand of Arsenius that Athanasins cut from his dead body and used for nefarious magic!"

A gasp of horror went through the council. The evidence was passed among the judges and the council Fathers. When he viewed the black shriveled contents of the box, the Bishop of Caesarea winced dramatically for all to see. As the hand was carried past me, I caught a glimpse of it. Although it was withered and claw like, I could discern that it was really and truly a human hand and that it had been severed from a male body just above the wrist.

Indignation was written upon the faces of the council Fathers as they stared at me and pointing their fingers at the hand whispered among themselves. Eusebius of Nicomedia studied the hand carefully with a pained expression on his face.

I requested permission to speak. "It is a man's hand. Yes. But what proof is there that it is Arsenius' hand?" I would play the farce out to the bitter end. Very seriously, the Bishop of Caesarea nodded and asked, "Is there anyone here in the court who can identify the hand?"

Five—five Meletians came forward to testify that it was Arsenius hand. At this point some of the bishops who believed me innocent were beginning to suspect me—except, of course, those who knew that Arsenius was at that very moment seated securely in my roster of clergy between Paphnutius and Potammon right there in the courtroom.

It was time to call a halt to the proceedings. Smiling at Mark, I whispered, "Bring Arsenius forward now." To the count, I said, "I should like to call a witness on my behalf."

"Granted," he replied as Mark walked over to the Egyptian clergy and motioned for the mysterious figure to come before the court.

Most Worthy Count Dionysius, venerable bishops," I exclaimed with enthusiasm, "is there anyone here who knew Arsenius?"

A few admitted that they had known him, among them John Arcaph who was still in possession of the withered hand. I walked over to where he was standing.

"Now, John Arcaph" I said addressing him face to face. "I want you to identify someone."

I threw back the hood from Arsenius' face. Arcaph gasped as if he had seen a ghost. Utter silence was in the court as I continued my cat and mouse game.

"Is this Arsenius"

"It is," he mumbled.

"Very well. Let's see where his hand was cut off."

I flipped back the cloak and exposed his right hand and arm. A series of "ohs" and "ahs" broke from the council fathers. Dramatically I uncovered his other arm. Everyone plainly saw that Arsenius had two hands. John Arcaph was dreadfully agitated. I surveyed him and taunted.

"Did Arsenius have three hands? If so show me the place on his body where the third hand was cut off."

Pandemonium hit the Council as John Arcaph, in complete confusion, fled from the courtroom with no one trying to stop him. Dionsyius called for order.

"Silence!" he shouted banging on the desk in front of him. Eusebius of Nicomedia rose to his feet. All the Arians became quiet to hear what he would say. The duplicity of the man was incredible! How he could keep a straight face as he cunningly accused me of using magic to produce Arsenius!

"You have witnessed for yourselves proof of Athanasius' evil magic! By the powers of magic he has procured this vision of Arsenius!"

Count Dionysius, obviously disgusted, waved his hand silencing him. "Enough! Proceed with the next charge against the accused."

The Bishop of Caesarea then called Ischyras to stand before the Council.

"What is your name?"

"Ischyras of Irene Secontauri in the Mareotis, a country region just outside Alexandria."

"What is the charge you wish too make against the accused?"

"One day," began Ischyras proudly flourishing his newly acquired bishop's robes, "one day when I was celebrating the Holy Sacrifice, Macarius and Athanasius rushed into my church and assaulted me. They overturned my altar and smashed my chalice." Even though he lied, he looked me brazenly in the eyes. I took one step towards him and boldly began to expose him.

"You say you were a priest when Macarius visited your home in the Mareotis. Yet, I have no knowledge of your ordination. You were not ordained by the Catholic Church or by the schismatic Meletians whose bishop you now claim to be." I waited for those present to absorb what I had said, before turning from Ischyras to face the court. Loudly and confidently I proclaimed, "Ischyras is not a priest!

The Bishop of Nicomedia began to protest.

Sweat broke out on Ischyras' brow as he stammered, trying to exonerate himself.

"Colluthus—the one you call heretic ordained me."

"Colluthus is not and never has been a bishop. He has no power to ordain you or anyone else. Any ordination made by Colluthus is invalid. The man is no priest!"

Ischyras began to squirm, redden, and yelled in his distress, "You have beaten many priests. You stole the corn that was to be given away free to the poor. I *am* a priest and you desecrated my altar!"

Eusebius of Nicomedia jumped to his feet, waved his hands wildly until the count recognized him. Then he said, "Most Worthy Count, I humbly request that we adjourn until tomorrow morning."

"Granted!" The Count adjourned the council. The Arians needed time to patch up their plots.

When the council reconvened and as soon as all the bishops were seated and in order, a woman was ushered into the courtroom and brought directly before the chair of Dionysius. Since, she was standing quite close to me, I could observe her well. By her appearance—cheap makeup on her face, gaudy clothing, and bold posture, I guessed that the Arians had found her in some street of Tyre and had paid her to perjure herself in a last desperate effort to have me deposed.

"What complaint do you wish to make against the accused?" the count asked.

"I am a consecrated virgin of the church," the woman said emotionally. She sighed deeply, daubed at her eyes, and added, "At least I *was* a virgin until Athanasius violated me."

The council went wild. Dionysius called for order. Sobbing loudly, the woman frantically ran her hands through her long hennaed hair. At the top of her lungs, so that even the lay people gathered outside the closed doors of the council chamber could hear her, she accused me. "Athanasius raped me! He summoned me to his study one day and raped me!"

This was more than I had bargained for. I was at a loss for words. Before I could think of anything to answer to this new lie, Mark ran to the woman and standing with his face in hers menacingly said to her: "Do you mean to tell this court that I raped you?"

"Yes, you did, Athanasius! You are an evil and wicked man!"

Slowly I walked over to Mark and the woman.

"Madam, *I* am Athanasius. I want to know who paid you to tell that lie about me."

My eyes burned into hers. Her face turned crimson. She began to cry—this time in earnest. Before I had a chance to question her further, a soldier came and removed her from the room. That was the last I saw of her.

All their plots failed. Still determined to try fresh ones, they renewed the charge that I used violence on the Meletian priests, bringing in fresh witnesses. They also drummed up another charge. In their determination to depose me, they insisted that I was not validly consecrated a bishop, because I was ordained before the canonical age of thirty. When they saw that they were making no headway with that charge, Eusebius of Nicomedia hit upon a new scheme. He suggested that the council send a committee to the Mareotis to gather fresh evidence. Fresh evidence, indeed! They wanted to go to Egypt in my absence and fabricate a fresh plot.

The Bishop of Caesarea quickly agreed to what Eusebius of Nicomedia had proposed. "I believe the Bishop of Nicomedia has an excellent idea there," he announced. I ask that Theognis, Maris, Macedonius, Ursacius, and Valens go at once to Egypt and obtain the true facts in the case. Ischyras will also accompany them. Macarius will remain here with Athanasius in Tyre."

The injustice of it! The accuser was permitted to accompany the committee and the accused was denied that right. Paphnutius was outraged. Dragging his hamstrung leg slowly and painfully behind him as he made his way to my side, he asked the Bishop of Caesarea to recognize him that he might speak in my defense. Denied recognition, Paphnutins yelled at the Bishop of Caesarea furiously. "How did you manage to get out of prison during the persecutions? You were imprisoned, as was I. I lost my eye and the use of my leg and you came out uninjured. Did a pinch of incense before a pagan altar set you free unharmed?"

Eusebius of Nicomedia jumped from his chair. He bounded before the count. "I ask for an adjournment," he demanded looking from the count to the Bishop of Caesarea and then back again to the count.

"Adjourned!" shouted the count who got up immediately and left.

There could be no justice for me at Tyre. While I was still a free man, I decided I would leave Tyre, go to Constantine and throw myself on his mercy. I would appeal to Caesar even as Blessed Paul had done.

Instructing Paphnutius to take charge in my absence, I took Mark and went under cover of night to the harbor where providentially we found a ship ready to hoist anchor and sail for Constantinople. Without anyone being aware of our departure, we left Tyre that very night. No one had the slightest chance of stopping us once we were at sea.

I had to find a way of approaching the emperor personally. However, I was afraid if I went through the customary ways of seeking an audience, I would be refused and sent back to Tyre. If I were sent back to Tyre, I might even receive the death penalty, depending upon the quality of the new plot that they were hatching against me.

In Constantinople, Mark and I found a villa near the imperial palace, where from our window we would be able to observe the movements of Constantine. Unfortunately, he was not in the imperial city when we arrived, since he had gone on a hunting party in the country. We had no choice but to bide our time and wait for his return.

Word came from Egypt that the committee from Tyre had arrived there with a military escort. Seeking the help of the apostate Prefect of Egypt, Flavius Philagrius, they convinced him to go with them to the Mareotis where they all entered Ischyras' house. With military threats, they began concocting their plot against me. My own clergy were not to be permitted to testify in my behalf.

After Constantine returned to the imperial city, we watched for our opportunity to approach him. When I learned that he was to travel down a certain street one day, I went there and waited, hiding in the shrubbery until he was right beside me. Before he knew what was happening, I jumped from the bushes, frightening his horse by my sudden appearance—so much so that it reared up on its hind legs.

"Out of my way beggar!" ordered Constantine.

He too was startled by my sudden appearance. No doubt, in my well-worn robes, I did resemble a beggar. Drawing his sword, a soldier aimed for my heart, waiting for one word from Constantine to run me through.

"Clemency! Justice! I beg of you!" I disregarded the sword.

"Out of my way, beggar!" Constantine motioned to the soldier. "Seize him!"

Two soldiers bore down on me. I am slight of build. The soldiers, one at each of my elbows, lifted me from the ground so that my feet were dangling in mid air. I was justly angered. With my face growing as red as my hair and with my blood on fire, I bellowed at Constantine. "Thus you treat the bishops of the Church of God?"

The soldiers must have been good Catholics, for when they heard that they had laid hands on a consecrated bishop they dropped me, as if they were burned, releasing me so suddenly that I fell in the mud. Rising to my full stature and with eyes ablaze, I addressed the Emperor boldly.

"I am Athanasius, Archbishop of Alexandria!"

Upon hearing who I was, Constantine sighed deeply and asked, "Why do you persist in harassing my peace with your contentions and disputes?"

"I am accused of murdering a man who is alive. I am accused of desecrating the altar of a man who was ordained in defiance of the decrees of Nicaea and who is no priest. The trial at Tyre is not just. I appeal to Caesar!"

With the vein in his bull-like neck pulsating rapidly, Constantine drew the reins on his horse and prepared to ride on.

"Hear my case. Call my accusers before your justice. Decide my case. That is all I ask."

Kicking his heel into the flank of his horse that wore the nails of the crucifixion in its bridle, he rode away at a gallop without another word. Prayer, continual prayer was my only recourse. I spent all my days praying in the Church of the Holy Apostles that Constantine had built in Constantinople. One afternoon, while I was there deeply absorbed in prayer, Mark came looking for me. His eyes were sad and I knew he had not brought good news.

"The Council of Tyre has deposed Your Piety. They said that your flight was proof of your guilt."

I learned that the bishops left Tyre and went to Jerusalem for the dedication of the Great Martyrium Church built on the site of the crucifixion. A comforting letter from Paphnutius assured me that the Church of Egypt did not accept my deposition. As long as I lived, my clergy would consider me the rightful Archbishop of Alexandria.

When news came to me that Constantine was not satisfied with what took place at Tyre, a flicker of hope stirred in my soul. He summoned the bishops who met there to appear before him and give an account of the justice of their decisions.

The day appointed for the bishops to make their accounting to Constantine, I went also to the imperial palace. To my surprise when I entered the hall chosen for the synod, I saw that only six of the clergy answered Constantine's summons. Across the large empty room where we waited for Constantine to arrive, I recognized Eusebius of Nicomedia, Maris of Chalcedon, Theognis of Nicaea, Ursacius, and Valens. The last two mentioned had only recently entered into the Arian affair. Young though they were, they had not been too young to go on the committee to the Mareotis and stir up more contention. My guess was that they were hoping for bishoprics as a reward for their machinations.

Constantine entered the Synod solemnly with a few soldiers. Mounting his throne and impatiently calling on Eusebius of Nicomedia, he demanded of him the reason why the other bishops had not come to his synod.

"I dismissed them, Your Most Exalted Goodness." Eusebius bowed profoundly and added, "There is no need to harass you with the wearisome details of the Meletian troubles."

Boldly Eusebius walked to the foot of Constantine's throne. Eying me with bitter hatred he said, "We have far more serious charges to consider. Ones that have nothing to do with Church affairs."

Constantine was aroused. With mouth agape, he listened most attentively to Eusebius' every word.

"When our committee went to the Mareotis to investigate the Meletian affair, we found," he paused and savored the suspense he had evoked and then repeated "we found Athanasius is guilty of treason!"

Treason! The death penalty! I sank into my chair and closing my eyes communed with God. I would have to defend myself on the spot—against I knew not what—without witnesses—without time to consider my defense. I looked at Mark; his eyes were filled with fear. Tracing the sign of the cross on my body, I waited to hear the latest lie invented by my enemies.

Bowing with mock gravity, Eusebius hissed, "Athanasius is plotting to destroy Your Exalted Imperial Person. We uncovered a plot in Alexandria." Constantine's face was flushed. His eyes were bulging, as he demanded that I explain.

Pleading my innocence, I cried out, "Truth is my only defense. I am ignorant of what Eusebius is saying."

Eusebius dropped on his knees before Constantine. "Without the grain that comes to Constantinople from Egypt your city will starve. If you do not give the people their free grain, they will revolt. Athanasius has stopped all grain ships from leaving Egypt," whined Eusebius. "He plans to starve the imperial city!"

As he uttered this new calumny, the face of Eusebius was the picture of perfect honesty. "Athanasius is very wealthy and has the money and power to destroy Constantinople in this way," added Eusebius seeing that the emperor had been touched in a very sore spot.

"It is preposterous," I protested "Absolutely preposterous! I know nothing of grain ships. My only business is saving souls!"

In vain, I pleaded my innocence. With lips curled in anger Constantine hurled my sentence at me. "By order of Constantine, Victor Maximus Augustus, I banish you to Treveri in Gaul!"

I was expecting the death penalty. Somewhat relieved I sank back into my chair. I had done everything I could to fight the Arian madmen and will continue to do so as long as I live. As long as I live!

The sentence struck Mark even harder than it did me. I turned to him and whispered, "My son, we will do the will of God!"

Despite the difficulties that journeying by winter would occasion, I left Mark in Constantinople and set out in the dead of winter on February 5, 336 for Gaul. The soldiers, whose task it was to take me safely to Treveri, took a land route, after crossing from Constantinople to Europe, and proceeded westward into Macedonia. The mountain passes of this region were all but impassable. Even Saint Paul found it impossible to journey from Corinth to Thessalonica in winter. Yet, step by step we edged our way up the snow clad peaks and down again, day after day, until we reached the Dalmatian Coast. In all honesty, I believe an old man or a man in poor health would not survive such a journey as ours. Once I was even buried under a small avalanche of snow.

When we finally reached Treveri, a letter was waiting for me from Mark. Eagerly I welcomed news from my secretary. With hungry eyes I read the letter.

"To our Most Venerable Bishop Athanasius of Alexandria, Mark, his secretary sends heartfelt and warmest greetings in Christ! Your Piety requested that I write relating the latest happenings in the imperial city concerning the Arian heresy. Arius is dead! After your Piety was deposed, Arius returned to Alexandria. He caused such a commotion there, when your loyal suffragan bishops refused to receive him into communion, that Constantine ordered him at once to Constantinople. Upon his arrival, Eusebius of Nicomedia was on hand to welcome Arius and present him to the emperor as a faithful adherent of the Nicene faith. Eusebius demanded that Bishop Alexander of Constantinople give Arius communion, threatening that venerable bishop with deposition if he refused.

"Bishop Alexander prayed constantly in the church, Irene, the Peace of God, that either he would die or else Arius would die before he would give communion to such a wicked enemy of Christ. They say the holy bishop watered the floor around his altar with his tears.

"Constantine had Arius come to the imperial palace. He asked him if he agreed to the decrees of the Council of Nicaea. Arius replied that he did and signed a statement to that effect. As a further proof, the emperor demanded that he confirm his signed statement with an oath. I heard that Arius made the oath practicing his customary duplicity. They say that he wrote his true opinions on a piece of paper and carried it under his arm and then swore that he really held the opinions to which he had signed his name.

"Satisfied by this deceit, the Emperor commanded the Bishop of Constantinople to give Arius communion the very next day. With great gratification, Arius left the palace with a large following of Eusebians and paraded through the streets of Constantinople, attracting much attention. I am certain that you recall Constantine's forum where the column of porphyry is located–the one bearing the statue of Constantine and containing the relic of the true cross. Well, when Arius approached this column where the relic of the true cross is, he was seized with great pain in his stomach and violent spasms and a pressing need to evacuate his bowels. I would not mention such things, Your Piety, especially in a letter except that they are an integral part of the story. To continue—Arius hurriedly inquired as to where the most convenient place for him to relieve himself was located. Directed to a public toilet in the back of the forum, he ran there at top speed. When he did not emerge after what seemed a reasonable length of time, some of the Eusebians went in after him. They found him still sitting on the seat. He was quite dead. With the evacuations, he had suffered a severe hemorrhage, and his bowels protruded and his smaller intestines and parts of his liver and spleen as well fell out of him.

That, Your Piety, is the exact account of the end of Arius. It was uncanny, for only a few hours before, Constantine told Arius that the Lord would punish him if he perjured himself.

Now everyone, who passes by, points to the place where Arius died. Those who go back into the colonnade, compelled by the urgencies of nature, and enter the public toilets where Arius expired, tell one another not to make use of the seat on which Arius died. No one will sit on and it—a public toilet—remains the memorial of Arius in the imperial city. It is a perpetual memorial to the memory of Arius, for quite a few curiosity seekers go to the forum just to stare at the place where Arius burst asunder and his bowels gushed out just like what happened to Judas.

"It is plain to see. The wages of sin is death. Someone tried to start a rumor that Your Piety had him poisoned, but no one believed it. As soon as further developments occur, I will keep you informed. Mark."

Constantinople seemed far away. Treveri was a delightful city, the capitol where the emperor's son Constans established his royal residence. It was also the episcopal city of Bishop Maximinus, whom I believe the Church will one day proclaim to be a saint. I found him to be quite charming as well as holy.

When I arrived at the episcopal residence of Maximinus, I was totally exhausted and suffering from a severe respiratory ailment. My clothes were also threadbare and patched. Nevertheless, Maximinus greeted me as he would have greeted Christ himself. When I introduced myself as Athanasius of Alexandria, he threw his arms around me and would have prostrated himself at my feet if I had permitted him.

"Yes," he sighed with sympathy "I have heard of your sufferings and your trials. What great joy must be yours knowing that Christ loves you so much that he gives you a great share in His cross."

I wasn't very joyful at the moment. I had a fever and a pounding headache. Gratefully, I accepted the hospitality he offered me—a suite of rooms overlooking the lovely Mosel River that meanders around the city. I think I slept for a week. After I was fully recovered, I welcomed a chance to serve God in my new home. For this reason, one morning I sought out my host in his study.

"I heard you preach at Nicaea," Maximinus told me when I volunteered my services to his diocese. "I would be most happy to have you preach in our cathedral."

Preaching is duty about which I am most enthusiastic. I was quick to discover that the people of God in Treveri were eager to hear me talk about our Egyptian monasteries. There were no such establishments in the West. I personally was living a monastic existence in Treveri. Having been relieved of the pressing care of my churches, I resumed the routine that I lived as a child in the desert, rising early to pray each morning, doing a small amount of manual labor during the day, but spending most of the time reading and writing. A great interest was enkindled among the people who heard me preach on monasticism. They were especially delighted when I spoke to them of my holy Father Anthony and of how he lived austerely, surrounded by his monks in the Thebais. However the monasticism of Pachomius, made more of an appeal to the Latin mind than did the hermitic life of Anthony, even though they found fascination in hearing of the miracles the holy hermit performed.

Fortunately, or rather I should say, providentially, Bishop Maximinus was on very friendly terms with Constans. Through his influence, I contrived to secure an audience with Emperor Constantine's son. I liked Constans and I think he liked me, for he promised to do everything in his power to help me return to my see in Alexandria.

The news I received from Egypt told me that no one had been chosen to take my place as archbishop. I also learned that Eusebius managed to drive the Bishop of Constantinople from his see to be replaced by the Arian Macedonius. The most important piece of news by far was the news of the death of Constantine.

Treveri went into deep mourning as Constans raced to Constantinople for the funeral and the reading of the his father's will that was to divide the empire between his three sons—Constantine, Constantius, and Constans, all born of his union with Fausta, Maximian's daughter, whom Constantine killed. For reasons that are not clear, Constantine also had his son Crispus by Minervina killed. Some say that it was because Fausta, Constantine's wife, accused Crispus of making love to her. Others say that Constantine's mother Helena loved Crispus dearly, and avenged his death by persuading Constantine that Fausta had yielded to Crispus

Another letter came from Mark who was still in the Imperial city: "To Athanasias, Archbishop of Alexandria, from his secretary, Mark, Greetings,

"I hasten to inform Your Piety that the emperor who banished you is now dead. Many are praying that your return to Egypt may be soon forthcoming."

I said amen to that prayer and continued reading.

"The Emperor fell ill shortly after his sixty-fifth birthday. He decided to take the cure at the warm baths of Aquyrion. Since the waters there did not seem to help him and his condition grew worse, he went to his palace at Nicomedia. Summoning Eusebius to come to his side and to remain with him, he requested the sacrament of baptism from his hands. I am convinced that Constantine did not know that Eusebius did not hold the faith of Nicaea, so cleverly had Eusebius managed to deceive him all these years. Wearing a white robe, Constantine received the sacrament with true humility, repentance and great joy. He never donned the imperial purple again, insisting that he would die in his baptismal robe avowing he received much more in being baptized than in being crowned Augustus.

"He entrusted his will to Eusebius, charging him to deliver it to his son Constantius, when he came to Constantimple. Devoutly, on Pentecost, May 22, in this year of our Lord 337, the emperor died.

"Placed in a golden coffin, the body of Constantine, was borne with great solemnity by a dozen black horses to Constantinople where it was laid out on a great bed in the palace, surrounded by an honor guard of soldiers. Day after day the people of the city filed past, paying their last respects to their first Christian emperor.

When Constantius arrived, he arranged for the funeral, having his father's body laid to rest, as he wished, in the great Church of the Holy Apostles that he constructed for that purpose. I, myself, attended the funeral. In fact, almost everyone in the city was there. The streets were lined five and six deep with people straining to get a glimpse of the funereal procession as it made its way from the palace to the church."

In closing, Mark said he hoped that soon we would both be back in Egypt. I wrote to Mark and directed him to go at once to Alexandria and open my office there. I felt that Constans would be faithful to his word and help me get home again, now that he was Augustus. I did not have long to wait. In July when young Constantine arrived in Treveri, Constans persuaded him to write a letter to Egypt reinstating me. However, my troubles were far from over. They were just beginning!

I left Treveri with young Constantine, accompanying him as far as Sirmium, where he was to meet with his brothers and divide the empire in accordance with their father's will. Constantine was to take Africa and Gaul; Constans was to receive Italy and Illyricum, and Constantius, the East and Egypt. Two of Constantine's nephews, Dalmatius and Hannibalian were also given parts of the empire to govern. The former was given Thrace, Macedonia and Greece; the latter received Pontus and Armenia. As events worked out, the nephews did not have long to live. When the struggle for ascendancy broke out among the heirs of Constantine, the army slew all of Constantine's nephews, except the children Gallus and Julian, the sons of Constantine's brother Julius Constantius and Basilina, Julian's mother, now a good friend of Eusebius of Nicomedia, whose evil schemes she helped perpetrate. When Gallus and Julian were left orphans, Eusebius of Nicomedia was entrusted with their upbringing and education. Is it any wonder that Julian became an apostate!

Young Constantine did not have long to live either. Chancing to invade the domains of Constans, he was killed by his brother's soldiers, leaving only Constans and Constantius to share the rule of the Roman world.

When I was journeying eastward from Trier, I met Constantius for the first time at Viminacium. After I left Constantinople on my southward journey, I encountered him a second time at Caesarea in Cappadocia. The first encounter gave me a chance to become acquainted with the man who was to become my arch-persecutor. The second encounter afforded little opportunity to talk with him, because he was hurrying to the Persian frontier, lest the enemy seize the death of Constantine as an occasion for battle. Constantius reminded me more of his grandfather Maximian, who had been such a violent persecutor of the Church, than he did of his father Constantine or his grandmother the saintly Helena. When I talked to him, he would not even look at me. He had the annoying habit of always staring straight ahead when talking to anyone. He gave you the impression that he was looking at something in the distance and not paying attention to what you were saying. Already an Arian at my first meeting with him, he spoke very enthusiastically of Eusebius of Nicomedia, who baptized his father and delivered his father's will to him.

Constantius' wife, who was named of all names—Eusebia—had been completely captivated by the bishop of Nicomedia. Furthermore, the Arians were able to convert all the palace eunuchs at Nicomedia to their heresy. I could see that the Church of Christ would be in danger if Constantius took it into his head to play the part of "bishop" outside the Church, as his father had done. What would happen if the emperor were to decide that he would rule on points of doctrine in the Church?

After I left Constantius at Viminacium, I went to Constantinople, curious to learn at first-hand the state of the Church in the imperial city. When Alexander was Bishop of Constantinople, the Arians did not dare to profess their beliefs, especially because Constantine pledged himself to uphold the decisions of Nicaea. When Alexander died, the people of Constantinople split on the issue of who his successor was to be, with the Arians supporting Macedonius and the faithful backing Paul, who was consecrated bishop of the imperial city during a period of time when old Constantine was not in residence there. When Constantine returned he turned on Paul, at the instigation of Eusebius, sending him in to exile in Pontus.

Now that Constantine's sons were allowing me to return to my see, many in Constantinople hoped that their rightful bishop, Paul, would be returned to them. Fearful of such an occurrence, the Eusebians were making insidious accusations against Paul. When I arrived in the imperial city, the Arian Macedonius was filling Paul's see, but already Eusebius was casting an evil eye on the bishopric of New Rome. It wasn't long after I returned to Alexandria that I heard that a synod was called at which the holy bishop Paul, that great confessor of the true faith, was deposed and Eusebius was made Bishop of Constantinople. Expelling Paul from the Church, Constantius sent him in chains to Singara in Mesopotamia where he was to live in exile. Later he was transferred to Emesa; still later he was banished to Cucusus in Cappadocia, near the deserts of Mount Taurus where his enemies confined him in a very dark place and waited for him to die of starvation. When after six days he was still alive, they strangled him to death by their own hands. Such are these savage men who plot to destroy me!

After arriving back in Alexandria November 23, 337, I waited until the warm Egyptian sun set before I left the ship. Wrapped in a heavy cloak so that no one would recognize me, I made my way through the night to the archiepiscopal residence. Because the Arians had grown stronger in my absence and were certain to protest my return, I told no one when to expect me.

Quietly I entered the house, as if I had left only the day before. Even though I was gone for more than two years and four months, I walked into my study and found everything just as I left it the July morning I sailed for Tyre. Picking up the hand bell from the desk and ringing it as hard as I could, I called out, "Where is everyone?"

"Your Piety!" It was Mark who recognized my voice and shouted out to me from his room upstairs. Within minutes Mark, Macarius, and Paphnutius were surrounding me, with broad smiles on their faces, looking at me as if I were an apparition.

"If you had let us know when you were coming," Macarius apologized, "we would have been at the docks to meet you." He had grown thinner and his face had an ascetic appearance that it did not have before the trial at Tyre.

Grasping the hand of Paphnutius, whose one good eye shone like the Pharos in the harbor, I said, "After what happened in Constantinople I wanted to keep my arrival quiet."

Paphnutius nodded knowingly, "The Arians have been causing disturbances in Alexandria ever since they heard you were going to return. Dissolute youths are causing minor violence among the people of God."

Young Mark had matured, since I had last seen him. Having filled out the heavy frame of his bones with strong muscles and a slight amount of corpulence, he no longer seemed as tall as he did. He was so happy to see me that he squeezed my hand so hard I thought he would fracture it.

"We heard what happened to Paul of Constantinople," Mark told me. "We assure you, Your Piety, you will never be treated that way in Alexandria. We shall protect the bishop God has given us—with our lives."

"I'll settle for a little supper tonight," I replied lightly, but I knew we were in for serious trouble.

Word spread fast that I had returned. Saying that they shared my suffering and accounted my trials as their own, the suffragan bishops of Egypt, Pentapolis and the Libyas and the priests of Alexandria came to welcome me home. My faithful clergy told me that it was the happiest day of their lives when we all assembled at a great banquet held in my honor.

Having grown much stronger, the Arian party was showing resentment everywhere over my return. Rioting became frequent. One afternoon in broad daylight, a dozen or so Arian malcontents came to the archiepiscopal residence and threw rotten vegetables at the windows and doors. Naturally, we notified the civil authorities. The prefect, Theodorus, who was friendly toward the Church—he was a faithful parishioner in Macarius' parish, the Quirinus Church–sent men to quell the riot. In the process, one of the Arians was injured.

With loud cries, the Arians protested the injury of the youth, stirring up even the pagans against Theodorus. When more riots resulted, Theodorus took stricter measures against the youths who were mainly responsible.

The most damaging thing the Arians did that winter was to spread the rumor that my holy Father Anthony had deserted me and was preaching the Arian heresy. Because of the pressing duties of the care of the churches, I could not visit Thebes right away. Actually I had not seen the holy hermit since before I sailed for Tyre. Even though Paphnutius was an able administrator during my absence, many things were demanding my personal attention.

I approached Mark one day on the subject of Father Anthony.

"You have heard what is being said about the holy hermit of the Thebais?"

"Yes, Your Piety, everywhere the Arians are bragging that he is one of them." A deep frown creased the usually serene face of my secretary. "It's a lie, but there are many who believe it. I am alarmed at what such a lie will do to the people of God who regard the hermit as a saint." Mark looked at me questioningly to see what it was I wanted of him.

"You will go to the Thebais. Tell my Father Anthony what is being said of him. Ask him to sign a statement, affirming his faith in the creed of Nicaea and supporting me."

Mark left at once to carry out my orders. When he returned a few days later, he burst into my study with a big grin on his well-tanned face.

"Well," I demanded. "Where is the statement I sent you to get? You look like you have spent the past week sun bathing on the beach."

I knew he had a surprise for me, but I was not prepared for anything as amazing as it turned out to be. With childlike joy, Mark raced to the door of my study and motioned for someone to come in. I couldn't believe my eyes. It was my father in God—the holy Anthony. Mark retired and left us alone to talk.

My holy Father Anthony was now almost ninety years of age. Although he was wizened and 'stooped ever so slightly, with a firm step and clear eyes, he approached me with arms outstretched. Calling his name, I embraced him. In so doing I felt the hair shirt that he still wore under his tunic. Recalling that I was his bishop as well as his son, he abased himself before me. I blessed him. Rising to his feet he looked down at me with authority. His blue eyes were filled with determination as he said, "I have come to help you, boy."

"They say that you have deserted me and have gone over to the enemies of Christ who deny the blessed Trinity." I felt like a child, so awe inspiring was the presence of Anthony now that he was on the threshold of the Beatific Vision. Light seemed to surround his entire body. His face glowed, illuminated by the fire that burned within his soul. He drew the sign of the cross slowly, deliberately on his body.

"From what I have heard, they are no longer content with denying the Lord. They are also preaching that the Holy Spirit is still farther from the Eternal Father than Christ."

Declining the comfortable chairs by the window, he sat down on the hard bench beside my desk.

"How can it be, Father, that priests and bishops are preaching heresy?" I pushed back my chair from the desk and waited to hear what he would say.

"Do you remember the parable of the wheat and the tares?" he asked softly.

I nodded.

"Our enemy the devil never sleeps. He always sows weeds in the Church of God. There will be a reckoning. The sheep will be separated from the goats." Tapping his foot on the stone floor for emphasis, he exclaimed, "Inwardly, these Arians are vicious, devouring wolves."

"What are we to do? Even the See of Constantinople has fallen to the Arians. The emperor is Arian." I greatly valued the advice of this man who lived so close to God and was almost ready to depart this life.

"Uphold the true faith! Even if the whole world falters and becomes Arian, You, Athanasius, must remain unmoved. You will preach the Trinity like the Blessed Paul—in fasting, in sleepless nights, in trials, in persecutions, in season and out of season, whether stoned, or scourged, or shipwrecked. You must be the Apostle of the Trinity! And—always remember, Blessed Paul said that apostles are sent into the arena to fight like men condemned to death."

The blue eyes of my father burned into my soul as he continued. "Alone against the world—you will stand firm—supported by an invisible army of monks at prayer. Always remember, heresy is the work of the devil. Our wrestling is not against flesh and blood, but against the spiritual forces of wickedness on high. The holy monks hidden away in the deserts are the army of defense that will give you strength. Like a mighty general you will lead the Church of God to victory! The devil will be defeated and future generations down to the end of time *will* be given the true faith—the cornerstone of which is belief in the Father, the Son and the Holy Spirit!"

Leaning forward, I pleaded, "And you, Father, you will pray for me when you go forth from the earth to dwell in the Trinity?" I lowered my glance from his penetrating stare that saw into every nook of my soul. I remembered that when I was a child, he promised me that if I were faithful to prayer that even in this life I would behold the Three Persons of God.

"My son," the old man whispered, reading my thoughts, "you have seen the Three in One, the One in Three!" He smiled seraphically and joyfully at the intuitive knowledge that informed him of the state of my soul. I nodded. It was not easy to speak of the vision of the Trinity. My holy father continued to study my soul

"I can see your soul very plainly," he informed me gently, "From time to time you see one of the persons of God—most often Christ, in your soul. At other times you glimpse the Holy Spirit. Sometimes borne on the wings of the Holy Dove, you have flown to the celestial regions where the Eternal father dwells with Christ resting in His bosom and you have beheld, as though in a glass darkly, the three Persons of the Trinity all at the same time. It is the greatest grace, my son, that a man can experience in this life."

His voice was almost inaudible now as he continued. "Suddenly you are caught up in that ineffable embrace in which you feel the love of the Three Persons of God—each distinct from the Other—flooding into your being and your feeble mortal heart melts with love. Your spirit rushes out of itself as you embrace the One in Three. Most blessed is the man who under the impulsion of divine grace elicits from his soul that perfect act of adoration—that over-flowing act of love—for the Three Persons of God whom the soul sees and loves as One."

I remained silent not knowing what to say.

"You, Athanasius, my son, you have experienced this on occasion. When you become more advanced in the ways of the spirit, it will become the perpetual state of your soul. Then the only thing that will separate you from the Beatific Vision will be the thin veil of your flesh which will chain you to this world, as long as God has work for you to do here."

He cleared his throat. His train of thoughts took another course. Speaking in a louder voice he continued. "Speaking of doing the work of God, reminds me of the reason I have come here to Alexandria. He has work for me to do here."

I looked up at him. He was the most vibrantly alive person I have ever known. Now he was almost ninety years of age and had traveled a great distance in the July heat and he was informing me that he had work to do in Alexandria. Astonished, I listened as he told me he intended to spend the next two days preaching in the parishes of the city.

"That is," he said, humbly inclining his head, "if you will give me your permission to preach."

"Please, Father, Please!"

Indefatigably he went from one parish to the next with great crowds of men, women, and children following him everywhere. All their lives the people had heard of the holy hermit, but only a few had managed to get a glimpse of him when he came to Alexandria in the days of the persecutions when the holy Bishop Peter was marty-red. Now all were determined to satisfy their curiosity about the old monk. Even the Greek philosophers begged for a chance to talk with him, or just to touch him, so impressed were they by the wisdom the Holy Spirit infused into his soul. My flock fell in love with the holy recluse. They wanted him to stay forever with them. To their entreat-ies that he remain in Alexandria, he answered them very simply.

"A fish cannot stay out of water very long. A monk cannot stay away from his solitude very long. If I were to stay in the company of men too long, I would no longer be what God has intended me to be. I would become useless to you—useless to God—useless to myself."

With impassioned eloquence he preached in the cathedral about the Three Persons of God. His preaching, born of sanctity, caused everyone that heard him to rejoice in the true faith. I was touched deeply by the miracle he worked, just as he was leaving the city on July 2. God has never chosen to work miracles of healing through my ministry and so I stood in awe when a woman came towards us yell-ing, "Wait! Holy Father, My child is ill!"

Laying down his water jug, Father Anthony, calmly surveyed the woman and her child that was screaming in her arms and kicking its little feet convulsively. With great faith, the woman laid the child on the ground at the feet of the monk, asking him to heal her daughter who was now rolling in the dust and babbling incoherently.

Without a moment's hesitation, my father reached down, touched the child and pronounced the holy name of Jesus. It was as simple as that. Instantly, the child was healed. Blessing us all, the hermit turned nonchalantly and started off towards the desert.

We had struck a solid blow for the true faith in Alexandria. Being greatly chagrined by the witness of the desert saint, the hard core of the Arians in the city retaliated by agitating politically against The-odorus, whose term of office as prefect was due to expire the end of August. Because they accused him of maltreating Arians in the city, he was recalled when his term was over.

To replace him, Flavius Philagrius was sent to Alexandria to be the new prefect. Since he was the apostate who took part in the Mareotic investigations with the Arians sent from Tyre, this was bad news for us. Sending Philagrius as prefect of Alexandria was an Arian victory and their first step towards seizing the churches of the city. I realized at once that Eusebius was ready to attack me again. I say Eusebius without mentioning that he was Bishop of Constantinople for the other, Eusebius Pamphilus of Caesarea, had died by this time and there is no longer the need to distinguish between them.

The arrival of Philagrius in the city was a day of rejoicing for the Arians. They celebrated it by attacking one of my priests as he was walking near Cleopatra's needles in the heart of the city.

Paphnutius broke the next bit of news to me.

"An Arian bishop has arrived in Alexandria," he told me observing me intently with his one good eye.

"Who is he?" I was curious to know what sort of strength Eusebius was capable of showing in my see.

"Pistus!" replied Paphnutius with a look of incredulity.

"The one who was excommunicated at Nicaea?" I could not believe that the Arians would have the unparalleled audacity to send someone who had been excommunicated by over three hundred bishops of the church.

"Yes. It is he. Secundus, whom we removed from his bishopric in Libya and who was deposed at Nicaea, consecrated him. He is already in Alexandria trying to see how many followers he can muster."

We were standing on the steps of the great Dionysius church, named after one of the former bishops of Egypt, when we had this conversation. As we were observing the people who were just leaving the Church, I exuded confidence to Paphnutius.

"The sheep know the voice of the shepherd. They will not follow the hireling."

"But," protested the old confessor limping up the stairs into the church, "they say you have no right to the See of Alexandria, because you were deposed by a church council and never reinstated by a council. They have even sent a letter to his Holiness Pope Julius relating to him all the lies they have told about you in an attempt to get him to approve Pistus in your place."

That was alarming news requiring immediate action.

"Summon all our bishops at once."

I rushed back to my study for solitude to think, pray and plan a course of action.

The time of crisis was fast approaching. That night the Arians staged a tremendous riot in Baucalis in which an unknown assailant struck down one of my priests and almost mortally wounded him. When the episcopate assembled in the Church of Theonas, I greeted my bishops with a heavy heart.

"My brothers in Christ," I began, "it is doubtful that I will be able to remain in Alexandria much longer. The enemies of our Savior are making an all out attempt to remove me from my see. In the event that I should be forced to leave Egypt suddenly, I want you to hold fast to the faith—no matter what anyone might say or do. Hold fast to your belief in the Trinity. Even if you were to hear that I have become an Arian—hold fast and do not believe it. I assure you such a statement would be but another Arian lie.

"We are fighting for our all. God is testing our faith—our hope—our love. He is trying our fortitude—our patience, and our generosity with Him. Let patience do its perfect work in you. Let me remind you of the words of Blessed Peter the Apostle in the second letter he wrote to the churches. 'False prophets were among the people, just as false teachers will be in your midst. Secretly they will spread destructive heresies among you, even denying the Lord himself.' You have witnessed the birth of such a destructive sect right here in Egypt. That heresy is now spreading like gangrene throughout the entire Church. Have you ever noticed that the Catholic

Church of Christ never bears any name but Christian, while the false teachers call themselves "Donatists," "Lucianists," "Sabellians," "Eusebians," or "Arians," or something similar? They even disown the Lord who redeemed them, said Blessed Peter, thus bringing swift destruction upon themselves. Many will follow their shameful ways and will bring even the truth into disrepute.

"Why do you wonder in your hearts when you see Christ who is the truth maligned by the Arians? The Holy Spirit speaking through the apostles has told you that such things would happen. Listen again to Saint Peter. 'These men are blasphemers who do not understand what they do. They are like dumb animals and they will perish.' You can be sure the Lord will separate the sheep from the goats. How many times have you heard the Arians mock and deride the mystery of the Trinity, because their weak and feeble minds cannot comprehend the ineffable Godhead? These men, says Saint Peter, are 'wells without water and vapors driven by a storm. Blackest darkness awaits them.'

"Beloved bishops of the Church of God in Egypt, in conclusion, I exhort you with the words of St. Peter: 'My dear friends, since you are aware of these things, be careful that you are not led into the error of lawless men and fall from grace. Rather grow in grace and the knowledge of Christ, our Lord and Savior. May he be glorified now and evermore.' Amen."

With a standing ovation, lasting a full five minutes, my clergy demonstrated their support of me. Showing great devotion, they all reaffirmed their loyalty to me and solemnly promised to uphold the true faith at the cost of their lives.

I knew that the Arians would not be content until they had taken my life. Great trials lay ahead of us. Winter progressed. The new year arrived. A few weeks later I was notified that a council had assembled in Antioch and deposed me, with no precedent for such action, sending another bishop to replace me. The Bishop of Alexandria has always been chosen from among our clergy in Egypt. Determined to remain with my churches as long as I could, I immediately sent a letter to His Holiness in Rome relating to him all that was transpiring.

The first part of Lent, Philagrius, the prefect, issued an edict to the effect that I was to be replaced by someone called Gregory of Cappadocia, soon to arrive and take over my see. On the twenty second of the Egyptian month, Phamenoth, that was Sunday March 12, 339, the middle of Lent, Mark and I went to the Church called Dionysius where I was invited to preach. After the sermon, we remained that afternoon with the pastor of the church and even stayed for our evening meal with him, before returning home rather late to the archiepiscopal residence. Since neither moon nor stars could be seen in the sky overhead and a storm was threatening over the sea, it was quite dark. When we had almost reached the main entrance of our residence, I heard something rustle in the shrubbery.

"Watch out, Piety! Watch out!" Mark yelled.

I jumped just as the blow fell. A club grazed my left cheek, striking my shoulder with a thud. I spun on my feet. Two men in black cloaks, with their faces masked, were bearing down on us. One of them jumped on Mark, the other on me.

"You are going with us," the bigger fellow snarled at me in Coptic between clenched teeth. He grabbed my wrist. Although I am small of stature, I am nevertheless strong. Using a trick I had learned as a child, I jerked my arm in such a way that my entire weight forced his thumb to open and he lost his grip on my wrist. Wrenching myself free, I tripped him with my foot, so that he went sprawling into the crotons that line the walkway in front of the house. Before he could recover, I bounded for the door and threw it open. Mark, who is a very big man, had also managed to free himself and was right behind me.

As we entered the open door, an object whizzed past my ear. When the door was safely closed and bolted behind us, I saw that the object was a dagger. It had pierced a wooden table and was standing and vibrating on end.

"They meant to kidnap me!" I exclaimed in unbelief.

"Or else kill you on the spot!"

Mark went to the windows and peered out into the darkness.

"I think they are gone now."

"They will be back. They are determined to get me. They have just gone for more men." Intuition told me this was true.

"They will never get you as long as I am alive." Mark drew the dagger from the table. "A few inches closer to your head—," he broke off thinking about what might have happened.

"Go, pack your things, Mark. We are moving out of here as soon as I tidy up the office and pack a few things of my own." I was not safe as long as I remained in the archiepiscopal residence.

"But where will we go?" he asked nervously.

"Let me worry about that," I ordered stuffing the important records of the church into a chest.

A few minutes later we were ready to leave. Cautiously we peered from all the windows on the ground floor. When we were quite certain that there was no one near the house, we slipped out the door into the deep, dark shadows that quickly swallowed us up. Carefully we made our way to the Cathedral–the great Theonas Church.

I slept very little that night, kneeling for hours before the altar of God in my cathedral where I was scheduled to baptize many the very next day. A large number of catechumens expected me to baptize them in preparation for the great Pascal feast that was drawing near. One of the most blessed joys I have known as a bishop is baptizing the catechumens in preparation for initiating them into the mysteries of the Body and Blood of Christ in the Eucharist at Easter. I anticipated that there might be trouble during the baptisms. Although it was well known in Alexandria that I would be in Theonas on March 19 to baptize, I had no intention of disappointing the candidates for baptism, even though it might provide my enemies with an opportunity to attack me.

There was a larger number to be baptized that year than any other, since I had become archbishop. Proceeding with the ancient rites of the Catholic Church, I began the baptisms at the appointed time. That day, one hundred or more pagans died to sin and were born to newness of life in Christ. It wasn't until I finished with the last baptism that the trouble broke out.

A large mob of agitators came storming into the church. They would have rushed right into the sanctuary and seized me, for I was praying there, thanking God for the grace of so many baptisms, at the moment of the unholy intrusion. Before the mob got half way to the chancel railing, I fled the church, eluding them the way that Christ eluded those who sought to take him in the temple. With Mark close at my side, I mounted my horse. Before the mob was aware that were gone, we vanished like phantoms in the night.

"Where to now, Piety?" Mark's face was strained with worry.

"The foxes have dens but the Son of Man has nowhere to rest His head." I sighed as our horses sped down the stone streets of old Alexandria. Rounding a curve in the narrow street, we found our passage suddenly blocked by an old man and a camel.

"We have no time to wait, old fellow!" yelled Mark tossing the man a coin.

The old man hugged the walls of the houses lining the street. We squeezed by him.

"The Scripture says when we are persecuted in one town we should flee to another," Mark remarked, suggesting that we should leave Alexandria.

"I shall stay as long as God wills. I am not yet inspired to leave."

"Where are we going then?"

"To Macarius and to the Quirinus Church," I whispered lest Arian ears might be listening.

Although my presence could mean danger to him, my old friend Macarius, who suffered so much for me at Tyre, welcomed me as a brother. As we sat talking at dinner that night, I noticed that Macarius' wrists still bore the scars from the chains he wore during his imprisonment. There were some monks present at Macarius' house that night. I still remember the solemn way in which they volunteered to accompany me everywhere I went, to protect me with their lives from mobs that might again try to seize me. We did not yet realize how serious the situation had become.

On March 22, Gregory arrived in Alexandria with a large company of soldiers. Imagine—a bishop—if you could call him that—entering his See under the aegis and protection of soldiery. The soldiers moved right into the archiepiscopal residence with him, even accompanying him into the cathedral the morning he proclaimed himself to be Archbishop of all Egypt, Thebes, Pentapolis and the Libyas.

It is even yet painful for me to remember the horrible things that happened when Gregory arrived. After stirring up the heathen mobs against the true Church, Philagrius, the apostate, sent them into the churches with swords and clubs to attack the people who were observing Lent in preparation for the Pascal mysteries.

They set the baptistry of my cathedral on fire! They stripped naked holy virgins consecrated to Christ and raped them right in the cathedral! The virgins who resisted found their lives endangered. They trampled monks underfoot, committed murder, and blasphemed the name of the Lord in his sanctuary. They even burned the Holy Scriptures that are to be found in every one of our churches.

All our churches reported these happenings. Stirred up by Philagrius and the Arians, the heathen mobs took off all their clothing and did all kinds of impure things in the baptistry of one of our churches.

Such was the entry into Alexandria of that enemy of Christ, Gregory, who was to replace me as archbishop. So pleased was he with the outrages committed against the Church that he gave our churches over to the mobs to be plundered. All over Alexandria churches were robbed. The mobs drank the altar wine or poured it on the ground. Doors were ripped off their hinges. In one church the chancel railing was torn loose and carried away to decorate a pagan house. With obvious satisfaction, Gregory watched as our priests had their flesh ripped and scourged.

On Good Friday, Gregory forced his way, together with the governor of Egypt, into one of my parishes, taking with him a mob of soldiers and heathens. When the people of God showed resentment at this intrusion in their worship service, Gregory had the governor order the virgins scourged, before all assembled. They unleashed all their ungodly fury against the chaste spouses of Christ! They beat them mercilessly, destroyed their Psalters, and even dragged away some of the consecrated virgins by the hair to prison. During these raids that Holy Week, I was the one they were trying to find. The governor and Gregory who were trying to smoke me out visited one parish after another in such fashion. Each parish so visited was turned over to that Arian madman. My priests were denied entrance to their churches, unless they would agree to take communion with the Arians. Far worse than in the days of Diocletian was this persecution of our people, because in the former time, the faithful could receive the sacraments as they fled the terror. Now that was no longer possible.

Although they had not yet detected my presence at Quirinus Church, I knew that at any moment they could strike. I imagined that they might choose the Easter vigil as the time when they would attack. A few hours before the vigil was to begin, Macarius, extremely agitated and excited, burst into my room where I was praying.

"Your Piety!" he cried in alarm, "the governor has made an indictment against you. In the name of the Egyptian people, he has charged you before the emperor with such crimes that they will kill you if they catch you."

"They'll have to catch me first!" I grinned at him. When he saw that I was calm in the face of the news he brought, he relaxed and waited for my orders.

"I am sailing for Rome. I am taking you and those two monks, who have been chaperoning me around Alexandria recently, with me. Mark is also coming along." I patted Macarius on the shoulder to reassure him. "We are going to see His Holiness Pope Julius. The heretics will not take the See of Alexandria away from the Catholic Church!"

Heaving a sigh of relief, Macarius smiled back at me. "It's about time!" He took strength from my courage.

"Yes—it *is* about time. If I remain in Egypt, I can do no more for my flock. We shall post loyal parishioners around the church tonight during the vigil—just in case. If the mobs and Gregory come, the horses will be waiting. We will make a run for it. Mark, make the arrangements at once."

"Yes, Piety. I shall take care of it at once."

When the hour for the Easter vigil service arrived Macarius, Mark, and the two monks who guarded me accompanied me into the church. Many of the people who had assembled were openly weeping because of the murders that had been committed, the altars desecrated, and the virgins who had been defiled. I made my presence as unobtrusive as possible to prevent violence from being leveled against the people of God, in case the governor should arrive searching for me.

We were halfway through the Easter vigil when Mark came to report that soldiers surrounded the church.

"Escape is impossible!" Mark's voice trembled. "They are lined up in battle formation!"

"God forbid that the people should suffer on account of me!"

I had an idea. It was worth a try. "Mark," I ventured, "give the closing prayer and then start the recessional psalm."

When the chant of the recessional psalm began, the people rose from their benches, filled the aisles, and made for the doors. Motioning for Mark to follow me, I joined Macarius. The three of us mingled with the people as they pushed down the aisles and out of the church. In the confusion of the dispersing crowd, we reached our horses where the two monks were waiting. We rode away under the very nose of Gregory who rushed into the empty church in search of me and to take possession of it.

We spent the night and Easter day in the home of one of Macarius' parishioners who would not be under suspicion of hiding me. Easter day, I devoted to writing a circular letter to the bishops everywhere in the universal Church, calling on them to make my cause their own.

Easter Monday, disguised as Greeks, we made our way to the port where we boarded a ship and set sail for Rome. As I watched the Pharos of Alexandria fade from sight on the horizon, my heart was filled with bitter tears. The bride for whom Christ died—the fair church of Egypt—had been seized by anti-Christ and had been reduced to a pitiful state. I thanked God that I was not alone. In a short time, I would see His Holiness and, perhaps, even Hosius and the other bishops of the West. They would know what to do with these lawless men who make traffic of the title of bishop! Alas! It was impossible for me to know the harrowing experiences that lay ahead of us.

CHAPTER 4

❁

*W*e rented a house on the Janiculum within walking distance of the Basilica that Constantine built in honor of the Apostle Peter on the very site of his martyrdom. From the window of my room, I had a magnificent view of Rome. Eager to begin at once to explore the city of the apostles, I appointed Mark as my guide, since he had visited the Eternal City previously. We set out to visit all the places hallowed by the apostles and the martyrs. Naturally the first place we visited was Peter's tomb, where I prayed for grace that I might follow his heroic example and be a holy bishop of the Church of God in the face of persecution. I grew to love that church during my stay in Rome and often went to pray at the tomb of Peter. Constantine enclosed the remains of Peter, the Apostle, in a worthy sarcophagus and placed it in a crypt under the basilica. I felt close to Peter as I prayed there.

Departing from St. Peters, we crossed the Tiber near Hadrian's tomb, heading for the Circus that is nearby the Palatine. It is a holy place where many shed their blood for Christ. Eagerly I pressed Mark to take us to the tomb of Rome's other apostle. With great devotion I knelt in the basilica Constantine erected as a final resting place for the body of Paul on the very spot where Paul had been beheaded for his faith in Jesus Christ. As I prayed there, I knew that the day might come when I, too, might taste the executioner's sword.

As we left the pine grove where Paul was executed, the monk Ammonius begged permission of me to return to our house on the Janiculum.

"I have seen Rome, Your Piety. Now that I have visited the tombs of the apostles, please let me retire and be alone to think and to pray."

His eyes were pleading with mine. He drew his cowl closer around his face as if trying to hide himself from the Romans who, finding him a curiosity because of the peculiar attire that monks wear, could not refrain from staring at him.

"First you must meet His Holiness Pope Julius. I want the Pope to see both you and Isidore."

I remembered how during my first exile in Treveri everyone was interested in learning about monasticism. Upon hearing this Ammonius cast his glance to the ground. Without a trace of emotion, he bowed submissively. When I mentioned going to see the successor of Peter, with childlike simplicity, Isidore's face beamed with eagerness. Macarius smiled as Ammonius tugged at his cowl and chuckled.

"Come on, old fellow, you will have plenty of time to pray later on. I am afraid we are going to be in Rome a long time."

Cheerfully Ammonius followed at my elbow as Mark led us to the Lateran Palace, the residence of the bishops of Rome that the saintly mother of Constantine gave the pope. Making our arrival known, we were ushered by a deacon into an antechamber where we were asked to wait until his Holiness could see us.

Twenty minutes later, I was ushered alone into a study furnished with great simplicity in much the same way that my own study in Alexandria is furnished. There was huge desk burdened down with the usual tremendous amount of correspondence that a bishop has. At the other end of the room a small well-stocked library beckoned invitingly. Just as I was about to reach down to pick up an intriguing parchment, the door opened and a small thin man wearing bishop's attire entered.

"Your Holiness," I exclaimed with the customary formalities one makes upon greeting such a personage.

I noticed that although he was a small man, his hands were strong as he clasped mine in friendship.

"We are greatly honored to welcome Your Piety to Rome." His eyes sparkled as he smiled. "We have heard of the sufferings which you have endured for your faith in the divinity of Christ and in the Nicene Creed. We commend you." His eyes were quick and intent as they studied my face.

"You have heard, Holiness, that a usurper has been sent from the court with soldiers and has driven me from my chair in Alexandria?" I took the seat he offered me in front of the desk where he was seated.

He nodded. "I even know that you left Serapion of Thmuis in charge during your absence." He smiled warmly. "You are no stranger here in Rome—the Church of Egypt is very dear to our heart. Although I have never met you before, Hosuis has told me of your struggles in Alexandria with the Arians."

"All the work that we accomplished at Nicaea under his leadership is being subverted. I fear lest the things that have happened at Alexandria to me and to Paul of Constantinople might happen—even here at Rome. I fear that the whole world will one day soon find itself Arian." I shook my head sadly. Pope Julius did not appear to share my fears.

"Constans our emperor here in the West is a true and loyal member of the Catholic Church. He has pledged himself to fight this Arian madness—to assist us in upholding the faith. As long as he lives we have nothing to fear in Rome." Julius spoke with assurance.

"Ah, but Holiness, he is mortal. What would happen if he were suddenly to die today? Constantius would then rule the world and he is Arian. While we still have time we must fight this madness—this heresy which eats its way like a consuming plague." Color was rising in my cheeks.

Calmly Julius replied, "I have responded to the Eusebians' request for a council. I sent two of our priests–Elpidius and Philoxenus to summon them. When they come, we shall hear their complaints against you and your complaints against them. Truth will conquer." He drummed his fingertips on the table for emphasis.

I could see that His Holiness Pope Julius was not yet aware of what kind of men these Arians were. He did not yet realize that they are completely lawless enemies of Christ and teachers of apostasy who are insensible to shame and who are past masters at fomenting atrocious schemes and fabricating evasions. Praying silently in my heart that he would learn before it was too late, I sat in silence waiting to hear what else His Holiness would say.

"Your Piety should have come to Rome sooner," sighed Julius. "But you can rest assured of one thing. Christ will be with His Church until the end of time and the end of the world. The gates of hell shall not prevail against it. And what are the gates of hell if they be not the lying jaws of heretics!"

Folding his hands on the desk in front of him, he pensively pondered the problem of my expulsion from Alexandria.

After a few moments, he said, "You will be returned to your see. I will use my influence with Constans. Once before he persuaded his brother to let you return. Perhaps he could do it again."

I thought for a few seconds about what he said before replying.

"Such tactics require much time to produce results. The question is what am I to do meanwhile?" I said this more to myself than to Julius.

Stretching forth his hand to me in fellowship, Julius replied. "There is much to be done for Christ right here in Rome. We shall keep Your Piety busy. I can assure you that the old Rome of the Caesars is dying. You can help bury it. A new Rome is being born—a Christian Rome. Paganism is in its death throes. The young pagans today are sickened by the corruption of their elders. They are looking for Christ without even knowing whom they seek. And alas," he sighed deeply, "our Catholic people have become lax, now that they are no longer persecuted. They have taken on many pagan ways. We need saints in Rome today—just as we needed them in the days of Nero and Diocletian."

Julius tugged pensively at his thin black beard. Leveling his penetrating glance on me he asked, "What are these monks that I hear live in your deserts?"

This was a subject on which I could speak with enthusiasm. I spoke at length of my Father Anthony and of his holy life in the Thebais. I told him of Pachomius and of the cenobitic monasteries he had set up in my archdiocese. I must confess I was proud to present to Julius a picture of our church in Egypt, showing him that it was strong, vital, and holy, in contrast to the lax and lukewarm church he pictured as existing in Rome. When I told him how the monks live and pray and work together all for the glory of God and for the strengthening of the Church, he listened with genuine interest. When I became breathless from talking, he exclaimed,

"Would that I had such souls in Rome! They are the fruit of your persecution, the strength of your martyrs, and the pillars of Egypt's Church."

"There are two of them right here in the Lateran." I was referring to Isidore and Ammonius who were waiting for me in the antechambers.

"Two monks?" Julius seemed surprised.

"Yes. I brought them with me so that you could see them for yourself."

Julius had the two monks and Mark and Macarius ushered into his study. With the simplicity of children they knelt at the feet of Julius and waited for his blessing. I could see that the artlessness of Isidore and the profound spirit of recollection of Ammonius captivated his Holiness. The unusual attire that distinguished them from the clerics attracted his attention. Isidore—coming from one of Pachomius' communities—was wearing, as is their custom, his woolen tiara adorned with purple nails. Ammonius, one of Anthony's monks, wore his sleeveless tunic and animal skins with great dignity.

"Tell me," said Julius to Ammonius after he had bestowed his blessing on him, "tell me—what is the significance of your attire?"

With modestly downcast eyes, Ammonius explained that a monk wears animal skins to remind him of the great contemplative Elijah. The tunic has no sleeves in order to instruct the monk that his hands ought not to be prepared to do evil deeds. Pointing to his cowl Ammonius told His Holiness,

"The cowl serves to remind me that I am to be as innocent as a baby, since cowls are the garments of infants."

"And what is this girdle and scarf?"

"It serves to remind me that I should always be ready to do the work of God."

"And so you shall!" exclaimed Julius. "By God's Providence, Egypt has sent us her bishop and her monks. The workings of Providence are always significant in every detail. It is not without reason that you have come! You must share with the churches of the West the graces God has showered upon Egypt."

With that, His Holiness ordered us to preach and teach in Rome and to spread the flower of monasticism everywhere we went in the West. In conclusion, he told us that we would in time be completely vindicated of the charges made by our enemies against us.

It was as a result of the enthusiasm of the Romans for more knowledge about the monastic life, that I began at this time to write a biography of my holy Father Anthony. While in Rome, I spent all my free time writing on this work. I always employ my free time in writing no matter where I am.

With the passing of the months, other exiled bishops began to appear in Rome. I saw Paul of Constantinople who had received worse at the hands of the Arians than I had. Marcellus of Ancyra in lower Galatia, Asclepas of Gaza, and Lucius of Adrianople also came and laid their cause at the feet of Julius.

Each time that I saw His Holiness, and I saw him frequently, I continued to tell him that the Arians would stop at nothing to gain control of the entire Church. Julius made plans for a council for the following summer, but the presbyters that His Holiness sent to the Eusebians to summon them to the council were very long in returning to Rome. When they finally did return, they explained that the Eusebians detained them until January. The reply they brought back with them was a very shifty and devious one.

Early that same spring, the Eusebians sent a message to His Holiness to the effect that they did not think they would be able to be present at the council His Holiness called because the Empire was experiencing some difficulties with the Persians. This message was signed by the group of Arians who assembled in January of 339 in Antioch and who deposed me and sent Gregory to replace me.

Because the letter bearing this message was so acrimonious, Julius kept it a secret from everyone for a while, hoping that at least some of the Arians would come to the proposed council. When His Holiness finally showed me the letter, I was shocked at the contentious and unbecoming way in which the Arians addressed Pope Julius. With words of irony they pretended to honor the successor of Saint Peter, but their insincerity and arrogance were very obvious.

When it became evident that none of the Arians would come for the council, I think His Holiness began to get some idea of the sort of men the Arians are. Writing them a letter telling them that their refusal to come was very suspicious, Julius condemned the heresy of Arius in no uncertain terms. Chiding them for not coming to the council, he informed them that Arian ordinations are not valid in the Catholic Church. Putting aside all their reasons for not coming as vain excuses, he denounced the council in which they deposed me, declaring it to be unecclesiastical and uncanonical. Everyone knows that it is a sacerdotal law that whatever is transacted contrary to the will of the Bishop of Rome is invalid!

Finally, Julius held a synod of bishops in Italy in which I was completely vindicated of all the charges the Arians ever made against me. He wrote to the Arians informing them that I, and Paul of Constantinople, Marcellus, and Asclepas were all vindicated.

Waiting to see what reaction all this would have on the Eusebians, time passed slowly. In the summer of 341, two years after I had come to Rome, the Eusebians assembled at Antioch for the dedication of Constantine's Golden Church. At this meeting they considered the letter that his Holiness sent them. Eusebius himself was present even though it was just a few months before his death.

A new generation of Arians was arising. As they met in Antioch, they tried to formulate a doctrinal reaction to the Creed of Nicaea by making one of their own.

All told, they composed four creeds. Having, departed from the one true faith, they could not agree among themselves. It is always the nature of heresy to splinter into numerous sects.

Three years dragged slowly by without my being able to return to my church. From Serapion, I learned that the most atrocious crimes were committed against the people of God in Egypt. The letters he managed to secret out of Egypt were filled with grief. Suffice it to ponder only one of them.

"To His Piety Archbishop of Alexandria, Athanasius, from his suffragan bishop, Serapion—health in the Lord! Since your departure for Rome, the atrocities inflicted upon our clergy are beyond belief. Potammon is dead, dying a glorious martyr's death in a most ignominious way. Seizing him one morning as he came from the altar of God, the enemies of Christ beat him so severely that they left him for dead. When one of his deacons found him hours later, he was still unconscious. Although they managed to revive him, a short while later, he breathed forth his holy soul to God.

"Many bishops have been imprisoned. Others who have been in the episcopate a long time have been forced to labor on the public works. Sarapammon has been banished, but so far Paphnutius has escaped the hands of the Arian lunatics, but he has to conduct his ministry from a place of concealment.

"Gregory—that usurping anti-Christ—demands that all of us have communion with him. Because the monks and virgins are steadfastly refusing to have anything to do with him, they are consequently beaten and kicked. Christian burial was even denied the aunt of one of our bishops whom Gregory cruelly persecuted.

"Everywhere Gregory goes, he is accompanied with military pomp and power, always boasting of his influence with the governor. Of course, we know it is Constantius who maintains Gregory in the Church of Egypt. When the holy Father Anthony wrote to Gregory accusing him of his wickedness, saying that he would suffer much wrath if he did not cease persecuting the Christians, Gregory gave Anthony's letter to Duke Balacius, who spat on it, and then threw it contemptuously away. Strangely, General Balacius died a short time later. He was riding on his way to Chaereu, the first halt on the Nile with Nestorius, the Prefect of Egypt, when one of his own horses attacked him. It was the one Nestorius was riding that bit Balacius, dismounting him. His thigh was torn so badly from the horse's bite that they took him straight back to the city where he died three days later.

"There is a wailing over the length and the breadth of Egypt. We long and groan for the expulsion of anti-Christ and for the return of your Piety. We yearn for the peace of Christ. How long, O Lord? is the prayer of every heart. God speed you to us!" Signed, Serapion.

My soul grieved at the thought of what was befalling my sheep. Persecution is an invention of the devil. Truth is not preached with swords and spears—or by means of soldiers. Of all persecutions the worst is that which comes from Christians who do not have the spirit of Christ. Such persecutors are truly the allies of the devil! Their conduct is inexplicable. The devil is anti-Christ and always prowls about seeking whom he may destroy, but why should anyone who calls himself Christian persecute his brothers in Christ? What is in the soul of man that makes him want to be as a god? How is it possible for men to assert themselves over their brothers, to exalt themselves over all, and at the same time to regard themselves as humble and holy!

No martyrdom is more cruel than one inflicted in the name of God. Oh the agony of soul—the sleepless nights—I have known because of these Arian madmen! By persecution the devil thinks to destroy the household of faith. All persecutions are not as violent and open as the Arian persecution or the pagan persecutions—but even persecution in its milder forms is just as insidious. By persecution I mean any molesting or disquieting of souls. Woe to those in authority who use that authority to destroy the peace of Christ in souls and to rupture that charity which is the bond of perfection.

Weary of trying to reason with the Arians, Julius placed all his hopes in Constans' ability to prevail over his brother to obtain my return to Alexandria. Finally, his appeal to Constans was heard. I was summoned to Milan where Constans was preparing to depart for his campaign against the Franks.

Protasius, the Bishop of Milan, welcomed me at his residence. It was he who took me to the imperial palace, even accompanying when Eugenius, the Master of the Palace, took me to the veil of the imperial chamber where such audiences are held. At Treveri I talked to Constans through the traditional veil. At Milan he drew the veil aside and admitted me to the intimacy of his chamber and a face-to-face encounter.

Constans resembled his father with the thick neck of the Flavians and the same lion-like eyes of Constantine. From his grandmother Helena, he inherited a virtuous temperament. Casting his princely dignity completely aside in my presence, he even invited Protasius and me to have lunch with him. I can honestly report that Constans ate sparingly like a bishop. During the course of the simple meal, Constans remarked to me with a winning smile. "I am pledged to uphold the faith of Nicaea, Your Piety."

"May God grant you many years!"

I knew that if he died, we would have no one to serve as mediator between Constantius and us. I studied him carefully observing that he was modestly dressed as befits a Christian emperor.

When the lunch was finished and we were still at table, Constans' face was fairly aglow. Obviously he had something he wished to say—something that he had been saving until the proper moment. After studying our faces for a few seconds, he told us what was on his mind.

"I have written to my brother Constantius requesting that a general council—an ecumenical council—such as was held at Nicaea be called to settle the dispute that has exiled Your Piety from Alexandria."

Perhaps an ecumenical council might help, I thought to myself. I committed the whole affair to God. When Constans went to Gaul, I stayed on in Milan. After Constans finished his campaign against the Franks, he summoned me once more, this time in Treveri.

Because winter was not far distant, I made haste to go to Treveri. Crossing the Alps and arriving at my place of former exile, I found many old friends on hand to welcome me. I rejoiced to see Maximinus who greeted me with his customary tranquility.

"My most persecuted brother in Christ—once more Treveri has the honor of sheltering you. Not only you, but others are here for the same reason."

As my host began taking me to the room in which I stayed when I visited him previously, he called loudly so that his voice could be heard all over the episcopal residence.

"Hosius! Our old friend Athanasius has arrived at last."

When I saw Hosius bounding into the room, arms outstretched to embrace me, my joy knew no limits. Despite his almost ninety years, he was still spry of foot and clear of vision, stooped, but yet vigorous. Now that age had made his skin very white and almost transparent, the scar on his cheek, a witness to the persecution he had experienced, stood out more vividly.

"What brings you to Treveri away from your fair Cordova?" I asked the old confessor whose face was lit with pleasure as he threw his arms around me.

"You have not heard?" he asked with a slight frown creasing his brow. "The ecumenical council of the Church will be held at Sardica when summer comes! I wouldn't miss it," he exclaimed. "There is still plenty of life left in these old bones!"

Nothing was to be done until summer! Separated from my Church and in exile again, I was to remain in Treveri. Because it was my duty ever since Nicaea to inform my people and the universal church of the date of Easter, I wrote my Pascal letter that spring in Treveri. Everyone in Egypt was still laughing at the error Gregory made when he tried to announce the date of Easter to them. Because they did not discover until the middle of Lent that they had begun the fast a week too soon, the Arians had to fast for an extra week. Yes, it was amusing.

Even though I was separated from my sheep by a great distance, I was with them in spirit. Exhorting them to follow the example of Blessed Paul and press on towards the crown of our high calling knowing that we suffer for truth, I gloried in my afflictions, because I knew they were bringing me closer to God.

Although God is always near and has promised to be with us perpetually, when enemies afflict us and persecute us, the Lord comes to us in a special way and imparts to us his peace and his life-giving waters. With joy we draw living water from the fountains of the Savior who was smitten for us. Winter gave way to spring. Spring blossomed into summer. All of the bishops assembled at Treveri set out for Sardica. From all parts of the empire, the members of the episcopate came to the city designated for the council, because of its location on the border between the domains of the two emperors. The Western bishops found lodging in the houses of the people of God, in the parishes, in the inns, in short, wherever they could. Mark and I found rooms in an old inn on the edge of town. Macarius and the two monks remained in Rome.

The first morning after our arrival in Sardica, Mark returned with great distress to the inn where we took lodging. He learned that the Eastern bishops arrived with their usual civil and military escort, accompanied by Count Musonianus and the ex-prefect of Egypt—the one who had caused me so much trouble—Flavius Philagrius.

Deeply troubled, Mark explained, "What is worse, the Arian bishops are lodging in the Palace Sophia of Constantius! I don't like the looks of it at all!" I noted that his hair was graying at the temples as he fretted over the news he was relating to me.

We both knew that none but great officers of the state are admitted into the Palatium. Even judges are not lodged there unless there is no Praetorium available. Yet—despite all this—the Arians were being specially favored in this way.

"Hosius will preside at the council," I remarked trying to give my secretary some confidence. "Philagrius will have no influence here. The council is to be strictly ecclesiastical."

"Guess whom I saw? He was wearing the most elaborate episcopal robes you have ever seen." Mark did not wait for me to venture a guess. "Ischyras!"

Ischyras! The one who so blatantly accused me of smashing his chalice. Later in a moment of remorse, he did write to me confessing that the Eusebians put him up to it. I suppose the vast church they built for him in his village made him relapse. Fortunately, I had with me the letter Ischyras wrote, repenting of the calumny he propagated against me and I intended to present it when the council assembled. With dismay, I learned that all the old charges that had ever been made against me were to be reviewed.

When the council convened, the bishops from the East were in the minority. Since Constantius was their sole defense, when they learned that the council was to be held without the civil authority having anything to do with it, they began to show dissatisfaction. Because the council was to be purely ecclesiastical, they asked for a postponement of several days. No doubt they wanted time to revamp their plots against me and perhaps hatch some new ones.

When we finally did assemble in council and Hosius opened the first session, Basil of Ancyra, the usurper, rose to his feet and told the presiding bishop that the Eastern bishops refused to be seated, until I was removed from the council. They had invented this ruse to keep from facing the issues at hand.

For several days, the council fathers debated as to whether I and the other exiled bishops should be allowed to be seated in the council. When two of their number came to Hosius, affirming that they wished to embrace the Nicene faith and give evidence against them, the Arians became very fearful. So much so that in the middle of the night, the Arian bishops fled the city of Sardica, leaving word with one of the priests of that city that they had to leave because Constantius was victorious in his campaign against the Persians. A flimsy excuse! Hosius wrote to them and told them that either they would come to the council or stand condemned of falsely accusing me. Since they had no intention of returning, we held the council without them.

I was completely acquitted and declared free from all blame. Letters to that effect were sent out to all concerned. We in our turn deposed Stephanus, Acacius, and George of Laodicea. I hoped that I had heard the last of George, a former dealer in pork that the Arians had raised to the episcopacy. Unfortunately, I was to learn a lot more about this butcher and his evil machinations in the months that lay ahead.

Upon fleeing from Sardica, the Eastern bishops went to Philippopolis in Thrace, where they wrote a letter denouncing what occurred in the council at Sardica. Incredibly they had the effrontery to "depose" His Holiness Pope Julius, Hosius, and myself and all the rest of the Western bishops who had been at Sardica! After venting their fury in this manner, they set out for Adrianople. When the people of God in that city refused to have communion with them, they went running to Constantius.

They got the retaliation they wanted. Ten of the laity of Adrianople were beheaded! I saw the tombs of these people just outside their city. Because of the refusal of the priests to hold communion with the Arian anti-Christ, the Bishop of Adrianople was also persecuted, bound in chains of iron on his neck and hands, and driven into banishment! The entire East experienced savage cruelties among the people of God who still opposed the madness of Arianism.

I passed the winter and the spring at Naissus. Having been completely vindicated, I wanted to return to Rome, because a letter from Serapion in Egypt ended all my hopes of going to Alexandria, at least for the time being. He wrote telling me that the harbor was being closely watched. If I were to try to return, I would be seized at the docks. My blood ran cold when I read in his letter, "The order has been issued that you are to be *beheaded!*"

Beheaded! The martyrdom of Blessed Paul was to be mine if I returned home. Heresy gave birth to calumny and now calumny was thirsting for murder. They wanted my head! They would not have it! It was not time for me to die. God still had work for me to do. I could not go to my death and leave the sheep of God without a shepherd to lead them through the hour of crisis that I knew to be fast approaching.

At the beginning of the year 344, just a few months after the late summer council at Sardica, Constans decided to take a hand in Church affairs by sending Vincentius of Capua and Euphrates of Agrippina as legates to Constantius. The message they bore to him did not mince words. Either he was to permit me to return to Alexandria or else Constans would regard the matter as cause for war.

Refusing to let the matter be decided so easily, the Arians fashioned one of their snares for the two legates. The plot which they invented in Antioch to enmesh Bishop Euphrates was the most brazen that they had hatched thus far. Although it was the holy season of Easter, that mattered not the slightest to the clergy of Bishop Stephanus of Antioch. The Arians hired a common prostitute and led her to the room where Bishop Euprhates lay sleeping. By stealth, they managed to get her into the room of the holy bishop, leading her to believe that he had hired her. When she saw that the man she was supposed to service was a bishop, she screamed and refused, destroying the plot before it was really hatched.

During the investigation of the terrible commotion that was caused by the prostitute episode, the palace learned that the clergy of Bishop Stephanus hired the harlot. In an attempt to gloss over their guilt, the Arians called for an immediate council at which they deposed Stephanus, replacing him with another Arian. Contrary to Church law, the new Arian bishop of Antioch was a eunuch!

Incensed by the plot to discredit Bishop Euphrates, Constantius was furious. With the threat of civil war hanging over him, he wrote to Alexandria in August of 344, stating clearly that I was to suffer no more persecution in Egypt.

About this time word came from Serapion that Gregory, the Arian chosen to replace me as archbishop, lay ill and was dying. Word also came to me from Constantius, informing me that he wished to see me to discuss the question of my return to Egypt. Having no intention of walking into another Arian trap, I disregarded his letter. His orders to behead me—which he issued not too long before—were still fresh in my mind.

Even when Constantius wrote a second time requesting to see me, I hesitated. The thought that it was just another Arian plot to capture me was uppermost in my mind. When I received a third letter from Constantius promising my immediate return to Alexandria if I came to see him, I decided to go to Antioch.

Mark and I left Aquileia where we had been since Easter 345, going first to Rome where I received once more the blessing of His Holiness. Reunited with Macarius and the two monks, we journeyed to Treveri, because I wanted to thank Constans personally for pleading my case with his brother. From there we went to Adrianople, finally arriving in Antioch in September. Without further delay we went to the palace where we were welcomed warmly by the master of the palace, who took us to a luxurious apartment that was to be ours during our stay in Antioch. Never have I been extended such hospitality as Constantius offered to us at this time.

The next morning, I was escorted to the throne room where the emperor was awaiting me. In contrast to the modest attire of his brother Constans, Constantius, regally outfitted in the richest silks of purple, was wearing a white fur around his shoulders, and in imitation of his father Constantine, a blonde wig.

Constantius did not look at me. Instead, he kept his eyes straight ahead the entire time he spoke to me.

"Welcome, most venerable bishop."

I bowed before him in the customary manner.

"Our benign clemency has taken notice of your unfortunate situation. We will not allow you to be tossed to and fro any longer. Our only question is this—why did Your Piety delay so long in appealing to our mercy?"

Inadvertently, my hand rose to my throat. Remembering his order to behead me, I did not answer his question.

"Well, in any event, you are here now—at last." The tone of his voice was honey-sweet like nectar. "I shall write at once for you to be given free and undisturbed passage into Alexandria."

It would not be that easy for me to return to my see.

Boldly I spoke out. "As long as my enemies are not corrected and punished for the false accusations that they have made against me, they will be free to do the same things again after my departure from here. Summon them. Expose their conduct, I beg of you."

"That will not be necessary. "I, Constantius, promise Your Piety that I shall never believe any more such accusations against you."

He sealed his words with an oath, calling upon God to witness what he promised. I was satisfied, knowing that the threat of civil war that Constans plagued him with had much to do with my restoration. I certainly did not attribute it to any great change in the heart of Constantius. I knew him too well for that.

I hurried on my way to Jerusalem where I wanted to visit the holy tomb of Christ. When I arrived, Bishop Maximus of Jerusalem, much to my surprise, summoned a council to welcome me to his city. I was truly honored by them. I proceeded by land southward from Jerusalem towards Egypt. My people–clergy and lay people alike—met me at a hundred miles distance from Alexandria and escorted me home amid great rejoicing. I wept unabashedly when I entered my cathedral for the first time in seven years and knelt at the altar to pray. I had been gone since April 16, 339.

Paphnutius was on hand to welcome me. Poor old Potammon must have watched our restoration from heaven. Only one face was absent—that of my holy Father Anthony. If he was still living, I promised myself that I would go soon to Thebes to visit him. I was forty-eight years of age, in the prime of life and eager to resume the care of the flock that the Good Shepherd had entrusted to me. Little did I suspect the horrendous trouble that was brewing.

I gave thanks unto our Lord God for the wonders he wrought and for the assistance he has given. Although he has chastened us sorely, he has not delivered us over to death. He brought me from exile and united me again with my sheep. Life is like a great sea. It seems that the wind blows us across this sea, but in reality each one directs his course with his free will. If one takes Christ as one's pilot, one will, in time, arrive at heaven, our homeport. As there are many storms and waves on the sea, so there are many trials in our lives. If we have faith, we do not faint under trial, but exercising our senses in self-control, we grow stronger in faith. We pass through fire and water, and when God wills, we find relief and refreshment. We take delight in our infirmities and with the blessed Paul rejoice always and give thanks in everything.

Great was our joy at the profound and wonderful peace that prevailed in the churches under our care. Because of the persecution they had endured and also because they were so very thankful that it was over, a great renewal was taking place among the people of God, who had become holy from their sufferings. Many young women renounced marriage to become spouses of Christ. Denouncing the pomp of this world to become monks, young men rushed into the desert in droves. Countless numbers of married people asked to have their marriages dissolved so that both the man and the woman could embrace the monastic life. Christian virtue was practiced with intensity never before known in Egypt. The fervor that was born as a result of the Arian persecution far surpassed that which arose as a result of Diocletian's blood bath.

Dear faithful Serapion, who managed admirably well during my absence, turned over the archiepiscopal residence to me. After the death of Gregory, he took possession of the residence and had everything in readiness for my arrival. In the days that lay ahead, he was to become my right hand. Although he was younger than I, he learned discretion and holiness from my Father Anthony. Consequently, Serapion had the wisdom of a man twice his age.

"It is a great blessing to have Your Piety with us once more," Serapion greeted me. His voice was very soft when he spoke.

Since the night the dagger was thrown at me, this was the first time that I entered the residence. Walking across the entrance chamber to the table where the dagger struck, I reached down and stroked the deep gash the blade cut in the polished brown wood

"A souvenir of the reign of Gregory."

"Those days are gone forever, Piety."

Serapion's warm brown eyes were full of trust and confidence. I could not, however, share his feeling of security. I knew that Constans could die at any hour and leave me at the mercy of Constantius! I tried to explain my feelings.

"Constantius surrounds himself with Arians. All the eunuchs of his palace are Arian. As a matter of fact, the chief of his eunuchs is even named Eusebius."

When I mentioned the eunuchs, I noticed that a half smile played at the corners of Serapion's mouth.

"Don't scoff at these mutilated men. They are powerful! If Constans were to die…" I left the sentence unfinished.

"Ah Piety, never again will the faithful allow you to be expelled. Never will they tolerate such outrages again. They are solidly behind you. At your bidding, they would willingly take up arms to défend their faith and your person."

I paused a moment before speaking.

"Truth is not preached with swords and soldiers. We are making progress. Two of the Arians have recanted their heresy. Valens and Ursacius are the two of whom I am speaking. You probably remember them as being sent by the council of Tyre to the Mareotis with Ischyras."

"Yes, Piety, I do remember Valens, but the other one…no." Serapion shook his head. "I also recall that Valens was a stubborn, outspoken, unrelenting enemy of yours."

"People can change."

In the secret recesses of my mind, I wondered if perhaps Valens merely found it politically expedient to recant his true beliefs now that Constantius reinstated me. Since the death of Eusebius and the old Arians, Valens wielded a great deal of power. Suddenly in one stroke, he relinquished it all. Consequently, he went to Pope Julius and told him that all the accusations the Arians made against me were just so many lies and fabrications.

Stroking his neatly trimmed beard, Serapion pondered the matter before speaking. "I wonder what Acacius, the Bishop of Caesarea, will do now that Valens has recanted? Acacius is, like his predecessor, only a political Arian. Valens, on the other hand, was more Arian than Arius—yet he has deserted their cause."

I shrugged my shoulders. "I suppose you heard who was chosen to be Bishop of Antioch after the terrible scandal in which the Arians introduced a harlot into the room of Bishop Euphrates?"

"Another Arian—at least so I hear, "replied Serapion pensively. "By the name of Leontius, I believe."

"Correct. But there is more to it than that. Leontius had himself castrated so he could be free to sleep with a woman who calls herself a virgin! Her name is Eustolium. The very idea! As far as he is concerned, she is a wife. Eunuchs! They hate Christ more than anyone else. Since they cannot have a son they deny God that right."

I walked to the windows of my study so that I could watch the waves breaking on the beach where I observed the tide was ebbing. Abruptly I changed the subject.

"Father Anthony, he is well?"

"Ah, yes, of course. Serapion smiled warmly at the mention of the holy hermit. "Hale and hearty at ninety-five, he is too holy to become ill and too strong to die for a long time to come. He sent word by one of the monks that he wants you to visit him. Ah, Your Piety, there are times when I wish—I wish that I were still a monk back at Pispir with him instead of..."He stopped speaking in the middle of the sentence and sighed. I could read his thoughts. Once I too had expressed the same desire to be back at Pispir.

Instead of donning the robes of a bishop, I noticed that he continued wearing his monk's tunic. As I studied him, I saw in Serapion something of the spirit of Anthony who taught him the ways of God. I decided to have him continue residing at the archiepiscopal residence. I needed him—both as a fellow minister of Christ and as a companion.

During the early weeks after my return to Alexandria, there were many people who came to see me. One of the most delightful visitors was a holy layman by the name of Frumentius of Ethiopia. I recall him as if that meeting were only yesterday.

Glancing up from the book I was reading, I expected to see an Ethiopian. Instead I saw a fair skinned young man of about thirty-five years of age that addressed me in fluent Greek.

"You are from Ethiopia?" I was truly curious.

"Originally, I came from Tyre."

I listened patiently as Frumentius told me his life's story. His uncle Meropius, a Tyrian by race, was a philosopher who decided to travel to Ethiopia many years ago, taking with him young Frumentius and his fellow kinsman, Edesius. When they arrived by ship in Ethiopia, they tried to put in at a harbor to purchase necessary supplies, not realizing that a short time previously the treaty that the empire made with Ethiopia was violated. The Ethiopians seized the philosopher, killed him and all of his party, with the exception of Frumentius and Edesius.

"Because we were so young they had compassion on us," explained Frumentius. "They sent us as a gift to their king." With gestures and acting out everything that occurred, Frumentius related how Edesius was made a cup bearer and entrusted with the custody of the royal records. In time, the old king died, leaving the government to his wife and infant son.

"The queen begged us to stay and help her. So, we took up the task of ruling Ethiopia." Humbly he inclined his head as he spoke.

"Had I known that I was entertaining a head of state," I apologized," I could have managed more solemnity. But I am not one to stand on protocol. The ways of the court are foreign to me." I gazed in wonderment at the blond young man with the seraphic face whose blue eyes spoke to me of virtue and holiness of life.

"Holy Father—I am but a child of the Church!"

I was pleased with his response and urged him to tell me more of his story.

"There were no Christians in Ethiopia," he continued. "It was my great desire to see our Savior loved and worshiped by the pagans in my care. When ships put in at our river harbor, I exhorted all the Christians who arrived in our land to stay, select, and occupy a place of worship. Before long we had a house of prayer and the Ethiopians were learning about Christ."

My amazement kept increasing.

"Ah! Since there were no priests or bishops for your people, God chose you, a layman, to be the Apostle to the Ethiopians! May He be praised and glorified forever!" I liked this young Frumentius with his straight posture and his pure blue eyes.

"That is why I came to Your Piety. The young prince is now old enough to run the government. I am free to do as I please. I came to beg Your Piety—in the name of my people–to send bishops and priests to Ethiopia."

I laughed with joy. The inspiration of God flooded my soul with light.

"Frumentius, you will be the Bishop of Ethiopia!"

The following Sunday, in the great Theonas Cathedral, I ordained him a priest and consecrated him as a bishop of the church of God. Later, I blessed him privately when he was ready to return to his country.

"Please, Your Piety, you must come to visit us in Ethiopia some-day."

"Some day I shall," I promised.

The inspiration of God whispered in my soul that one day Frumentius would give me refuge when those who would seek to kill me in Egypt would hunt me down like a wild animal, invading even the tombs of the dead to find me.

It was about this time—just a few months after I returned from exile—that Pachomius died. A delegation came from Tabenne, bringing the sorrowful news that their holy founder died on the fourteenth of Pachon, in the year of our Lord 346. An epidemic they explained spread through the monasteries claiming many lives. Faithful Pachomius, who cared for his spiritual children in their illness, himself succumbed. The monasteries were still flourishing and growing stronger, however, they proudly reported. I gave them my blessing and my wholehearted support.

I had another visitor soon after this. I was taken completely by surprise when Mark announced that Arsenius was waiting outside my study to see me.

"Show him in."

I walked towards the door to meet the old Arian whom I was once accused of murdering and cutting off his hand. A fat little man, with his brow creased with lines of worry, nervously made his way into my study.

I couldn't resist asking him, "How are you getting along now that you lost your third hand?"

He blushed and without further ado threw himself at my feet. Covering my hands with kisses and with tears streaming down his cheeks he begged my forgiveness.

"Piety...forgive! Forgive me! I have sinned and I am truly sorry and I am repentant."

I peered into his soul. "Is this a confession you are making to me as a priest of Jesus Christ?" I asked with compassion.

"Yes" he sobbed.

I said nothing.

He began making a recital of all his sins especially of those against the true faith and against me, his bishop. When I lifted my hand in blessing and said, "I absolve you," Arsenius heaved a great sigh, rose to his feet, and started towards the door.

"My son..." I called after him.

He turned towards me uncertainly, not daring to raise his eyes. He waited for me to speak.

"Christ needs you, Arsenius, and," I added softly, "I need you."

He glanced at me furtively and then looked out the window.

"The church in Hypsele—" I watched as his face began to brighten—"the church in Hypsele," I repeated, "needs a bishop."

Arsenius stared at me in amazement. "You mean you can forgive—Christ can forgive—everything?" he stammered.

"My son" I said, as I laid my hand on his shoulder "When Jesus forgives, he blots out the entire sin as if it never happened."

Tears were beginning to flow again, running down his cheeks, following the creases of his wrinkles.

"Thank you, Piety!"

"Don't thank me," I protested. "Thank Jesus who died for your sins."

Hypsele found a true pastor in the repentant Arsenius.

It was necessary to make other appointments to the episcopate. I appointed a coadjutor for old Artemidorus in Panopolis, because he requested help due to his old age and infirmity. With great sadness I chose a successor to my old friend Potammon. Sethroitis needed someone to take his place, so I sent Orion. From this time on, I began to fill the vacancies in the episcopate with monks. Consequently, the bishops under me became solidly loyal and strong in holiness. There were no more Arians to be found in Egypt, except for a handful of lay people in Alexandria who were no threat to our peace and harmony. Once everything was in good order and I felt free to leave Alexandria, Serapion and I mounted our horses and set out for Chaereu, the first halt on the Nile on the way to Thebes.

From one end of the desert to the other, word spread of our trip to the monks at Pispir. When we were still fifty miles distant from the community at Thebes where I lived as a child, two monks who were sent out to meet us greeted us. Ammon and Dracontius welcomed us, not only on behalf of Anthony's monks but also on behalf of all the countless communities of monks in the desert—communities of both male and female ascetics.

"Your Piety," said Dracontius with great solemnity, "twenty thousand monks are awaiting your arrival at Pispir. When it was learned that you were coming to visit the Holy Hermit, monks and virgins began arriving by the score."

Ammon nodded, seconding everything Dracontius was saying. Serapion, who knew both Dracontius and Ammon intimately, blurted out impulsively, "We have been looking for men, Your Piety, who will make good bishops—well, Dracontius is a true scholar and a leader of men. He would make an excellent bishop."

"Never!" cried Dracontius in alarm.

I was surprised to hear him speak so vehemently. I was also surprised at the strange turn the conversation had assumed.

"Would it be so unpleasant as all that," I asked, "to feed the people of God?"

"No," he answered softly. "It's not that. The idea is simply distasteful to me."

Patiently I explained to Dracontius, as we journeyed to Pispir, that the episcopate has its rewards. I reminded him that it was established by the Savior himself and pointed out to him that he would never have known Christ, if there had been no bishop to baptize him. I explained that a bishop's office is not an occasion of sin and that one can be both an ascetic and a bishop.

Not seeming convinced, he merely smiled and pointed at the large army of monks who were coming down the road to meet us. They had built a bishop's chair for me and placed it on a platform that they were bearing on their shoulders. When they were amassed around me, they dropped to their knees and would not rise until I mounted their chair and permitted them to bear me the rest of the way to Pispir.

When at length they put me down again, I was in an assembly of thousands of monks. I greeted them with great joy. "Glory to the Father and to the Son and to the Holy Spirit!"

Twenty thousand voices thundered back the response. "As it was in the beginning, is now and ever shall be down through the ages of ages!"

Since it was Sunday, they requested me to offer the Holy Sacrifice and to give the Body and Blood of Christ to the throng that, fasting, waited my arrival. At an altar in the open air, I began the ancient liturgy handed down through the ages of time since the apostles. The first lesson from the Holy Scripture was read and then followed by a psalm. Like angelic choirs, the monks chanted the words of David. The second lesson followed and then another psalm was chanted so beautifully that it must have made the angels glad. I gave the blessing for the dismissal of the catechumens and to any penitents who were to leave before the Holy Sacrifice proper began.

How wonderful the liturgy sounded with the swell of twenty thousand voices making the responses to my prayers. I gave the kiss of peace. Two monks brought the oblations to the altar. With profound peace, I read the diptychs, the second collect and the prayer for the people. Dracontius poured water on my hands. When they were purified, I began with joy the Eucharistic prayer, thanking the Eternal Father for creation, for the garden of Eden, for the Incarnation, praying that we might join the choirs of angels who praise God and say—"Holy, holy, holy, Lord God of Hosts." The monks sang this refrain.

I continued the prayer, praising God the Son who having been made man took bread and blessed it. I pronounced the holy words of the institution. The glorified Body and Blood of Jesus were once more on the altar before me as I elevated the Mysteries for all to behold. As I listened to the monks repeat together the words of the prayer the Savior taught us, I thanked the Lord for the holy men of prayer he had given me. With the help of a large number of deacons, we began to communicate all those assembled.

I found great happiness in looking into the upturned faces of the monks who knelt waiting for me to give them the Body and Blood of the Lord. The greatest joy of all came when I gave Christ to my Father Anthony who had waited until over half of the multitude had communicated before approaching the altar. His face glowed with divine light as, lost in God, he turned and disappeared into the crowd to make his thanksgiving.

Later that day, I went to the cell of the holy hermit who was still rapt in God when I arrived. Since he did not hear me knock at his entrance, I let myself in and stood beside him laying my hand on his shoulder. With a seraphic smile he greeted me in a whisper.

"Welcome, Athanasius, my son."

"Tell me about God, Father," I asked the way I had done when I was a child and had surprised him in his contemplation.

"God is all love."

Sighing with a tremor in his voice, he returned to his heavenly vision. Until, at length, he was ready to speak, I knelt beside him sharing his prayer. Then I asked him about visions. I wanted to know how one could discern true ones from false ones.

"The vision God sends," he replied, "is not filled with distractions. It comes very quietly and gently so that immediately joy—gladness and strength come to the soul. It is the Lord of Joy who comes to us. When he comes, the soul remains at peace and undisturbed and feels itself to be enlightened. Divine love possesses you. Willingly you would be wholly united to him—if you could depart with him, you would go at once."

So transfigured by grace and having the appearance of a celestial being, the holy monk, seemed no longer to belong to this earth. Pausing to consider his words carefully before continuing, he said, "But, my son, the devil's visions are filled with confusion. They cause fear and tumult in the soul. Confusion of mind—despondency—hatred for those who live the spiritual life—these are all signs of the devil's visions. The evil one produces fear of death in souls and the desire for evil things, hatred of virtue, and bad habits."

I was filled with wonderment at the holiness that shone from his eyes.

"By their fruits you shall recognize them," I remarked softly.

"Exactly. Sometimes a soul that is unaccustomed to holy visions will experience fear at the beginning of the vision, but God will immediately reassure the soul and the fear will be immediately taken away and in its place will come an ineffable joy—love—ecstatic rapture." Sighing deeply, he buried his face in his hands, and murmured, "Oh, how good our Jesus is!"

Once more he was engulfed in God. Silently I rose and left his cell, leaving him alone with Christ.

The next day, when he was more attuned to the things of this earth, I had ample opportunity to converse with him. Then I learned that Constantius had written to him, begging his prayers and his advice. At first, he disdained the emperor's letters, but at the insistence of the monks, he decided to answer them. Imploring the emperor to be merciful, just, and benevolent, he advised him to be more concerned with the coming judgment than with the things of this world, reminding him that Christ alone is the true and Eternal King.

I said "Amen" to that and returning to Alexandria, I was able to enjoy, for a time, respite from trouble. I am glad I did not know then the sufferings that lay ahead.

Perhaps more than he ever realized, Constantius needed prayer. Added to the grief the Persian war caused him, a fresh menace to his sovereignty arose. I head about it first from Mark who came rushing into my study after he returned one day from the shopping district of Alexandria.

"Constans is dead! Everyone in the street is talking about it!" He paused to catch his breath.

"What happened man? Speak up," I snapped, realizing that we were entering upon very perilous times.

"Magnentius—the Governor of the Province of Rhoetia murdered him! It happened in Gaul—January 18th." Mark studied my face to see my reactions to his words.

"God grant him eternal refreshment. And may God have mercy on us all!"

I wondered what Constantius would do. We heard from him shortly thereafter in a letter in which he begged me not to listen to any vain rumors from anyone who might try to alarm me, insisting that he wished me to remain as Archbishop of Alexandria. His reference to "vain rumors" gave me reason to believe that already the Arians approached him with the suggestion that I be once more exiled. All I could do was watch, wait, and hope that the promises he made upon his oath would be honored even though his brother was no longer alive to guarantee them.

For the time being, Constantius had more on his mind than bishoprics, because immediately Magnentius grasped the reigns of the entire government of Constans. Then another usurper arose–Vetranio, who had himself proclaimed Emperor by the Illyrian troops at Sirmium. Still another contender appeared in the person of Nepotian—a son of Constans' sister Eutropia. Organizing the gladiators, Nepotian set out to overthrow Magnentius. He failed utterly. Both he and his mother who was also the sister of Constantius were slain by the soldiers of Magnentius. Prepared to fight both Vetranio and Magnentius, Constantius proclaimed himself sole Augustus. When Constantius marched confidently into Sirmium, where Vetranio had established himself, and when the Illyrian troops saw Constantius arrive in power, they deserted Vetranio and greeted Constantius as sole Augustus.

I was most happy to learn that Constantius treated Vetranio with mercy as befits a Christian Emperor. Throwing himself at the feet of Constantius, Vetranio asked for clemency. Stripping him of the purple and of all imperial ornaments, the emperor told him to return to private life. He even went so far as to give him a large sum of money from the imperial treasury to provide for his future, advising him that it would be more fitting for an old man to renounce the cares and worries of imperial rule and to live a serene old age. Later, I heard that afterwards Vetranio wrote often to Constantius thanking him deeply for having spared him the cares of world rule.

Magnentius proved to be a more difficult opponent. I did not trust him even as much as I did Constantius. Had he not murdered his own master, Constans? Was he not faithless to his friends? In addition he blasphemed God by consulting poisoners and sorcerers and even violated his oath. Hoping to take advantage of the conflict that existed between Constantius and myself, he sent a group of ambassadors to Egypt en route to Constantius. When these men came into my study, I knew that they came to seek my support for Magnentius. One word from me and all the people of Egypt would support him against the Emperor, so strong was my influence among the people and even among the pagans who respected my kindness towards them.

Questioning Clementius, whom Magnentius sent to me, I asked him how Constans died. When I heard the cruel barbaric way in which he was slain, and when I remembered his kindness and his Christlike spirit, there were tears in my eyes. I wanted no part of the murderer's plot. I feared that perhaps Magnentius planned to invade Egypt. As the ambassadors he sent surveyed me, I exclaimed, "Let us pray for the safety of Constantius." With that I terminated the interview.

I ordered prayers in all our churches for the safety of the emperor.

On March 1, Constantius proclaimed his cousin Gallus as "Caesar," even bestowing his own name upon him. Threatened by Magnentius in the West, and needing someone to guard the East for him, he chose the son of his father's brother Consul Julius Constantius, who was put to death after the death of Constantine. Gallus had been spared because of his poor health, the thought being that he would die of natural causes.

I knew that Gallus was reared as an Arian, for he had been entrusted to the care of Eusebius of Nicomedia for his religious training. His mother, Basilina, was also an Arian, and helped to depose the true Bishop of Adrianople. Naturally my enemies felt their position strengthened by the ascension of Gallus to the purple.

Like dogs, Ursacius and Valens returned to their vomit. Like swine they returned to wallow in their former impiety. Denying their recantation of Arianism, they circulated the story that the fear of Constantius caused them to recant what they still believed in their hearts. Of course, Valens profited greatly by recanting. He was now bishop of the powerful See of Mursa. All over the empire the Arians were beginning again to raise their ugly heads and Serapion and I were concerned about what they might do in the future.

"Surely, Serapion, Constantius will not break his oath and believe any more false accusations against me."

"We shall watch and pray, Piety."

Watch and pray we did. Magnentius managed to make himself master of the city of Rome where he killed many members of the senatorial council. As Constantius advanced upon him with great armies, the tyrant Magnentius fled into Gaul. A number of battles were fought. Sometimes one had the advantage, sometimes, the other. Finally Magnentius was defeated at the fortress Mursa, causing him to flee deeper into Gaul. Near Mount Seleucus, Constantius utterly routed him. Alone Magnentius fled to Lugduna, where he killed his mother, his brother, and took his own life by falling upon his sword.

Valens of Mursa regarded Constantius' victory as an Arian triumph. Since all the old Arians were dead, except Secundus, a new generation sprang up, looking to Valens as their leader. More resolute than Eusebius, more Arian than Arius, he might be described as an ultra Arian, for he scorned the compromises the first Arians were willing to make.

I could see clouds gathering for the storm. When Pope Julius died in 352 after fighting the Arian madmen for twenty-five years, I lost a good friend and a great champion for my cause. Liberius, whom I was anxious to contact, succeeded him. Thinking that a delegation to Italy would serve the twofold purpose of sounding out both His Holiness Liberius and the emperor, I discussed the idea with Serapion, who agreed with me that there was cause for alarm. There was a rumor rife in Alexandria that Constantius had publicly announced his intention of bringing all the bishops to unity in matters of doctrine. On the 24th of Pachon, May 19, 353, Serapion, Bishop Triadelphus of Nicion, Apollo of Upper Cynopolis, and three priests from Alexandria set sail for Italy where Constantius was in residence in Milan. Four days later, an officer of the palace, Montanus, arrived in Alexandria with a letter from Constantius addressed to me. It was a strange letter that purported to be in answer to a letter which I had supposedly written to him requesting his permission to go to Italy,

Since I had not written the emperor, I suspected an Arian plot. However, Montanus' arrival with the letter caused no harm. When the people of Alexandria learned of his presence in the city they caused such a tumult that he fled in terror.

Since Constantius did not order me to come to his court, I decided to remain in Alexandria. I figured that Serapion and the others that I sent to Milan would be able to smooth out any difficulties that might arise.

When the delegates that I sent to Constantius returned in November, they had much to report. Not even waiting for Serapion to unpack, I followed him to his room and began plying him with questions.

"You saw Constantius?" I asked eagerly as I sat down on a chair.

"No, he refused to see us." His kindly gray eyes were very serious.

"I guess he has forgotten how he wrote to me after Constans' death. Then he expressed the desire that I trust in him the way I did in his brother."

"I am afraid he has forgotten." Serapion slammed his fist into his open palm. "Look!" he cried. "It's bad news, I'm afraid we are in for the worst!"

"Go ahead. Tell me. I'm ready for it."

"Constantius summoned a small provincial council at Arles. Everyone present agreed to the emperor's condemnation of Your Piety."

I took a deep breath. Without a trace of emotion I asked, "Did you see Pope Liberius?"

"Liberius' delegates were at Arles. They signed too—the same as all the rest."

"God forbid! But did you see Liberius?"

"Yes, we saw him. He desires to undo the evil work of his legates. The Council of Arles was very small–strictly provincial. Constantius decided to have you deposed at a great council in Milan. Liberius is doing everything he can to postpone it."

Sighing deeply, I confided myself into the hands of God.

"And what of Hosius, and the saintly Bishop Eusebius of Vercellae, and Lucifer of Sardinia and Hilary of Poitiers?"

"I did not see any of them. It is Your Piety that Constantius considers his greatest enemy. While he wintered at Arles right after he defeated Magnentius, he is rumored to have said that Your Piety was more to be feared and more detested by him than his archenemy Magnentius."

I kept wondering what sort of lies my enemies told him? Later I found out that charges were being brought against me, accusing me of turning Constans against his brother. First I was charged with speaking ill of Constantius to Constans. It was preposterous! Why Constantius knew that I never spoke evil of anyone. When he himself had interviews with me, did I ever breathe forth a single unkind word about anyone? No! I did not even speak evil to him about my enemies.

The second charge against me was treason. I was accused of corresponding with Magnentius. After I heard these charges, I passed many sleepless nights trying to decide what I could say to prove my innocence. Perhaps, I reflected, Constantius would remember his promise that he made me, saying he would no longer listen to or believe any accusations against me.

I decided to visit my holy Father Anthony. Since he often had visions of the future, I wanted to hear what he would advise. When I arrived at the inner mountain, he came out of his cell at the sound of my footfalls. Smiling at me with the tenderness of the very aged, he greeted me.

"I was expecting you today."

"You knew I was coming?" I was amused.

"Oh, yes," he replied with childlike simplicity. "My angel told me."

I entered his cell. Kneeling at his feet I poured out all the perplexity and anguish of my soul. When I had quite finished, he fell into deep thought and pondered all I had told him.

"Soon it will be Athanasius against the entire world!"

Pressing his handmade cross to his lips, he sank into a deep trance. I could see his temples pulsating under his shrunken marble-like skin. A groan escaped his lips. He began to tremble. I put my arms around him to steady him.

"What is it, Father?" I asked with alarm.

He did not answer. The vision he was experiencing caused him to weep bitterly. Large tears dropped from his face and fell on my hands that were still supporting his trembling, thin body. At length he opened his eyes.

"Oh my son, it would be better to die than to live and see such things come to pass." He burst into tears. How touching it is to see an old man cry.

"Wrath is about to descend upon the Church of Christ. Men who are like brute animals will grasp the Church from us." He spoke in whispers.

"What did you see, Father?" I urged him gently.

"I saw the altar of God surrounded by mules who were kicking to overthrow it! And Christ spoke to me, saying that his altar will be defiled."

Meditating on what the holy hermit had just said, I put my head in my hands. Gently he reached over and took my hand in his.

"Don't be sad, my son." With a seraphic smile that revealed his great charity he added softly, "Truth shall triumph!"

A few weeks later, I was alerted to what might be in store for me. Philagrius, the former Prefect of Alexandria, came to our city. Since I was not at home when he came to the archiepiscopal residence—I was visiting with Macarius at his church that afternoon—Serapion received him. When I did return, Serapion met me at the entrance, eager to speak to me. "Piety," he said with distress "truly you should not travel abroad so freely in Alexandria. In a city of over a million people, there are all kinds."

I knew at once something was troubling him. This was merely the preamble that he was giving me.

"What is it?" I inquired trying to read his thoughts.

"Philagrius stopped here this afternoon."

"Flavius Philagrius?" I doubted that it could be the same. "The apostate who follows the Arians around?"

"Yes, the same. Recently he was made deputy governor in Cappadocia."

"So? What did he want of me?"

"I don't quite know." Serapion's eyes narrowed to slits. "He told me that Paul has been deposed from his chair in Constantinople and that the Arian Macedonius is once more in control of the see."

"What happened to Paul?" I was afraid of hearing the worst.

"He is dead. He was banished to Cucusus—near the desert. They locked him up in a very dark confining place where they left him to die of starvation." Sighing deeply, Serapion signed himself with the cross of Christ.

"They are fiends from hell!"

With his customary monastic calm, Serapion laid his hand on my arm. "Piety, you have not heard it all. When they returned six days later they found him still alive. They pounced on him and strangled him to death."

I gasped. I thought I could no longer be surprised by anything these enemies of Christ might do. I was wrong. The murder of Paul stunned me. I understood why Philagrius had come to my office. The Arians hoped the recital of this story would unnerve me. This was merely—I discovered later—the first step in a plot to remove all my friends from their sees so that I alone would remain in opposition to their evil machinations. They thought to themselves, "We will see how long Athanasius will be able to hold out when he no longer has anyone to whom he can have recourse."

Things kept getting worse. Constantius revealed his true colors when he had Gallus killed—slain in cold blood! Then he placed his head on a pike in the center of the city for all to see. Next Constantius turned his wrath against me. Presenting in person my deposition to the bishops at a council that he summoned in Milan, he demanded that either they sign it or go into banishment. Protesting that there was no ecclesiastical canon for his action, a number of bishops, including Lucifer of Sardinia and the holy Eusebius of Vercallae, insisted to him that the entire council was without precedent. He hurled these words at them: "Whatever *I* will—regard that as a canon!"

When the staunch supporters of Christ then told the emperor that the kingdom of the Church belongs to Christ, not Caesar, and threatened him with the judgment of God, Constantius went into a rage, drawing his sword against the holy bishops.

Knowing that his wrath would soon overtake me, I waited for the blow to strike. It was not long in coming. In the month of Mesori, on the Egyptian calendar, August on the Latin, when we were in the midst of the most oppressively hot summer in a decade, I went out that morning onto the beach in hopes of finding relief from the heat. There was a breeze rippling the waters of the sea. As I sat on the sand watching the white clouds drifting by, I let the sea and the sky raise my thoughts to the contemplation of God. In the midst of my reflections that God is more mighty and more majestic than the sea and more infinite and mysterious than the sky, Mark came running down from the house waving his arms excitedly.

"Piety! The secretary of Constantius has arrived in Alexandria to drive you from the city!"

"Blessed be God!" I answered with great peace of soul. "If you have no further news, let me return to my contemplation."

Looking at me in surprise, Mark shook his head and hurried back to the house. I needed time to pray and be alone with God to learn what course he wanted me to follow. Finally, I rose, blessed myself in the name of the Trinity, and went up to the house where I found Mark and Serapion having a heated argument as to what we should do.

"What else have you heard?" I asked looking from Mark to Serapion who seemed to be better informed.

"The secretary, Diogenes by name, is trying to turn the local people and the judges against Your Piety so that *they* will drive you from the city." Serapion paced nervously back and forth from the window to the door of my study.

"He won't succeed," Mark insisted. "The people of God and even the pagans want Your Piety to remain. They will fight if necessary."

"But," interrupted Serapion, "the prefect has received an imperial order encouraging him and everyone else to insult Your Piety and to attempt to expel you."

I knew the prefect well. "You have heard from the prefect?" I inquired.

"Yes. Maximus told us that he will assist Your Piety in any way that he can." Serapion was wringing his hands as he continued speaking.

"But he warned me that the magistrates of the city have been threatened, if they refuse to hold communion with the Arians."

"So that's how it stands!"

After praying a moment, I stated our course of action with confidence. "For the present, we shall continue our usual way of life. We shall wait and see what Diogenes will do."

Daily, I kept expecting that Diogenes would come to our residence with a letter from Constantius. No letter came. Instead he chose another mode of attack. On the sixth day of the month of Thot, September 4, he hired a large mob of dissolute youths from the lowest classes of the city. With a few Arians, he stormed Dionysius Church. Intending to wrestle this church from my care and hand it over to an Arian pastor, he failed miserably, when our people rose up against him and drove him from the church.

Not conceding defeat, a few days later Diogenes stormed another church.

He was again driven away. Not dismayed, he continued storming churches until he finally wearied of it December 23, when he gave up and left the city. Since even the magistrates would not help him, he realized he was fighting a losing battle.

A short time later, we were curious to know what Constantius had in mind when we heard that he summoned his young cousin Julian, the brother of the dead Gallus, to Milan. Because he was only eight years old when his parents were slain, Julian was spared on account of his tender age. Reared in the palace Macelium in Cappadocia, he came under the influence of Eusebius of Nicomedia. Since it was hoped for a time that Julian might even become a priest, he was enrolled among the clergy and became a lector at the Divine Liturgy. When he went to school in Constantinople and mingled freely with the other students, a rumor circulated that the boy hoped to become emperor one day.

When Constantius heard that Julian hoped to be elevated to the purple, he demanded that Julian return from Constantinople to

Nicomedia. Learning that Constantius was fearful that he might be a threat to the throne, Julian shaved himself and became a monk, satisfying Constantius that he intended to continue in the Church. Upon the death of Gallus, Constantius, afraid that Julian might rise up against him, placed Julian under guard until his wife, the empress, interceded for Julian and Constantius granted him permission to study in Athens. When Constantius received Julian, November 6, 355, he proclaimed him Caesar, married him to his sister Helena, and sent Julian into Gaul as a general of his army.

Rumors began to pour into Alexandria. The bishops who refused to sign my deposition at Milan were arriving in all parts of the East and telling of Arian schemes that were afoot to destroy the true faith of Christ. Bishop Dionysius of Milan had been banished and Auxentius, a busybody and certainly not a Christian, was now occupying his see. Auxentius was made a "priest" by the usurper Gregory. He had no more right to the see of Milan than did an ape! Why he knows absolutely no Latin! He is a Cappadocian who knows only irreligion!

When Duke Syranus arrived in Alexandria on January 6, an attack, intended to be fatal, was launched against me.

"The Duke has brought with him a large force of the Roman legions," Mark reported with much agitation.

"Perhaps," suggested Serapion with monastic calm, "Your Piety should leave Alexandria before it is too late." His eyes had dark circles under them, betraying his loss of sleep.

I considered the matter carefully and prayerfully.

"I have not yet received an ultimatum from Constantius. We shall send Mark to Syrianus to inquire if he has brought any communication from the emperor for me."

When Mark returned from seeing Syrianus, who had no messages from Constantius, I sent Syrianus, a copy of the letter which Constantius wrote me in 351, advising me of his desire that I continue as

Bishop of Alexandria. I hoped that would forestall any action against me for the time being.

When our people caught wind of Syrianus' arrival, there were many rumors circulated regarding his intentions. He let it be known that he was in the city merely awaiting orders from the emperor. Evidently many people were receiving orders from Constantius.

One afternoon—it was late—near the dinner hour—Paphnutius came to our residence dragging his hamstrung leg behind him with great difficulty. He had aged considerably and the sight of his one good eye had grown dim with the passing of the years.

"Ah! Piety!" He took my hands in his. His voice trembled from old age and from emotion. "I have been ordered to subscribe against you. I have been ordered to hold communion with the Arians—or be exiled!"

I knew exile would mean death for the old confessor, who even in his declining months could find no peace from the persecutions that plagued him all his life. Since he was very weak, I wondered if perhaps Our Lord would call him home before the reign of terror arrived. I asked Macarius to take Paphnutius into his home and to care for him.

More of my bishops received similar threats from the emperor. Meanwhile Duke Syrianus lulled the people into a false sense of security by announcing that, by Caesar's life, he would do nothing until he heard from Constantius.

On Thursday night, it was, the 13th of the month of Mechir, I went to the Cathedral to preside over a service that was in preparation for communion the next day, Friday after Septuagesima. For this vigil service, the sanctuary was filled with a good number of monks, men that Serapion selected to safeguard my welfare. Halfway through the vigil service, I preached to the people, telling them that God is the ruler over this world. I remember my very words. "Unwittingly evil men work out the designs of the All Loving Providence of the Father. All things are for the best for those who love the Lord..."

At this point, I was interrupted by shouts outside our Theonas Cathedral and by the galloping of horses and the rattling of arms.

Mark, who was right beside me, explained what was happening. "Your Piety, the Cathedral is surrounded by about five thousand soldiers!"

Although the soldiers were banging violently on the doors of the cathedral, I calmly finished my sermon. Then I went to my throne in the apse and in a steady and strong voice, I announced, "The deacon will read the psalm with the people making the usual response."

It was not without reason that I chose a particular psalm. Just as Syrianus burst into the church with the notary Hilary, Mark chanted, "Give thanks to the Lord our God!"

"For his mercy is everlasting." Like a clap of thunder the people responded.

"Give thanks to the God of Heaven."

"For his mercy is everlasting."

"Who alone does great and wonderful deeds." On we continued with the psalm.

"Who smites great kings and slays them."

"'Who does not forget us in our abjection."

"Who frees us from our enemies."

The congregation suddenly realized what was happening. Someone yelled, "Flee, Your Piety! Don't let them take you! Flee!"

Soldiers surrounded the sanctuary.

"We shall not leave until His Piety is free," shouted the congregation.

The people shook their fists at the Arians who stood at the chancel railing whispering my name and pointing at me.

With great calm I rose to my feet, gave the blessing of dismissal, and said, "Very dear children, I, your Bishop, shall leave last of all. I desire that none of you be injured or hurt in any way. Go in peace!"

Obediently they began to file out. With his eyes bulging, the Duke was leering at me, probably already relishing the reward that Constantius promised for capturing me. Remembering the horrible death Constantius and the Arians gave the Bishop of Constantinople, the thought of falling into their hands was abominable to me. Perhaps they would also behead me and display my head on a pike in the shadow of Cleopatra's needles! These were my thoughts while the people were leaving the Cathedral. In minutes, I thought, Duke Syrianus would take me prisoner. I pictured myself becoming a martyr like the Blessed Apostle Paul.

When only a few worshipers still remained in the church, one of the monks who was in the sanctuary near me made a signal to his fellow monks. Suddenly monks surrounded me. They were pulling me—pushing me—dragging me from the sanctuary. Like a heap of ants they converged on me. I heard the Duke shout. Then a pain shot through my head and I lost consciousness.

When I opened my eyes again, Serapion was bending over me, fanning my face and sighing deeply. When he saw my eyelids flutter he cried, "Ah! Piety! Piety, did we hurt you?"

I lifted my hand to my head and groaned. I could feel a large egg-like swelling where something had struck me. Serapion rushed to get a cold wet cloth that he applied gently to the knot on my head, affording me some relief. I sat up uncertainly. I found that I was in a small windowless chamber alone with Serapion. When I saw his worried face, as he studied mine the way a mother does a sick child's, I burst out laughing.

"Old fellow, you amaze me!"

"You're all right?" he inquired nervously. Kneeling on the stone floor beside me, he examined the lump on my head.

"Never felt better," I replied. "Where are we?" I glanced around the unfurnished room.

"We are on the bank of the Nile. This is a subterranean chamber that was used as a rainwater reservoir," he replied quietly as if it were a common occurrence for bishops of the Church to hold their meetings with one another in reservoirs.

"You amaze me, more and more, the longer I know you. I can see why my Father Anthony recommended you so highly. How did you manage to secrete me here?"

It was his turn to laugh. "Can't we monks have a few secrets from our archbishop?" he quipped.

Growing serious, I announced to him a decision I made. I felt like a general at the head of an army calling out the orders for the day.

Respectfully, Serapion listened to what I had to say.

"I am going to go in person to pay a call on Constantius!"

CHAPTER 5

S ince I could not believe that Constantius was so base as to go back on his word, I left Alexandria going first into the Nitrian desert and then setting out across the Libyan desert headed for Italy, determined to have a face to face interview with the emperor. When we stopped one night at a colony of monks, Mark and I learned that Lucifer of Sardinia, Eusebius of Vercellae, and even saintly Hilary of Poitiers, and countless others had been driven into banishment. The little monk who told us these things had the wide eyes of a child as he anxiously related the dreadful news.

"Hosius of Cordova has been banished!"

"Hosius! Not the ancient and venerable Hosius!" I could not believe what I was hearing. "He was a very good friend of Constantius' father."

"He has been banished, nonetheless," replied the monk. "Have you not heard what the emperor did to Pope Liberius?"

I shook my head and confessed that I was ignorant of recent events in Italy.

"He—too—is banished."

The monk registered surprise that I had not heard any of the things he told us. Many of the exiled bishops had come to Egypt, and word had spread of these events like wildfire from one colony of monks to another. Horror struck, I listened as the monk told me that the Arians decided to make an Arian out of His Holiness Liberius—the Roman Pontiff, the Bishop of Rome, and the successor of Saint Peter! They reckoned that if Pope Liberius became Arian the whole world would become Arian. Raising accusations against Liberius to Constantius, they hoped to destroy the pope and the true Catholic faith!

Sending a eunuch to the Lateran with letters and gifts, Constantius commanded Liberius to subscribe against me. When the Pope steadfastly refused, the eunuch—Eusebius, by name—became furious. In his rage, he went so far as to threaten His Holiness severely! When the eunuch saw that his threats against Liberius could not influence him, he returned to the palace where he then persuaded all the rest of the mutilated creatures in the palace to prevail upon Constantius to persecute the pope. Letters were sent to the Prefect of Rome to persuade His Holiness to leave Rome and go to the court. That failing, the pope was to be persecuted violently.

Not daring to venture out, and unable to receive any visitors, Liberius was consequently a prisoner in the Lateran. Trying to force the Pope to do his bidding, the emperor threatened and wrote letters to various commissioners. When none of his schemes worked to his satisfaction, Constantius, in desperation, had his soldiers lay hands on His Holiness and drag him to the court! Undaunted, Liberius rebuked Constantius for persecuting the Church. All to no avail, for Constantius sent Pope Liberius into banishment—just like he did all the rest of the bishops who opposed the Arian madness.

The enormity of the Arians! Liberius, the Roman Pontiff, banished! Hosius, that Abraham-like old man exiled! Perhaps—perhaps—my mind raced—if I could hurry and get to Constantius, I could convince him that I am innocent of any evil. Perhaps I could even persuade him that he had done wrong in banishing Pope Liberius.

The next morning Mark and I rose early and traveled without resting that day, until we reached Cyrenaica, where we took a room in an inn. While I waited in the room, Mark went out into the streets of the city to see if he could hear of any fresh developments in the critical situation in which we found ourselves. When he returned a few hours later, he was deeply agitated and troubled.

"Piety, you can't go to Constantius! You can't! He has written a letter to the people of Alexandria in which he calls you a 'pestilent fellow!'" Mark looked down at the floor, his eyes avoiding mine. "He says you are guilty of the most evil crimes and that you deserve ten deaths. In another letter that he wrote to the Ethiopians, he says that you are removed from your see and that George of Laodicea is coming to Egypt to take your place!"

"What else did he tell the Ethiopians?" I asked, wondering about Frumentius whom I had consecrated to the episcopate for Ethiopia.

"Constantius ordered Frumentius to go to Alexandria to see George and to let George determine whether he was worthy to be made a bishop or not. He warned the Ethiopians lest Your Piety might go to them and 'corrupt' them." Mark's face reflected the inner turmoil that he was experiencing over these events.

"Yes," I agreed. "Going to see Constantius is out of the question." What else could I have expected from a man who had slain his uncles and his cousin? "Did you say George of Laodicea is coming to take over the see of Alexandria?" It was hard to comprehend it all.

"Yes. He has already left Antioch and is on his way to the court at Milan to receive his orders from Constantius."

Mark paced the floor the way he always does when worried. What do you know of George?" he asked.

"I met him once—years ago when he was a priest in Alexandria. My predecessor had to depose him for his irreligion. He became a pork contractor in Cappadocia—an embezzling one at that."

Never dreaming that the Church would be reduced to such a state of affairs, I gave up all hope of reasoning with Constantius. Immediately, I wrote a circular letter to my entire episcopate directing them to hold fast to the faith—come what may. I especially warned them against signing any Arian creeds. Having written the letter, I mounted my horse and with Mark at my side headed for Pispir, riding as fast as we could, stopping only as was necessary for food and rest, until we reached the community of monks in the Thebais.

Upon our arrival at Pispir, the monk Ammonius, who accompanied me to Rome some years before, greeted us. When he informed me that Serapion had fled Alexandria, shortly after I had, and that he too had just arrived at Pispir, I insisted upon seeing Serapion at once. Needless to say, my suffragen was more than a little surprised to see me, since he thought I had gone to see Constantius.

"I heard of the appointment of George," I explained to him. "I came at once. I have given up any idea of seeing the emperor."

"Thank God you got the news in time!" exclaimed Serapion. "I was afraid you would walk right into their hands."

Since the time that I last saw him only a few weeks before, Serapion had aged ten years, his hair becoming quite gray almost overnight.

"What happened?" I asked with my eyes intently focused on his.

"Terrible persecution" he sighed heavily. "We went to the cemetery to pray at Easter. While we were at prayer, the general swooped down on us unexpectedly with more than three thousand soldiers armed with swords and clubs. They attacked the women and children." Serapion' s voice broke and there were tears in his eyes when he related the appalling story to me. "They stripped the virgins and beat them until they were unrecognizable. They took the bodies of those who died and fed them to the dogs."

"Enough! Enough! "I have heard enough!" I put my hands to my ears to keep out the sound of his voice.

I was to hear even worse things in the days that followed.

News travels fast up the Nile. The Prefect Maximus, who pledged me his help, was recalled from Egypt before his term of office was due to expire. The new governor, Cataphronius, accompanied by

Count Heraclius, arrived in Alexandria on June 10, unleashing immediately a new wave of terror.

I still found it hard to believe that Constantius was the wicked persecutor of Christ that I later found him to be. I guess I did not want to believe evil of the man.

When Count Heraclius brought with him a letter from Constantius, in which the emperor threatened the pagans of Alexandria severely if they did not begin to persecute my flocks, I realized the enormity of the man Constantius. He was wicked, nefarious, and pernicious to the core.

Soon after his arrival, the count announced that, by order of the emperor, all my churches were to be given over to the Arians. All the magistrates of Alexandria, including the functionaries of the pagan temples, were forced to sign an agreement to accept the appointee of the emperor as Archbishop of Alexandria.

After the vigil service of June 13 held in Theonas Cathedral, most of the worshipers had gone home and only a few women remained to pray, when the governor and the count decided to storm the church. Bringing with them the receiver general and a large mob of dissolute young pagans, they forced the frenzied pagans to stone the praying women, saying that Constantius had commanded it. Completely naked the youths burst into the cathedral bearing stones and clubs with which they murdered some of the women—right before the altar of God!

They tore the veils off the consecrated virgins and kicked them brutally. Since they knew the holy character of the spouses of Christ, they reasoned they could harm them even more with obscenities than with stones and clubs. Finding pleasure in the foulness of the pagans, the Arians even suggested obscenities to them.

When they tired of torturing the women, they set about wrecking the cathedral, taking the ancient wood altar railing, the wooden seats of the people, and the red curtains from the chancel railing and the entrance door and made a large bon fire of them in front of the cathedral. They were all set to sacrifice a heifer to the idol Alpis until they discovered that it was not a bull, but a young cow, that they found nearby.

When the fire in front of the cathedral was blazing with flames leaping high in the night, one of the youths rushed into the cathedral and brazenly seated himself upon the archiepiscopal throne and sang some licentious song. Then he decided to pull the throne from where it was fastened to the floor in order to drag it to the fire outside. As he pulled and tugged at the chair, it suddenly gave way and fell upon him with a sharp piece of wood protruding from the broken chair. It punctured the abdomen of the young pagan and pierced his bowels with his entrails falling out all over the sanctuary. After horrible suffering, he died the next day.

The official transfer of my parishes to the Arians took place Saturday, June 15. Still my enemies were not satisfied. Upon the pretext of searching for the "wicked Athanasius," they plundered the houses of the parishioners like degenerate fiends. Even the tombs of the dead were violated and ransacked with the excuse of searching for me. Many more bishops were driven into exile as Sebastian, the Manichee, took over the military command of Syrianus.

We saw Arians installed in all our chief bishoprics. Our priests were scourged and beaten when they failed to submit to the Arian "bishops." Still the new "Archbishop" of Alexandria failed to appear.

Finally, one morning my holy Father Anthony appeared at the door of my cell. He still looked well and healthy despite his almost one hundred and five years. As he made his way into my cell, his vision was still clear and his step was still firm, although he had grown thin and had shrunk in stature, as people usually do when they live to be very old. Although he looked as if the first gust of wind might blow him away, the only concession he made to his advanced age was using a staff when he walked.

"Father Anthony, you shouldn't have come. If you wanted to see me, I would have come to your cell in the inner mountain".

With a quiet smile playing at the corners of his mouth, he surveyed me serenely. "I came to get the blessing of my bishop—and to say goodbye." With much difficulty, he knelt for me to bless him.

"But," I insisted, after I had blessed him, "I am not going anywhere—not just yet. Soon perhaps, but not immediately."

He dropped his staff in the corner and I helped him into a chair. His eyes lit up as he replied, "I am going away soon."

I dropped my hands to my sides and questioned him with my eyes. I began to realize slowly, but with certainty, that my holy father was telling me that he was going to die soon.

"You are going away?" I spoke softly and waited for him to elaborate.

"I long to dissolve and be with Christ." At the thought of being more closely united to God, Father Anthony's face became radiant with light. "Soon I shall see face to face—soon I shall know as I am known."

As was his habit when speaking of God, he slipped into a gentle ecstasy with his radiant face reflecting the beatitude of his soul. Then to my amazement his joy gave way to another emotion. When his face became troubled by the vision he was seeing, he arose from the trance in an instant.

"You must leave here at once!" Tugging at my sleeve he explained why. "Gorgonius—the Commander of Police—and Sebastian are on their way here to take you prisoner. They will be here very soon! You must hurry!"

"But where shall I go?" I demanded more of God than of the holy monk.

"With me—to my cave in the inner mountain. The cave is very deep and dark. You can hide there until they give up looking for you." He reached for his staff and rose nimbly.

Outside the cell I signaled to Ammonius to bring the horses and to accompany us.

"Hurry!" insisted Father Anthony. "Hurry! We haven't much time! They'll be here any minute!"

Kicking our heels into the flanks of the horses, we began the long and difficult ascent of the mountain. When we reached a plateau, we could see in the distance a cloud of dust on the horizon. Already the vision that Father Anthony saw was being realized. Knowing that the horses of Gorgonius and Sebastian caused the cloud of dust, we did not wait for them to get any nearer, but disappeared into the labyrinth of caves that honeycomb the mountain.

I spent the night in the cell of my Father Anthony. As I related to him my concern for the churches in my care, we talked until far past midnight.

"All will be restored to Christ," he kept assuring me. "The true Catholic faith will prevail. Meanwhile you, my son, will become a saint. You will be tried in the fire—like gold."

I slept very little that night, awakening from time to time to discover that the holy hermit was kneeling at the other end of the cell, deep in prayer. From time to time, he would bless himself in the name of the Trinity and breathe forth the holy name of Jesus. I thanked God that I was privileged to have such a man for my spiritual father. Without his prayers to sustain me, I would never have been able to do the things I have done. Even now, since he has departed this world to join the blessed in heaven, he still prays for me.

The next morning I returned to the community of monks and to my own cell there. The police were gone, but Dracontius, whom I some time previously consecrated a bishop, arrived during the night and was waiting to see me. He quickly explained the situation of the Church in Alexandria.

"Piety, I have been banished to the desert at Clysma. Philo has been sent to Babylon and Adelphius is coming to Thebes. All the episcopate is loyal to Your piety…"

I interrupted him. "You mean they are loyal to Christ and the true Catholic faith!"

"Even Paphnutius has been exiled!"

"Paphnutius! Why he could barely manage to get around! He was so old and frail. How could the Arians have been so heartless as to drive an old confessor who was blind in one eye and hamstrung in one leg into exile in the desert?"

Dracontius shuddered.

"I know. He took a coffin with him for his burial as did many of the others who were too ill or too old to last long in the desert."

"But whom have the Arians found to replace so many bishops of the church in Egypt?"

"Heathens! Pagans! They have taken heathen youths and have ordained them and made them bishops!" In alarm Dracontius added, "Why one of the new bishops is even a bigamist!"

"It is appalling!"

Tugging at my graying beard, I tried to remember how the holy hermit Anthony had assured me that all would be restored to Christ and the faith. However, worse things were yet to happen. All summer and fall we expected the arrival of George of Laodicea. November came and yet he did not appear.

In late autumn, Ammonius, the monk, came in the middle of the night to my cell and stood by my bed, calling my name. When I awoke, he whispered that my holy father Anthony lay dying. I rose at once and went with him to the inner mountain. When I entered the cell of the holy hermit, my soul was deeply grieved. In the dim candlelight, I could see that he was stretched out on the bare earth on the floor of his cave. Instead of his sheepskin and the garment that I had given him, he was wrapped in a grave cloth—a shroud.

"I have come too late," I sighed dropping down to venerate the remains of the saint.

When I was kneeling beside him, I could see that a flicker of life still animated his thin, emaciated frame. Drawing in a short, shallow breath, his eyelids fluttered ever so slightly.

Ammonius handed me the sheepskin and the garment that my holy father had worn. "Father, wants you to have these."

I took the sheepskin that he had used as an instrument of penance. Removing my tunic, I put the sheepskin on my own body. It was then that I realized that Father Anthony was watching me, smiling at me, pleased that I had taken up his instrument of penance as my own.

"My son—don't let them take my body away from Pispir."

I drew closer to him so that I could hear every word that he might speak. His voice was quite faint. Ammonius and another monk, who was standing nearby, were both weeping openly. I took my father's hands in mine. They were cold as death. His fingertips were bluish and his breathing became heavy and labored.

"My son...don't let them take my body to Egypt."

I said nothing but pressed his hands firmly to reassure him.

"I don't want my body venerated as a relic. I want to be buried in an unknown grave. Please. I want to dissolve and be with Christ."

A smile flickered across his face.

"It shall be as you wish." My throat tightened as I spoke. He closed his eyes a moment and rested before he could gather strength to speak again.

"You will remember me," I whispered in his ear, "when you appear before the throne of God?" I thought of how much I would miss the wisdom, counsel, and the moral support of my father in God.

He nodded. "When I go to God, I will be of more help to you and to the churches than I am now. Let your faith grow strong, my son, in the hour of trial. Christ will win the victory over Caesar."

He was growing weaker. When I laid my finger on his lips to urge him to rest, he opened his eyes that were very clear and blue as they gazed wistfully into mine.

"I am going soon, my son."

Still holding his hands in mine, I pressed them to my lips. "We will meet in heaven."

"In heaven!" His voice was barely audible.

"Jesus," he whispered. With eyes shut, face radiant with joy, he was in ecstasy—already closer to heaven than he was to earth. When a tremor passed through his body, I could feel the force of his spirit as he rushed up to embrace the Three in One, leaving behind his worn out body like a cast off tunic. All the sadness I had felt at losing him gave way to profound peace. My heart told me there was great rejoicing among the angels now that Anthony was wholly in the Trinity. My heart sang with joy! I could feel the prayers of my holy father as he interceded for me before the face of God! With renewed hope I rose up and went to face the future.

The colony of monks at Pispir greatly mourned the passing of Anthony, the beacon light that gave their spiritual lives direction. As their bishop, they turned to me in their grief. I did all that lay in my power to comfort them and bring them closer to God.

Now that God had called me once more to the desert, I tried to take advantage of the silence of the sand and the sky and of the long starry nights to grow in union with the Three Persons of God. Even Mark had adopted the tunic of a monk and was consumed with zeal for spiritual perfection. Many times we sat watching the sun sink into the desert and the moon rise over the palms while we spoke of God.

As a result of the persecution we endured, Mark had grown very serious. To him the Arian madness was something of a personal problem deep in his soul. The fact that such things could happen to the Church disturbed his faith.

"Why can't the Arians see the truth?" he demanded of me one night. "St. Paul wrote very clearly about the person of Christ."

I sensed that his soul was profoundly distressed.

"Ah, my son, without a pure mind, a man cannot comprehend the words of the saints."

He thought about this for a moment. Then glancing up at the stars overhead, he asked, "You mean their sin makes them blind?"

"Yes, Mark, a pure soul reflects God, but an evil soul is like muddy water. Light will not penetrate it. The road to God is within us. If you have faith, you will see God in your soul."

I remembered how my holy father had instructed me about prayer and the vision of the Trinity. Now Mark and the monks at Pispir, even Serapion, were turning to me for spiritual guidance. Something was still distressing Mark. I peered into his soul and could see that he was not at peace.

"Something is troubling you," I ventured, as the chill of night began to fall on the desert.

Involuntarily Mark shuddered.

"Yes, Father. You are right. Something is bothering me." He looked away from me.

"Would you like to tell me about it?"

"It's the Arians. I hate them! I hate them! I hate them so much that my soul aches from the intensity of it." He waved his hands with emotion.

"But Christ says we must love our enemies!"

The moon hid behind a cloud, hiding his face.

"That is why I am troubled. I cannot love them. I wake up at night and remember how they scourged my fellow deacon Eutychius and condemned him to the mines at Phaeno, where no one can live more than a few days. They beat him. They wouldn't even permit him to have his wounds dressed before he set out towards the Dead Sea. He died on the way." There was catch in Mark's voice, as he thrust his face into his hands.

He had spit out the poison. Peace would not be long in coming.

"He was a close friend?"

"He was my brother!" There was bitterness in Mark's voice. "My half brother. My mother was married twice." He turned his head from me. I was sure that there were tears on his cheeks.

"Since Christ rose from the dead conquering death, death is so weak that even little children can mock death himself as being dead."

I thought of the joy my holy Father Anthony had found in death.

"Our salvation is effected in the hour of affliction. Your brother—I am sure—forgave his murderers and won the palm of martyrdom. Let your love overcome the evil of the Arians."

Mark shifted restlessly on the sand dune where we were sitting. "That's just it! I don't love—I don't have charity!"

I was determined to bring peace to his soul. "Let Christ be the judge of that. Place your heart in the hands of Christ." I smiled at him in the moonlight.

"How, Father?" He seemed self-conscious.

"Meditate continually on the words of Christ and you will grow in love."

I was giving to him one of the secrets of my own soul.

The Arians continued to propagate their nauseous and abominable doctrine throughout Egypt. Although they called themselves Christians, they had no king but Caesar. They gnashed their teeth against Christ and called upon Constantius to persecute us. We had hoped that perhaps the arrival of George would see some mitigation of the atrocities that were being committed by the Arians against our churches. Perhaps, we reasoned, George would put an end to the dastardly attacks on the people of God by the civil authorities and by the pagan mobs they wielded. We were wrong. Dead wrong.

George arrived in Alexandria February 24, 357, the third Friday in Lent, with armed force and full military pomp and strength. We soon learned that George had the temper of a hangman!

A week after Easter, the virgins of Christ were thrown into prison, bishops were led away in chains by the soldiery, and orphans and widows were robbed of their meager provisions. The week after Pentecost when the people of God were praying in the cemetery, Sebastian, taking a large number of troops armed with swords, bows, and darts, swooped down on them. He built a fire and, threatening the virgins with the fire, he tried to make them say they were Arians. When they refused, they were stripped and beaten so that they were unrecognizable. He then seized forty laymen and flogged them with a rod that was covered with thorns, embedding the thorns in their flesh so that many died in agony. Christian burial was refused the dead! Resorting to a surgeon's knife for the removal of the thorns, the ones that survived were in greater agony. They were all banished to the Great Oasis.

Secundus, who was bishop of Libya before he was deposed by the Egyptian episcopate, wasted no time in returning to his church, now that George was archbishop. Because one of the priests of Barka refused to submit to him, Secundus and his accomplice kicked the priest to death. It was the middle of the holy season of Lent.

Hearing all these things I came to a decision. I called Serapion to my cell and announced to him my plans.

"I am going to Alexandria! My sheep have need of me."

"But—Piety," he protested. "The madmen will kill you. Then who will care for your flock?"

"Before they can kill me, they will have to catch me first!" I was already packing my few belongings.

Night had fallen when I entered Alexandria. I was alone, refusing to permit anyone at Pispir to accompany me. It would be hard enough for one lone bishop to find a place to hide from the Arians' sharp eyes, I advised Serapion, who expressed great eagerness to return to Alexandria with me. I had no idea of where I would go or what I would do, but I was confident that Providence would guide me, for I was convinced that it was God's will that I return to my see.

In a city of over a million inhabitants, it is easy to get lost from sight, especially if one knows the city the way I know Alexandria. Shrouded in darkness, I walked briskly down the narrow, winding, back streets, where I felt no one would be able to recognize me in the night. I decided to go to a residential section, not far from the cathedral, where I knew the people to be loyal Christians.

After strolling slowly past about fifty houses, I felt inspired to knock on the door of a modest home. I had nothing to rely on except inspiration. If I chose the wrong house…well, I decided not to think about that.

The door swung open, revealing a beautiful young girl silhouetted against the lamp light of a cozy sitting room.

"Good evening," I ventured. "Someone suggested that you might have a room for rent."

She hesitated a moment. "I don't rent rooms."

"I'm sorry. I must have been mistaken. I was sure this was the house."

I turned to go.

"Wait!" she called after me.

"Yes?" I turned to face her.

She looked me over very closely. "Come in, please."

Once inside the house when the door was safely closed behind me, she smiled and said, "You are welcome here. You will be safe here." She recognized me.

"Do you know me?"

Her beauty was breathtaking. "Yes, Your Piety. You baptized me." She lowered her eyes and smiled shyly. Her polished copper hair fell in a cascade of curls on her shoulders. I guessed her to be no more than eighteen.

"What is your name, child?"

"Sophia." She smiled again. I could see her straight white teeth.

"Sophia—that means 'wisdom.'" I looked at her more closely. Her eyes were soft like the petals of an orchid and they were as deep as the night skies. Peering into her soul, I said, "Our Lord told a parable once about wise and foolish virgins." I could see that I had touched the heart of her being.

"How could you tell that I am a spouse of Christ?" She seemed surprised. A slight blush made her more beautiful. "I am wearing ordinary clothing. I am not wearing my veil. How did you know that I am a virgin consecrated to Christ?" Her eyes were troubled that I had hit upon her secret.

"My child," I said raising my hand in blessing. "Do not be afraid, Christ sent me to your home. He it was that revealed your secret to me."

She seemed reassured. Leading me to a chair she exclaimed, "Oh I wish I could wear my veil openly the way I used to, so that everyone would know—but the Arians would beat me and—and I don't know what else they might do to me—if they knew." Then as if to apologize she added, "I felt that the Divine Spouse wished me to hide from them."

"You did right to flee from them. No one flees from those who are gentle, kind, and humane, but from these who are cruel and evil. Our Lord hid when his persecutors sought him. When his hour had come he no longer hid. Sometimes we must be preserved in time of peril for the sake of many souls."

She listened to me intently. "I think I understand." Her eyes crinkled into a smile. "I want to preserve Your Piety in this evil hour, for the sake of the many souls who are on the verge of being lost, now that George has taken away our churches."

I was eager to know what was happening to my people in Alexandria.

"Are the people of God being deceived by the Arian madmen who tell them Christ is a creature?"

"A few are going to the Arian communion. The rest of us gather in our homes in small groups to pray. The Arians think we are merely having a social gathering, so they don't molest us."

She folded her hands and perched herself on a small foot stool at my feet as I sat in the chair she gave me.

"Are you certain that you wish to—'preserve' me—as you expressed it?" I studied her face. "The penalty for hiding me is death." I spoke solemnly.

Her eyes met mine. Without a moments hesitation she replied. "I am ready to die for Christ!"

"You just might have that opportunity!"

She changed the subject. "Ah, Your Piety, will you give Christ to me? Will you offer, the Holy Sacrifice here in my house? It has been so long!" She sighed deeply. "We have no priests. Thank God, you have come back to us."

"Thank God," I repeated. Softly, I added, almost in a whisper, "I will give Christ to you every morning."

Her joy was emblazoned on her face. Then with a catch in her voice she spoke. "Father, the Arians have even desecrated the Holy Sacrament. They have trodden it under foot."

"May God forgive them!"

Since they did not believe in the divinity of Christ, they could not believe in his Presence in the Eucharist. I smiled at her to comfort her. "I have plans—wonderful plans for the future. I will tell them to you tomorrow. I am very tired now."

Almost sixty years old, I was beginning to feel the accumulation of the years. Sophia led me to a large room on the second floor that belonged to her father before he died a year previously. In the room, she told me, were some of his personal effects and clothing that I could freely use. She suggested that people upon seeing an older man living in her house would think it was her uncle from Heliopolis.

When I awakened the next morning, I found that Sophia had improvised an altar in one of the bedrooms that she turned into a chapel. Like a child she awaited my approval. There were even fresh flowers on the altar.

"It is such a beautiful cathedral!" I thanked her.

Without a word she knelt before the altar and waited for the Holy Sacrifice to begin. Together we prayed the ancient liturgy. Once again the curtain of time was drawn aside and we were present on Calvary.

I could see at once that Sophia had a true contemplative spirit. She lived to pray. Prayer was her life as it is mine. After communion she remained a full hour motionless in prayer.

I had been in Alexandria only ten hours and already I had a cathedral and a flock of one. I had much for which to be thankful.

Something had to be done to provide priests for my sheep. After breakfast I disclosed my plans to Sophia. I suggested that perhaps she could invite some of her friends to share the Body and Blood of Christ with us. I knew how much the people needed to be fed with the glorified Body and Blood, Soul and Divinity of Jesus.

At once Sophia suggested the names of several that she could trust. I was especially eager to meet some nice young men who might possibly be candidates for the priesthood.

"There is one young man that I know. He would make a good priest. His name is Peter and he is afraid of nothing. When we were children, he would do anything on a dare."

"When can I meet him?"

I was helping her clear the dishes off the breakfast table. Dropping the dishes down on the table she said eagerly, "I'll go right now and fetch him."

Brimming over with hope, she flitted out the door before I could say another word. Half an hour later she returned with the young man. As he entered my presence, he was quite serious. In his eyes, I could detect a resoluteness of purpose that is rare in one so young. His poise was also admirable. I remembered how awestruck I was the first time I had encountered His Piety Alexander. Persecution had given me a gaunt appearance and with my gray hair and beard I supposed I was considered a rather formidable old man by the upcoming generation. Nevertheless, Peter was at ease with me and completely straightforward in his manner of speaking.

"How old are you, my son?" I laid my hand on his shoulder.

"I am twenty, Your Piety," he answered with a manly thrust of the jaw.

Twenty seemed to be very young to be entrusted with the care of souls—but yet, I knew that young men were often more daring and fearless in the face of danger than more mature men.

"I am afraid you are too young for the mission I had in mind for you, Peter." I was testing him.

"I won't always be twenty, Your Piety," he countered with a smile that disarmed me.

"Well, perhaps." I pretended to consider, but already I had decided that God had plans for Peter.

That very day, I began preparing him to become a deacon. Reminding me of myself years before when his Piety Alexander was educating me for the service of God, he had an eager mind and a responsive will. As the days went by, I spent as much time with Peter as I could. I found him to be so submissive to my direction that I was able to ordain him within a matter of weeks.

It was a great joy for me when Peter first offered the Holy Sacrifice. I was blessed. I had a "cathedral" and one priest. Before long I was to have twenty-five young priests like Peter—all unknown to the Arians. Secretly my new priests made their way among the people with the Mysteries of grace.

Arianism could not last. Strictly negative in its outlook, it was but a protest against the Catholic religion and had nothing creative to offer. If the government ceased supporting it, I was certain that it would disappear in time.

Having found lodging for Serapion and Mark in the homes of two of my secret clergy, I sent for them to join me. I kept Mark busy writing letters that I intended to have circulated far and wide, among the people of God. One afternoon as I knelt praying before the altar in our lovely little cathedral, Sophia informed me that Serapion was waiting to see me. I had instructed him to come to my residence only when it was urgent, and preferably at night so that the police would not spot him.

Drawing the sacred sign of the Savior's cross on my body, I left the chapel at once to meet Serapion, who was deeply agitated, instead of enjoying his customary monastic calm. Nervously he tapped his foot on the faded green carpet, as I entered the sitting room where he was waiting. I questioned him with my eyes.

"Hosius has become an Arian!" He blurted this out without preamble.

"God forbid!"

What had they done to the old confessor to induce him to deny his faith in the Trinity? Serapion's eyes were wide and troubled. "The news just broke. One of the monks from Pispir came and told me. The Arians assembled at a council at Sirmium and prevailed upon Constantius to recall Hosius from his banishment so that they could force him into signing the blasphemy that they invented and which they call a 'creed.'" Lowering his voice to a whisper Serapion continued, "They beat him until he signed!"

I had thought that nothing could break the spirit of Hosius. To me he had seemed invincible.

"But if he signed under force—it means nothing."

"It means," retorted Serapion bitterly, "that the church has been reduced to a pitiful state! Arianism has replaced Christianity as the official religion of the empire. When the pillars of the Church—men like Hosius fall…"

"Wait!" I interrupted.

I could see that the forced submission of Hosius was having the psychological effect on Serapion that the Arians hoped it would.

"We must try to be understanding with Hosius. We must remember that he is a hundred years old. Perhaps his mind is failing."

"Nevertheless," replied Serapion, not to be consoled, "the fact remains that we are alone—you and I against the world! How can we fight such a losing battle?"

Defeat was written in his eyes.

"My son," I said gently with my hand on his arm. "God is never on the losing side in any battle. Always remember that we are on the Lord's side. The bark of Peter is being tossed to and fro on some tempestuous seas in this Arian storm, but Serapion, never forget that Christ is sleeping in Peter's boat! And with one word he can silence the winds and still the tempest. We are not alone. Christ is with us!"

I learned from Serapion further details of what had transpired at Sirmium. There appeared to be a widening breech between different factions of those who met there and composed the blasphemous creed denying the Trinity. Being lost in heresy, they found it impossible to agree on only one creed, and had found it necessary to compose three of them.

I kept informed of events in the Church all over the empire. It became more and more evident to me that the enemy camp was dividing into three factions. Valens of Mursa was carrying on in place of my old enemy, Eusebius of Nicomedia, and was the head of the party that was made up of the bitterest adversaries of the true faith. The Anomoeans, as they were now called, were ferociously opposed to the doctrine of the divinity of Christ and the coessentiality of the Three Persons of God and were on the verge of becoming a scandal to the more conservative Arians.

In 350, Leontius of Antioch ordained one of the pupils of the Lucianists a deacon and permitted him to preach. Aetius was his name. Well, Aetius was not afraid to proclaim in a loud voice all the irreverent and blasphemous conclusions that resulted from his belief in the Arian view of Christ. Consequently, such a wave of protest broke out in Antioch that Leontius found it necessary to suspend Aetius. Shortly after George of Laodicea intruded himself into my see, Aetius made his way to Alexandria.

Valens was dedicated to imposing an Arian creed on the whole Church. Since he was first and foremost a politician, he knew that in order to achieve his ends he needed the help of the more conservative Arians who were the second discernible faction emerging in the Arian camp.

Acacius, the leader of this second group of Arians, was then Bishop of Caesarea, having succeeded Eusebius Pamphilus, in addition to assuming his ideas. Eusebius of Caesarea had not been a true Arian. Neither was Acacius. He was a man without convictions and a political Arian above all else. He also tended towards conservatism, but he showed an evident revulsion for principles of any sort. He even went so far as to appoint a very orthodox bishop named Cyril. When he found out Cyril's true beliefs, he quarreled with him. Although Acacius' real beliefs were hard to determine, I was certain of one thing. He was in accord with the policy of Constantius to unite all elements of the Church in subservience to the State. If he succeeded, it would be the death knell of the true faith of Christ!

The creed that Hosius was forced to sign at Sirmium was the triumph of Arianism under Valens and the Anomoeans. It proclaimed the sole Godhead of the Father, the subjection of Christ to him, and forbid the terms of the "same essence" or of "like essence" as being unscriptural. The devil is always ready to quote scripture when it is to his advantage. Nowhere in the Scripture does it say that Christ is of the same substance of the Father, shouted the Arians. Therefore they declared the Nicene faith in the Trinity and the consubstantiality of the Father and the Son to be false. The conservative Arians maintained that Christ is like in substance or essence to the Father. At Sirmium the phrase "like in substance" was denounced and condemned and the conservative Arians were ordered to keep silent.

A rumble of dissatisfaction among the conservative Arians began to reach my ears. If I could only reach the minds of these men, I reasoned, I could convince them of the truth. A third party headed by Basil of Ancyra was beginning to emerge. They condemned Arianism at the Ecumenical Council at Nicaea only to join the Arian ranks afterwards. In point of numbers, they made up the largest party among the Arians. They were anti-Sabellian and conservative and in a modified manner were followers of Origen. Actually, their own beliefs were confused, not very well defined, and generally very hazy.

Since Basil of Ancyra was well educated and honorable, the blasphemy of Sirmium united a large number of conservatives around him creating an informal reaction against the ultra Arianism of Valens and the Anomoeans.

In 358, I observed with great interest that Basil of Ancyra invited twelve bishops to a church dedication in Ancyra. At this time, he drew up a synodal letter in which he proclaimed the essential likeness of Christ to the Father and cast anathemas at the Anomoeans. Basil and his followers then went to Constantius' court where they gained an audience with the emperor and achieved the ratification by a council of a creed that was in opposition to the creeds of Valens. When Valens, who happened to be present, was forced to sign, war broke out among the Arian ranks.

I was horrified to learn that Pope Liberius had also signed the conservative Arian creed! Because they threatened him with death, out of fear, he signed his name to this false creed! Serapion was completely distraught by this news.

"We are doomed to failure, Piety!" He moaned, took a deep breath, and sank into a chair. He put his face in his hands and mumbled, "Pope Liberius is an Arian. Constantius urged his Holiness to declare that Christ is not of the same substance with the Father. And he signed! He signed! The pope signed the false statements!"

It did look bad. I had to admit that. I remembered what my Father Anthony had told me. "You must be," he said, "the Apostle of the Trinity, my son. No matter who yields or submits, you will stand unmoved!" I closed my eyes to pray. My Father Anthony seemed very near at that moment. I could almost hear him whisper to me, "There are Three equal Persons in God—the Father, the Son, and the Holy Spirit."

Opening my eyes, I surveyed Serapion calmly and exclaimed, "Blessed be the glorious and adorable Trinity!"

Slowly Serapion lifted his head from his hands. There was new confidence in his eyes when they met mine. "Praise to the Father and to the Son and to the Holy Spirit down to the ages of ages." He clenched his fists resolutely. "Amen! I am with you, Piety—all the way!"

I shook my head and corrected him. "You are with God, my son."

We sat in silence a few moments. I was praying and I am certain my suffragan was doing likewise. Finally I spoke.

"We are making progress here in Alexandria. George has failed. The pagans hate him for the cruel treatment he has shown them. They don't like the law he made forbidding them to worship in their temple. Our people will have nothing to do with George. He has control of the church buildings, but the souls of the people of God are in our care and our secret priests are doing an admirable job of ministering to them."

"But, Your Piety, if they catch you…" He hesitated and then decided to leave the sentence unfinished.

I smiled and read his thoughts. "You are afraid that they would force me to sign one of their creeds—the way they forced Hosius and Pope Liberius?"

He nodded and looked away from me.

"We have enough to worry about the evils of this day. We shall not worry about the future. Besides they will never catch me! They will never have the chance to try on me the tactics they used on Paul of Constantinople, Hosius, and Liberius. I tell you, my son…"

I was interrupted by a loud shout that came from the street in front of the house. I walked to the window and glanced out. A large mob of people was suddenly gathering, making so much noise and commotion that I remained peering out the window to see what was happening.

What I beheld was truly strange. Making its way down the street passing the house was a bizarre and macabre procession, led by George of Laodicea on horseback. In his hands, George was carrying of all things—a pagan idol! Behind him was a long line of common laborers in dirty clothing. Each one of them was carrying in his hands a human skull. I turned to Serapion and shrugging my shoulders said, "Now I have seen everything."

I mopped my brow. It was a hot day even for August.

Serapion who was still looking out the window retorted, "There is something you missed."

Returning to the window, I saw someone in the crowd following the procession pick up a rock and throw it at George, grazing his ear. Turning a deep shade of red, George gestured violently with the idol that he was carrying and yelled at his assailant.

"Pagan swine!"

The mob, further enraged by George's anger, began pressing in on him with clubs. In fury, George tossed the idol into the surging mob, lashed his horse, and rode away with clouds of dust swirling behind him.

Once George was gone, the mob grew quieter. Still the lugubrious procession bearing the human skulls continued winding its way down the street. I sent Sophia to inquire discreetly as to what was taking place. It didn't take her long to find out and return to tell me.

From Constantius, George received a plot of ground on which a pagan temple, now in ruins, once stood. Deciding that it would be an ideal site upon which to build a church, George set about clearing the land of the remains of the pagan temple. In the process he uncovered an adytum that had once served as the inner sanctuary of the pagan temple and into which none but the priests of Mithras were allowed to enter.

In this particular temple, the priests of Mithras had not been content with sacrificing bulls and using the bulls' livers and other entrails for divination and foretelling the future. The adytum contained human skulls of men, women, and children. They had offered human sacrifice to the detestable Mithras! George, who was already hated by the pagans, because of his intolerance of them had the effrontery to insult the modern pagans by parading these skulls from ancient times through the city streets of our great modern city. No wonder George whipped his horse and fled for his life.

This was only the beginning of trouble. That night, August 29, 358, Peter came to me with the news that a mob of pagans had stormed the Dionysius church where George was conducting a service. George had to flee from the church to save his life! The pagans were determined to have his blood.

Because my Arian successor alienated everyone in Alexandria, there was nothing left for him to do but leave Egypt. In defeat, he sailed from Alexandria on the second of October.

Young Peter, the first of my secret priests, was overjoyed with the news that the usurper was gone. With great enthusiasm, he said, "Now Your Piety can publicly resume your duties."

"On the contrary. George has forced me to leave Alexandria. Constantius will be expecting me to come to Alexandria and resume my episcopal duties. No house in the city will be safe. The police will search every corner of the city looking for me now."

The news of my coming departure troubled Sophia, because she hated to see me leave. There were tears in her deep blue eyes when I broke the news to her.

"Have I failed you, Father?" She asked biting her lip.

"No, child, and I shall not fail you. I must go away for a time."

Taking her chin in my hands, I lifted her face and looking into her tear stained eyes, I promised, "I will be back...and soon!"

We left Alexandria just in time. A few days later, I received word that the police were searching for me just as I had predicted. They broke into a private home in one instance where they found a virgin's cell and tortured the virgin whose name was Eudaemonis.

Recalling the invitation of Frumentius to visit Ethiopia, I decided to take him up on his offer of hospitality and go there. Refusing to comply with Constantius' demands that he present himself in Alexandria and submit to George, the usurper, Frumentius remained loyal to Christ.

Since I needed a secretary for the great amount of writing I was doing, I took Mark with me. In addition to maintaining a vast correspondence, I was writing discourses against Arianism, hoping with these writings to convince the conservative Arians of the truth concerning the person of Christ. After I left Alexandria, the people of God regained control of the churches on October 11. They held them until Sebastian returned from the country and restored them to the Arians.

When Lent was drawing near, I decided to go once more to the Thebais, because I wanted to prepare my soul in silence and in prayer for the celebration of the feast of the resurrection of Christ. Because the cell of my holy father Anthony, a place permeated with his spirit, was unoccupied since his death, I took up residence there. Often too I would visit his grave to pray and beseech him to pray for me and for the churches in my care.

News began to filter into Pispir of a council the Arians were planning to hold at Nicaea. The reason they gave for desiring a council was that they wanted to consider the faith regarding our Lord. Both Valens and Acadius were anxious to convene a general council of the bishops once more in Nicaea. I perceived at once that they were intending to establish a second creed of Nicaea—an Arian creed to replace the true one. Since Basil of Ancyra, the leader of the third faction of Arians, was opposed to convening at Nicaea, he prevailed upon Constantius to hold the council instead at Nicomedia. Edicts were sent out far and wide summoning the bishops to appear.

As the bishops were speeding to Bithynia for the council, word came that the city of Nicomedia had been destroyed. Even nature rose up to protest the planned repudiation of the true faith by the heretics. So suddenly and so violently that no one had been able to flee to safety, an earthquake of tremendous proportions shook Bithynia, killing the Bishop of Nicomedia and one of the bishops from the Bosphorus. It was rumored that the cataclysm caused great damage even as far as Nicaea and Constantinople. Fires followed the quake. The news of the destruction of Nicomedia stopped the bishops on their journey to Bithynia, since it was impossible to convene there.

Seeing an opportunity to seize control of the situation, Valens persuaded Constantius to divide the council in two sections with the eastern Bishops under Acacius meeting at Seleucia—a rocky, mountain fortress in Cilicia where many soldiers were stationed. The western bishops were to meet at Ariminum. If the councils differed in their deliberations, then each was to send ten of its members as delegates to Constantius' court where all differences would be resolved.

In preparation for the twin councils, Basil of Ancyra, Mark of Arethusa, Valens, and my personal enemy George got together and drew up a creed. I quote it in part.

"The Catholic creed was defined in the presence of our master, the most religious and gloriously victorious emperor, the eternal Constantius Augustus, in the consulate of the most illustrious Flavii, Eusebius and Hypatius, in Sirmium on the 11th of the calends of June."

They prefixed their creed with the date of the current year showing that their faith dated from the reign of Constantius and not from that of Christ! They showed that their faith originated with them May 22, 359 and had not been handed down from Christ through the apostles. They referred to Constantius as "master" and although they denied that Christ is everlasting they called Constantius "eternal!" History will laugh them to scorn!

The councils met as scheduled. The western council affirmed the Nicene faith. The eastern council affirmed the beliefs of the Arians that they had stated at their council of the dedication at Antoch in 341.

From each council, rival delegations hastened to Constantius who was then residing at Constantinople. The delegates from the majority party of the western council were detained at Adrianople and in Thrace where Valens persuaded them to sign a revised form of the infamous dated creed. However, the date had been dropped and the creed revamped to express the ultra Arian views of Valens, who sniffed victory in the air.

Valens took the delegates back to their council and with threats and tricks forced the signatures of almost all the western bishops. A few refused to sign. Only too late did the majority of western bishops realize what they had done, for Valens deceived them by fraud, dissimulation, and manipulation.

Snatching the document of his victory, while the ink was till wet on it, the victorious Valens raced with it to Constantius. When he arrived, he found the Seleucian delegates were with the emperor, engaged in fiery debate. The bishops of the eastern council held to the creed of 341, denouncing the beliefs of Acacius and the compromises Basil of Ancyra wished to make.

Valens and Acacius were openly at war with the Arian conservatives; Constantius' court was the battleground. The fight ended with Constantius championing Valens and the ultra Arians. Backed by the threats of the emperor, Valens achieved the submission of the conservative Arians late New Year's Eve.

When they met in Constantinople for the dedication of a new church, Valens and the ultra Arians deposed the conservative Arians in January. The most perverse—the most corrupted of the Arians now had control of the Church of Christ! The whole world was on the verge of becoming Arian!

The enemies of Christ had not considered what turns Providence might take to upset their plans. At this time, having many scores to settle with Constantius, Julian, blaming Constantius for the deaths of his parents and of his brother Gallus, decided that *his* hour had come. Successful as the general of the armies in Gaul, a position Constantius had given him, Julian was well liked by the soldiers who admired his courageous and victorious stance. In January—the same month in which Valens thought himself to have the entire Church in his possession—the armies surrounded the house of Julian in Paris and in loud shouts proclaimed him emperor. To the bishops of Gaul, it was a providential opportunity to speak out in defiance of Arianism, extending their sympathy to the conservative Arians who had been deposed in large numbers by Valens.

I decided the time was ripe for me to return to Alexandria. Sophia welcomed me, as I knew she would. I remained in seclusion in her house biding my time. Like a general, I directed the affairs of the Church by the written word and the whispered command to my faithful secret priests. I was pleased to learn the Lucifer of Sardinia, a vehement defender of the Nicene Creed, and Eusebius Vercellae, a saintly bishop of Italy, had both gone in their banishment to Thebes. In all fairness to Hosius, I must mention that before he died, he once more affirmed his belief in the Trinity and repudiated the Arian doctrines he had been forced to sign.

I watched and waited to see what Julian would do. Constantius was in a difficult position. Since he was busy fighting the Persians, he was unable to turn his attention to Julian and to deal with him as he had with others who tried to wrest the reigns of government from his hands. In fact, he was having so much difficulty with the Persian campaign that he earlier ordered Julian to send him troops from Gaul. Having no desire or intention of going to the Persian war, the armies turned against the emperor, when they heard the order to march to the Persian front, and proclaimed Julian Augustus.

Deciding that Julian was a worse enemy than the Persians, Constantius signed a quick treaty with the Persian Shapur and started a westward march with his armies to meet Julian who was advancing with the forces from Gaul to attack him.

Daily Serapion kept me informed of the news of the empire. What the outcome of the conflict between Constantius and Julian would be was anyone's guess.

"I am betting on Julian," remarked Serapion. "He is young. They say he is as austere as a monk, sleeps on a hard pallet—never has heat in his rooms in winter."

"I, too, have heard rumors about Julian. They say that since his wife died he has determined to be a celibate," I observed. "But even if he overthrows Constantius, the chances are he will support Valens and the Arians. He certainly never has been an orthodox Christian and his parents were both Arians. He was tutored by the arch Arian himself—Eusebius of Nicomedia!"

I studied Serapion. He had aged. His hair was as gray as his eyes that peered out at me from under gray, bushy brows. Thank God for suffragens like Serapion! He was loyal through and through.

"Julian is well liked in Gaul, I have heard."

"I hear that he is just. They say that he has established a principle that a man is innocent until he is proven guilty."

I shook my head sadly. "That is a principle I wish Constantius observed."

From my chair at the window I had a clear view of the street below. Mark was approaching the house stealthily to be sure he was not being followed. Even though it was dark I could recognize his tremendous bulk since he had filled out considerably in recent years. He burst in the rear door of the house and came bouncing up the stairs two at a time.

"Piety," he called, almost tripping as he entered the room. "Julian has announced that he is a pagan! Julian is an apostate!"

Breathlessly my secretary told me that Julian had stopped at Sirmium on his march toward his battle with Constantius and openly professed his paganism.

"He's been a pagan for ten years," said Mark running his hand briskly over his balding head.

Serapion who was with me was taken back by this news. "All that time he has merely pretended to be a Christian?" he asked. Serapion whistled in astonishment. "Why," he continued, "Julian was even a lector in the church—read the scriptures to the people during the liturgy."

"Yes, that is true. Now we learn that he was initiated into the pagan mysteries years ago at Eleusis."

A return to paganism! I found it incredible!

"Why if Julian defeats Constantius…"

Mark interrupted me. "The pagans are dancing in the streets of Alexandria. A large number of devotees have gathered in the temples of Serapis and Poseidon."

We could do nothing but watch and pray. More news began to filter into Alexandria. Julian was boasting that his entire army was pagan. On November 26, Sophia returned from market with the news that George, the usurper, had returned to Alexandria and was once more living in the archiepiscopal residence.

"One of our priests saw him," Sophia told me with concern. "He was seen going into the Caesareum church."

"He must be betting on Constantius to win in his coming encounter with Julian," I remarked laconically. I thought about what Sophia had just informed me and then decided on a course of action. "Child, go at once to Peter. Warn him of the arrival of George. There will probably be a new round of persecutions now that George is back."

George had the temper of a hangman. I fully expected to hear of a recurrence of the atrocities that occurred when he first arrived in Alexandria several years before. One day passed, then two. Nothing happened to disturb the peace of the Church. Perhaps George was just waiting for an opportune occasion to make his presence felt.

Four days after George arrived, news came that was of colossal importance. Constantius caught a fever on his race to meet Julian. In the streets outside the house, the pagan mobs were screaming the news.

"Constantius is dead! The enemy of the gods is dead! Many years to Julian!"

Constantius, aged forty-five, succumbed to an illness—apoplexy—and died at Mopsucrene on November 3, 361 right after having been baptized by the Arian Euzoïus. The so-called eternal master of the Arians who interfered so much in the affairs of the Church was until the end an unbaptized outsider through it all!

The pagans went wild with excitement.

"Julian! Julian! Augustus! "

I thought their lungs would bursts with their cries. In the midst of the celebration someone remembered George who had a reputation for hating pagans.

"Death to the enemy of the gods!" someone shouted.

The mob took up the cry. Seizing George, they threw him into prison. However, the pork contractor turned bishop did not live to stand trial. In the frenzy of excitement over the ascension of Julian to the purple, the pagans stormed the jail, dragging George into the streets of the city. Right below my window, his body was torn to pieces. I prayed God's mercy on his soul as I stared in disbelief at the unrecognizable remains of the fat little man who caused such a reign of terror in Egypt. Trouble, terrible trouble loomed on the horizon for the Church and for me. I couldn't even begin to imagine the events that were soon to follow.

CHAPTER 6

❁

The whole world looked on as Julian became once more the devoted cousin, honoring the deceased emperor with a pompous imperial funeral. As soon as Julian was officially proclaimed Augustus, he announced himself to be Pontifex Maximus of Zeus and Helios, the sun god, ordering the restoration of pagan worship.

Julian detested Eusebius, the head eunuch and the chief of Constantius' royal bedchamber and the same Eusebius who had so brazenly threatened Pope Liberius. Blaming him for the murder of his brother Gallus, Julian had him immediately put to death and dismissed all the palace cooks and even the barbers. Without a wife he had no need of eunuchs and his meals were so meager he had no need of cooks.

From one end of the empire to the other, fear of persecution gripped the Church as we momentarily expected a revival of the terror that we had known under Diocletian. Fortunately, it did not materialize. Instead Julian, highly indignant, severely reprimanded the Alexandrians for taking the law into their own hands and murdering George, the usurper. When on the fourth of February an order was promulgated, commanding the restoration of the pagan temples in Alexandria, I expected to hear that, by order of the emperor, everyone was once again required to sacrifice to the gods. The great surprise came five days later when an edict was posted in all prominent public places in the city. Sophia was the first to see it and came rushing to me with the news.

"Your Piety!" She sounded very joyful.

I ran down the stairs to see what it was that had made her so happy.

"Julian has issued an order recalling all the bishops who were banished by Constantius! The Arians are forbidden to persecute us any more!"

She raced to her room only to emerge a few moments later when she had discarded her secular dress and appeared before me garbed and veiled as a consecrated virgin of Christ. Radiantly she smiled at me and waited for me to comment.

"Let's not rush, child. We must be cautious. We must be sure it is not some kind of trick. You are sure you read the notice carefully?"

I couldn't understand why Julian wished to recall the exiled bishops unless it would be to exasperate and harass the Arians who were very powerful in Constantius' court. As I sat there pondering the situation, some one knocked on the house door. It was Serapion. Boldly he walked into the house, looking quite pleased.

"I just walked openly through the streets of Alexandria in broad daylight right under the noses of the police! No one tried to stop me!"

He hobbled towards me. Of recent months he had taken to walking with a cane.

"You mean it is true?" I asked with my eyes keenly searching his.

He grinned boyishly and nodded, "Yes! Thank God!"

"We have no time to waste!" My mind was racing furiously. "Julian might change his mind when he discovers the plans I have for the future!"

I snapped out orders like a military chief. Serapion was at my heels.

"Go to Thebes! Go at once! Summon the bishops who are hidden away in the deserts. Tell them to come at once to Alexandria."

The faster my mind raced, the faster I paced the room. I almost tripped over Serapion who was eagerly jotting down every thing I commanded.

"By all means, find Eusebius of Vercellae and Lucifer of Sardinia. Find every bishop you can. Tell them to come at once!"

Serapion's mouth fell open in amazement.

"*We* are going to have a council!"

Serapion dropped his pen and just stood staring at me in disbelief.

"Hurry, Serapion. Don't just stand there. We are going to have a council to end all the Arian councils. We are going to undo the evil Valens did at Ariminum. Without Constantius to enforce their creeds, the Arians will vanish like a mirage in the desert. Truth shall prevail! We shall overcome their evil with good!"

"Yes, Piety." He dropped his cane and went rushing out the door without it.

I sent Sophia to bring me a tailor. I needed a full set of vestments and robes if I were going to return to Theonas Cathedral in triumph. Now that I was past sixty, I was beginning to look the way I thought a bishop should look. The red-headed youth that I was when elevated to the episcopate and who looked more like a country priest's curate than a bishop had given way to an old man with white hair and a long flowing white beard. I still walked straight with my head held erect without need of a cane. I had been bowed to the earth many times, but each time served only to make me grow stronger. The Lord of Glory continually renews my strength like the eagles. In victory, I would lead my clergy back to our churches, but the victory was not mine. It was Christ's.

I directed Mark to go to the archiepiscopal residence to prepare it for our return. When all was in readiness a few days later, Mark came for me. Together we walked the short distance to my official residence that was denied me all too long. It was almost six years to the day, since I had been home. When Mark opened the door for me, my heart beat a little faster as I walked into the old familiar world that I had known with his Piety Alexander, my holy Father Anthony, Potammon, and all the rest. Every piece of furniture served to remind me of people and events lost in the distant past. In the study, my books were still on the shelves. My desk bore a few scratches on its polished wood that weren't there when last I saw it. George had carved his initials in the rich polished mahogany. Outside of that, everything remained the same. I walked to the windows and threw open the curtains and let the sun stream it. With great peace of soul, I watched the waves rolling in on the sandy beach. Glancing out to sea, I saw a few gulls, hunting for fish, suddenly swooping down to make their catch. Yes, I had come home at last!

To make the homecoming more complete, priests and bishops that I hadn't seen for years began arriving. Agathus of Phragonis, Agathodaemon of Schedia, Adelphis of Onuphis, Hermion of Tanes, Marcus of Zygra and even old Arsenius of the three hands, and countless others came to the residence to see their archbishop and to resume their former duties.

The greatest surprise of all came one morning when I looked up from my desk to see a shriveled up old bishop standing in the doorway of my study. A big toothless grin illuminated his wrinkled face from ear to ear. Surely I was mistaken—it looked liked Paphnutius!

"No!" I rose from chair and walked towards him. "It can't be!"

"It's me—make no mistake about that, Piety!"

With the help of a staff he dragged his old bones and hamstrung left leg across the room.

"Can't see too well any more," he explained as he felt his way along," but couldn't miss seeing Your Piety back on your throne in Theonas!"

"Yes," I said with relish. "It will be a great day tomorrow—February 21, a date to remember."

The old confessor scowled and tapped his staff on the floor for emphasis. "Don't trust Julian," he hissed. "He is up to no good. It is only human nature for an apostate to turn and try to rend the Church."

"How well I know it! No one hates Christ the way an apostate Christian can!"

I motioned for him to be seated.

"Now tell me about yourself and how you survived being exiled."

I listened as the old confessor related his experiences of the past six years. Then he began giving me his opinions of Julian. I had to agree with him. I couldn't trust Julian.

"How long I will be allowed to remain, I don't know. I intend to use to the full every moment that I do have."

Though I had not meant it as such, Paphnutius took my words as a cue for him to leave, assuring me that he would be right in the front of the cathedral the next day for the festivities.

Theonas was packed with other bishops who felt the same as Paphnutius. Entering through the main doors of the cathedral, I walked down the aisle in solemn procession and took my place on the new throne that had been erected for the occasion. The echo of the bishops, priests, and deacons as they sang the processional psalm still lingers in my memory.

"I love you, 0 Lord, my power, 0 Lord, my foundation, my stronghold, my redeemer, my God, my rock of refuge, my protector, the horn of my salvation, my fortress."

"Praise be the Lord, I am safe from my foes. The swirling waters of death surged around me, the devastating floods overwhelmed me, the tethers of the underworld trapped me, and the snares of death overtook me.

"In my affliction, I called upon the Lord and cried out to my God; from his sanctuary he heard my voice, and my cry reached his ears. He stretched down from on high and clasped me, pulling me out of the deep waters. He saved me from my formidable foe and from my enemies who were too powerful for me. They assaulted me in the day of my catastrophe, but the Lord came to my aid. He set me free, and saved me, because he loves me.

"The Lord rewarded me according to my just dealings, according to the purity of my hands, he avenged me; for I kept the ways of the Lord and was not unfaithful to my God; for his precepts were all present to me and his laws, I put not from me, but I turned to him with my whole heart and I was on guard against all evil.

"O Lord, you truly illuminate my lamp. O my God, you brighten the shadows about me, for with your help I run against an armed horde, and by the help of my God I overcome all obstacles. God's way is unfailing and the promise of the Lord is enduring and true. He is a protector of all who take refuge in him."

Lucifer of Calaris in Sardinia and Eusebius of Vercellae were present in the cathedral that day. They had hastened to Alexandria to welcome me and to be present at the coming council to voice their belief in the Trinity. Asterius of Petra, Kymatius of Paltus, and Anatolius of Euboea arrived the next day. I invited them to stay in the official residence with me until after the council when they would return to their churches.

A rather abrasive and impetuous man, Lucifer expressed the view that the bishops who signed Arian creeds should be harshly treated, before being allowed to return to the Catholic fold. I, taking the opposite view, was in favor of treating them kindly and making the return as easy as possible for them. In his eagerness to visit the churches of the East and especially the church of Antioch, Lucifer announced that he could not take time to remain in Alexandria for the council, because he planned to hurry eastward to reunite as many of the heretics to the Catholic Church as he could, now that the Arians had fallen from power. Leaving a delegate in Alexandria to represent him at the council, he set off in haste for Antioch.

Eusebius of Vercellae also planned to visit eastern churches before his return to Italy. However, realizing the importance of the council, he determined to remain for it, before proceeding to Antioch.

Expressing his views and plans to me, he spoke with calm and resolute determination. "We must permanently destroy the Arian madness. As soon as I return to the west I plan to meet with Hilary of Poitiers, who has already held a council in Gaul reaffirming the Nicene faith."

Eusebius of Vercellae was a saint. I am convinced of that. When he spent the afternoon prior to our council alone with me in my study, I perceived that he possessed the virtue of prudence in an heroic degree. We both agreed that Lucifer of Sardinia had acted impetuously in rushing away to Antioch without waiting for the council to decide what course we should follow in reinstating the Arians.

With the Church in Egypt truly flourishing since my public return, all was in readiness for the council. During the season of Lent, the people of God in Alexandria fasted as they never had before, even without my having to reprove them, as I had done in past years for not fasting as devoutly and as faithfully as the people in other parts of the empire. At Easter, I baptized the largest number of catechumens in the history of my episcopate with even some Greek ladies of rank among those converted from paganism.

On the eve of the council, the first sign of trouble appeared. In a letter from Julian, posted in public places in Alexanderia for all to read, he stated that he had recalled the exiled bishops to their homes, but not to their bishoprics. He further insisted that since I had been accused of so many crimes, I should have requested special permission before returning. He commanded me to leave Alexandria at once or be subject to more severe punishment.

I couldn't possibly leave Alexandria until after the council. There were also a number of other affairs that required my personal supervision. To stall for time, I decided to appeal the order to leave the city, for with an appeal pending, the prefect would not enforce the order to exile me.

When the council met as scheduled, with all the bishops rallying around me, all my hopes were satisfied. First and foremost, we strongly and steadfastly affirmed our belief in the Trinity. Since it was evident that one of the chief causes of division in the Church was semantics, we proceeded to define some of the words that seemed to be sources of conflict. Some terms meant different things to different bishops. Some words upon translation from Greek to Latin or Latin to Greek take on a different meaning. Whereas many believed the same as the Catholic Church, they were separated from it because of misunderstandings of terminology. We set out to correct this.

We also had to deal with the problems arising in the church of Antioch that was divided by rival parties. The council decided to send a commission to Antioch to investigate the situation, but before the commission was able to act, I received a letter from Lucifer, who I was concerned would make matters worse in his impetuosity.

The letter read as follows:

"To Athansaius, Archbishop of Alexandria, Egypt, Pentapolis, Thebes, and the Libyas, Lucifer, Bishop of Calaris sends greetings from Antioch.

"Your Piety will be interested in learning of the state of the Church in Antioch. Meletius had not yet returned from exile at the time of my arrival here. Originally selected as Bishop of Antioch by the Arians, believing him to be one of them, he caused the Arians much consternation, because the day they installed him as bishop, he boldly preached the true faith, proclaiming his belief in the Nicene Creed and the Trinity! When the congregation of the laity applauded him wholeheartedly, his Arian deacon silenced him by holding his hand over his mouth. Unbelievable but true! Unable to finish his homily, Meletius held up three fingers to indicate his belief in the Three Persons of the Trinity.

"Since the Arians had exiled him, I took it upon myself to consecrate a new bishop for Antioch. It is now my pleasure to inform you,

Your Piety, and all the bishops assembled in council at Alexandria, that the new Bishop of Antioch is Paulinus.

"Persistent concern that pagan persecution will again overtake the entire empire, as in the days of Diocletian and other pagan emperors, haunts the Church of Antioch. We have heard many reports about Emperor Julian Caesar. They say he lives a life of philosophic simplicity amid the pomp of the imperial palace, where he lives and dresses like a monk. Never attending the theater and bored by the Hippodrome, he works at government business from the first rising of the sun in the morning until his candle has burned low in the midnight hours. He has even addressed the Senate, the first emperor since Julius Caesar to do so. Although he is an accomplished administrator, he is at heart a philosopher and by his natural disposition very religious. He has a great love of books and has even written some himself.

"From his writings, in which he reveals his true thoughts, it is clear that he is committed to commissioning a new paganism that will be patterned upon the Catholic Church, with himself as a bishop, so to speak, overseeing a large number of pagan priests to whom he writes pastoral letters. Pagan monasteries are also part of his plan.

"As chaste as a monk, Julian is urging the pagan priests to follow his example. Needless to say, Julian and his new religion are an enigma to the pagans who liked to cavort in the temples of Aphrodite, freely giving vent to their sexual passions.

"I shudder to write that Julian maintains that he has cleansed himself of his baptism into Christ by making bloody sacrifices on pagan altars. Glorying in the sacrifice of bulls, he is minting new coins here with the image of the bull on them. Even the pagans, in revulsion, find it abhorrent to see him covered with blood, contemplating the liver of a bull he has just sacrificed, as he attempts to foretell future events. You are well aware, that there are only a few places left in the world where animal sacrifices take place. Even though animal sacrifice is totally odious and revolting to the people of these modern times, Julian can be seen frequently at the Mithraic altar. Ironically, it is reported that one day as he examined the liver of the sacrificed bull, he clearly saw a cross surrounded with a crown.

"More than once has the cross been a source of embarrassment to Julian. The story is told that on one occasion when Julian was with his pagan philosophers and idolaters, he became suddenly unnerved and frightened by something that occurred. Inadvertently, he immediately made the sign of the cross on his body as any Christian might do in similar circumstances.

"I have learned that Julian intends to persecute Christ and His Church, but not in the bloody fashion of Diocletian. In Antioch, he has ordered the Christians to return any and all pagan temples that they have converted into churches and to subsidize all costs involved with the rebuilding of any pagan monuments or temples that have been destroyed. Since the churches of Antioch cannot raise the large amounts of money necessary for such projects, our churches are gradually being stripped of property, the gold and silver vessels of the altar, and the votive gifts of the people. For failing to provide the funds to rebuild the pagan temples, our clergy are being tortured and locked up in prison.

"The uncle of the emperor, also named Julian, is here in Antioch determined to take everything of value from the churches. When he grabbed one priest, Theodoritus, and mistreated him, the priest very bravely held to our faith and was killed by the sword. Thereupon, the emperor's uncle snatched the sacred vessels from the altar and desecrated them by throwing them to the ground. Blaspheming Christ with his tongue, and adding sacrilege to blasphemy, he sat on the sacred vessels! Something most unusual then occurred. Instantly his genitals putrefied with his flesh being consumed by worms. This is true!

Since he was the uncle of Emperor Julian, the physicians did all in their power to save him by attempting to draw the worms out. When they tried every drug in their pharmacopoeia, the worms merely went in deeper. Even the fat of rare birds was applied to no avail. When the worms penetrated more internally into his vital organs and his flesh was completely rotted, he died.

That is about all there is to report at this time."

I tossed Lucifer's letter on my desk. We had our troubles here in Alexandria too. Julian was busy trying to lead the people of God and the populace that was pagan in name only and did not practice any religion, back to the worship of the gods.

In the public square near the library, I saw the gigantic painting of himself that Julian ordered hung there. Portraying himself with the god Jupiter, descending from a billowing cloud and giving him the imperial crown and the purple, Julian calculated that in rendering the emperor homage the people would again be paying homage to Jupiter and the other pagan gods. In the painting, his hair was smooth, but his beard was shaggy. I recalled that once, in describing himself, Julian said his beard was full of lice. So much for Roman cleanliness! Greatly did he resemble Constantine, his father's brother. No doubt the artist was encouraged to make him look like Constantine. He had the same bull-like thick neck, straight nose, triangle-like mouth, and intelligent keenness in his eyes that I had observed on Constantine. The artist had painted him well.

Although there was no bloody purge as the summer wore on, those in our city who refused to sacrifice to the gods were deprived of their citizenship and public office and our Christian children were denied the right to attend the public schools. Finally Julian, wishing to raise money with the desire of financing a war against the Persians, levied a tax on all Christians. In theory, the tax was to be determined by the amount of wealth each one possessed. In practice, the local officials gouged whatever they wished from a defenseless Christian. When our people appealed to Julian of the inequity of the taxation, he jeered at them telling them that our God commands us to bear afflictions patiently.

A letter from Eusebius of Vercellae related that in many places councils were being held, patterned upon our Alexandrine Council, reaffirming belief in the Nicene faith. A bitter struggle was taking place, he informed me, to drive the Arian Auxentius from the see of Milan but to no avail. His holiness Pope Liberius was now staunchly supporting Nicene orthodoxy.   No doubt remembering his own weakness in signing the Arian creed, Pope Liberius was showing great leniency in reuniting with the Catholic Church any bishop who in time of trial had signed Arian creeds.

Sometime during the first week in October, Mark ushered into my study a strange looking fellow, who proceeded to introduce himself as a philosopher.

"Pythiodorus Trico of Thebes," he mumbled his name in his beard.

"What can I do for you?" I asked with my eyes widening at the costly fabric of his cloak, since I imagined philosophers to be modestly attired men in the manner of Socrates. The man who carefully sat his corpulent frame down into the chair across from me was wearing gold jewelry studded with rubies.

"There is very little you could do for me," he sniffed, wrinkling his nose nervously as he talked. "It is rather I who could do much for you, my good follow," He slammed his fat hand on his thigh for emphasis.

I raised my eyebrows and stared at him, waiting for him to explain.

"Have you not heard, my good fellow, that our most illustrious emperor has proven in his book *Against the Galileans* that your Scriptures are ridiculous and unfounded and—that your Galilean is an imposter—your Apostle Paul a fraud—and the martyrs are—"

I pounded my fist on my desk to silence him. My heart began to pound. Calmly I addressed my silenced visitor, who had been startled by the sudden and explosive sound of my fist striking the wood of the desk.

"If you have come to convert me, you are wasting your time!"

"I would not condescend to bestow my pearls on such swine as you. It is rather you, Athanasius, who is wasting time. I am here to insist that you waste no more time in leaving Alexandria! By order of my fellow philosopher, our dear Emperor Julian, I am authorized to tell 'the contemptible little fellow,' as Julian calls you, to get the hell out of town!"

Obviously, it was time to leave Alexandria once again.

"It is only a passing cloud," I said to Mark to reassure him, as we plowed our way once more up the Nile. "It will soon pass away." I was referring to Julian and his paganism.

We had made a hasty departure form Alexandria, since it was rumored that I was going to be placed under arrest. Over two weeks had passed, since Trico visited my office with the order from Julian that I leave Alexandria. We rented a boat at the riverside. Almost as soon as we pushed off from the shore and the oarsmen began slowly and rhythmically to pull the oars though the rushing green waters that give life to Egypt, I had the feeling that we were being pursued.

"Faster!" I insisted. "Faster!"

Mark kept glancing nervously over his shoulder down the river in the direction of Alexandria.

"It is funny," he said scowling. "I am sure the police are following us!" Since the riverbanks were lined with farms and I did not want to risk having anyone recognize us, I ordered the oarsmen to stay as far away from shore as possible. If the police were following us, they might proceed by horseback along the riverside and overtake us. I was sure, however, that no one recognized us when we rented the boat.

A farmer, standing in his field, waved his hand at us in greeting, in the manner people have of doing when they see travelers pass, although they do not know them. At the first station on the Nile, we put in to the docks to get food. Because it was mealtime, the oarsmen would go no farther without stopping to refresh themselves.

Mark and I went into the inn at the water's edge and sat down at a small table in a dark corner. The proprietor of the inn was one of those individuals that are always hungry for news. After our food was served, he invited himself to sit with us.

"Going far?" he asked propping his elbows on the table.

"No. Not too far," Mark replied politely but tersely.

"Well, if you go far enough, you might just see some excitement." Obviously the innkeeper was trying to arouse our curiosity and start a conversation.

Looking up from my bowl of broth, I said nothing as I studied his face. So anxious was he to relate his news to us that he needed no encouragement to speak.

"The police were just here half an hour ago. They are looking for some terrible criminal." The innkeeper watched to see the effect of his words on us.

"A criminal—you say?" Mark asked as he glanced at the innkeeper out of the corner of his eye.

"Oh, yes. A very wicked fellow from what the police say about him." The innkeeper blinked his eyes with excitement.

"Athanasius—they call him Athanasius. If you gentlemen are rowing up the river you had better watch out for him! He might be dangerous! There is no telling what a criminal might do when the police are closing in on him!"

"Thanks for the warning," I replied slapping down on the table one of Julian's newly minted coins bearing his image and that of a bull. With Mark at my side, I went to find the oarsmen in order to induce them to resume our trip at once. We found them reclining under a palm near the boat. I handed Mark a fistful of coins and sent him to pay them to return to the oars.

"Hurry," I ordered when once again we began to push our way through the swiftly moving currents of the Nile. "We have no time to waste."

Because we were traveling against the current, our progress was all too slow. I had decided to go to Tabenne and stay with Pachomius' monks until it was again safe to return to Alexandria.

Half an hour later, I noticed that there was a boat in the river behind us. Since it was a larger vessel than ours, it was moving more swiftly than we in the churning current. Nudging Mark, I whispered, "I think the police have picked up our trail!"

"With a boat like they have, we don't stand a chance of outrunning them." Mark said with anxiety

"I figure that we have perhaps half an hour before they will be along side us." I called to the oarsmen, "Faster!"

Mark tugged nervously at my sleeve and said "If we go ashore perhaps we could escape them in the desert."

We were approaching a bend in the river. Once we rounded that bend, we would be out of sight from our pursuers for a while. We could row to shore, hide the boat and make a run for it. Noiselessly, we glided around the curve through the swiftly moving water. The police had not yet drawn close enough to our boat to get a good look at us. From the distance, all they could tell was that a small boat was in the river south of them. I weighed the merits of beaching the boat and striking out across the desert. It seemed very risky because we did not have proper supplies for an extended trek in the desert. Beckoning to the head oarsman, I made my decision with the help of the Holy Spirit.

"Reverse our course. Turn the boat around. I wish to row back towards Alexandria!"

Mark was clearly upset and puzzled.

"Are you going to turn yourself over to them without even trying to escape?"

Calmly I surveyed my worried secretary and replied, "After all these years, you should know me better than that!" Laying my finger against my lips, I silenced Mark. I wanted to talk to God in prayer and I did not want to answer my secretary's questions.

"But, Piety…!"

"Pray! Pray!"

Without another word we changed our course, rowed northward, drawing nearer to the boat that was now approaching us very quickly. The figures on deck became discernable.

It's the police, all right," I whispered. "Be calm!" I placed my hand on Mark's arm to steady him.

As the police boat drew nearer, we could hear a bell ringing on board it. One of the police, the commander, stood at the prow waving his hands at us.

"Halt!" he shouted.

Instructing the oarsmen to row towards the police boat, we drew alongside the vessel in a few minutes time. From my seat in the prow of our little boat, I called to the police commander:

"Good afternoon. What can I do for you?" I smiled at him and added, "Always glad to be of assistance to the police."

More at ease, the police officer replied, "We are looking for a criminal. One Athanasius of Alexandria. Someone reported that he was headed south on the river. Perhaps you good citizens have seen him? Perhaps you could give me some idea of where he is since you have just come from south of here."

"Ah, so!" I exclaimed in my most friendly and courteous manner. "Yes, by all means! He is not far from here! I'll tell you what you should do. Just keep going right up the river the way you are headed! He is not far off!"

As the police officer ordered his men to start rowing again, I called out to him, "Good luck!"

When the police boat had rounded the bend out of sight, Mark whistled and showed his amazement and surprise. Not wanting our oarsmen to realize the significance of what had just occurred, I motioned for him to be quiet.

"Piety, I thought they had you this time," Mark whispered softly to me.

"We are not safe yet. Not as long as Julian is emperor."

I ordered our crew to row for the shore. Once ashore, Mark paid off the oarsmen and we walked to the nearest hamlet where Mark purchased supplies that we would need in the desert, while I remained out of sight. With ample water and food, we set out overland, following the Nile at a short distance from its banks, journeying southward by night and remaining hidden by day. Two days later, when we felt it was again safe to return to the river, we rented another boat and resumed our trip up the Nile. As we drew near Hermopolis in the Thebais, about one hundred bishops, priests, and monks were lined up on both banks of the river to welcome us, although it was night. I greeted the monks, whose faces glowed in the torchlight, with a few words from Isaiah.

"Who are these that soar as a cloud and as doves with their young?"

When I stepped from the boat, Abbot Theodore clasped my hand in greeting, while Orsisius, who had resigned as abbot in favor of Theodore, was beside him holding the bridle of an ass. In the glowing, golden light of the torches, I could see that the face of Theodore shone with the peace that the world cannot give and that passes all understanding.

"Ah, Theodore!" I clasped his hand in mine. "You are truly a 'gift of God' as your name indicates. How are you and all the brothers in Christ?"

He knelt for my blessing. "We are well, Your Piety, thanks to your holy prayers." He rose to his feet and pointing to the ass that Orsisius had with him said, "We have brought Coco. He is wearing his best bridle so you can ride the rest of the way to our monastery."

Orsisius, who had a way with animals, made the ass kneel at my feet as if it were begging my blessing. I couldn't help but laugh. Actually, I would have preferred to walk to the monastery with the rest of them, but remembering how our Lord rode on the donkey into Jerusalem on Palm Sunday, I acquiesced. Once I was mounted on

Coco's back, Abbot Theodore began our joyful procession toward the monastic community. In their eagerness to serve me, the monks crowded around me, as we made our way through the night. They almost set me on fire with their torches, so affectionately did they surround me.

The next day when Abbot Theodore proudly showed me around the monastery, he told me that the monks in the other foundations of Pachomius in the Thebais were eagerly awaiting my visitation also. Theodore had been the favorite disciple of Pachomius and under his direction the spirit of the founder lived on in the monks.

"All the brothers long for martyrdom," Theodore told me. His keen gray eyes shone with faith.

"Julian does not seemed disposed to making martyrs for the Church. Perhaps he has realized that the Church is merely strengthened by the blood of the martyrs," I remarked to Theodore who was busily weaving his basket of rushes, as we sat resting behind the monastery in the shade of a ficus tree. Although it was autumn the sun's rays were still quite warm.

Theodore pursued the topic of martyrdom by saying, "But on the other hand, Julian makes no effort to do anything about pagans who are putting Christians to death for the faith. In Gaza, a traveler who visited our monastery told me that three Christian brothers were martyred and Julian did nothing to reprove their murderers. The people of Gaza took the young men from their home and threw them into prison and beat them. A mob appeared and accused the three Christians of committing sacrilege in one of their pagan temples. They went wild, broke into the prison, and treated the three brothers very cruelly, dashing them to pieces on the pavement of the town, as they dragged them through the streets." Theodore crossed himself and added, "I was told that the pagan women took their weaving spindles and pierced the holy young men with them and that the cooks of the town took pots of boiling water and poured their contents on them." The abbot's fingers ceased from working on the basket. He sat gazing silently into the cloudless sky.

"Did the brothers remain firm in the faith until death?" I inquired.

"Oh yes. They did. They did not waver even though their flesh was torn from their bodies and their skulls smashed so that their brains gushed out on the ground."

I shuddered involuntarily, wondering how I would bear up in similar circumstances. Sobered by the thought, I glanced at Theodore and saw that he was smiling seraphically.

"They captured the monk Hilarian, too, but he fled. What a wonderful opportunity Hilarian wasted. He could have won the martyr's palm."

The abbot returned to plaiting the rushes firmly one around the other. I remembered the many times I had fled my persecutors.

"But our Lord commands us not to expose ourselves to persecution," I observed.

"All the same," replied Theodore staring at me with his steady gray eyes.

"Hilarian missed a wonderful opportunity!" Dropping his basket again, he continued, "Mark of Arethusa fled at first, when the pagans commanded him to rebuild or pay for rebuilding their temple that he destroyed."

"What happened?" I had not heard of his death.

"When, after he fled, he heard that others were suffering in his place, he returned and told the populace of his city that he was ready to suffer whatever they wished to inflict on him." Theodore's face glowed at the remembrance of what had become of Mark of Arethusa. He grew silent as if relishing the courage of the bishop.

"So? Did the pagans have the baseness to persecute one who so willingly laid down his life?"

"They did not scruple to inflict on him the worst treatment they could. They cut off his ears by tightening fine ropes around them.

Then the older schoolboys played ball with him, tossing his frail body back and forth until he was a mass of open wounds. Then they smeared him with honey and enclosed him in a basket made of rushes and placed him in the center of the town where all could mock him and the insects could devour his living flesh."

"God forbid! What fiendish things their hellish minds are capable of conceiving!" I did not find the same enjoyment in contemplating these atrocities that Theodore did.

"Oh? That is nothing compared to what happened at Heliopolis." Theodore waved his hand dramatically.

I would have preferred not to near what happened at Heliopolis, but fraternal charity refrained me from silencing Theodore.

"At Heliopolis near Mount Libanus, the populace seized the holy consecrated spouses of Christ. They stripped them naked before the multitudes and in their nudity made them the objects of public insult. After they inflicted them with many things, they shaved their heads and ripped their abdomens open and stuffed their bodies with the slop they usually feed the swine. Then they tossed the virgins to the swine—the beasts tore their bodies apart and devoured them with the slop."

Fighting off a wave of nausea, I jumped to my feet as quickly as my age would let me. Before he could say another word, I told him, "It is time for me to get ready to go to visit the other foundations!"

"But, Your Piety," Theodore called after me, "I haven't told you yet of how Basil of Ancyra was martyred proclaiming his faith in the Nicene Creed!"

I excused myself as fast as I could and rushed to find Mark. He was sound asleep in the cell assigned to him. When he awoke, he looked at me in bewilderment, when I told him, "Mark, my son, I don't think I have a vocation to be a martyr!"

We left that afternoon to visit the next closest colony of monks where we were to stay several weeks before moving on to the next monastery, a colony of women who were living the contemplative life. The women rivaled the monks in their fervor and many times surpassed them as they copied the monasteries of the men.

Winter passed as we traveled from one colony of monks to another. News came that Julian went with his armies to Antioch shortly after I left Alexandria. Planning war against the Persians, he dreamed of excelling Alexander and Trajan. Julian went so far as to believe that he *was* Alexander the Great reincarnated. Filling him with ideas concerning the transmigration of souls, the philosopher Maximus, who urged him on in his military exploits, assured Julian that he would far surpass the Macedonian in glory.

In Antioch, Julian brought the wrath of the populace down on his head, because he fixed prices, causing the merchants to flee from the financial ruin the emperor's low prices would cause them. The people of Antioch blamed Julian for the scarcity that resulted. Openly ridiculing him and his long beard, the people called him the "Bull Burner," because of his countless sacrifices to Mithras.

Leaving Antioch in a fury, Julian went to Tarsus. In an effort to maintain his pose as a philosopher, he satisfied his anger by writing a treatise against the people of Antioch calling it "Hater of Beards."

It was during Lent 363 that Julian set out across the Euphrates to attack the Persians. He stopped at Carrae where there was a large temple to Jupiter and offered sacrifices. With a great show of arrogance, Julian wrote a letter to Arsacius, the King of Armenia, one of the Roman allies, asking for his help in fighting the Persians. Boasting of his own prowess, he threatened Arsacius and blasphemed Christ in the letter, even though he knew that the King of Armenia was Christian.

Fearlessly Julian led his armies through Assyria. Everywhere he went, he permitted his armies to pillage and destroy whatever they wished, not considering that he would have to return by the same route. When he pursued the retreating Persian army, Julian was greatly distressed to find that the Persians burned all the crops behind them so that the Roman troops were on the verge of starvation. It was reported that Julian shared all the hardships of his men, eating their scant rations, marching on foot, and fighting with the front ranks at every encounter with the enemy.

Pressing onward in late spring, Julian laid siege to Ctesiphon near the Tigris. At this time, I was near Antinopolis when a messenger brought me a letter from Theodore, warning me that the police were once more on my trail. Theodore advised me to be cautious and to stay in seclusion, until he arrived with a covered boat in which to spirit me away up the Nile to Tabenne and safety.

When I sent Mark to scout the surrounding area to see if he could get any news concerning our pursuers, he was gone all day. The sun was setting in the west, when he returned weary and haggard. We were both getting old—almost too old—to keep escaping from those who would gorge themselves on our blood.

"Bad news?" I needn't have asked. I could tell just by looking at him that our pursuers were not far away.

"They were at the next closest monastery this afternoon. They will probably be here the first thing in the morning." Mark spoke without emotion.

"God's will be done." I sighed in resignation and went to my cell.

I slept little that night. I knelt on the cold stone floor by the windows praying until the moon crossed the heavens and was sinking behind the sand dunes on the distant horizon. One by one the stars began to disappear. When finally I could see someone approaching in the distance, I was trying to decide whether to go and hide in one of the tombs or else try to secrete myself in an abandoned cistern. Before I made up my mind which course to take, I realized that it was Abbot Theodore and Pammon who were coming toward the monastery. Theodore was doing as he said he would. He was coming to take me to Tabenne. I awakened Mark. We were ready to leave in minutes.

"Once more, I tell you, Theodore, you are truly a gift of God."

"The boat is waiting. Hurry, Piety!" He spoke in hushed tones.

We raced to the river. As soon as we were on board the covered boat, the crew pulled up the anchor and we were once more in flight. Since we were traveling against a very strong current, we seemed to make extremely little headway. Knowing the great relish that Theodore had for martyrdom, I decided that our chances of reaching Tabenne were fairly slim. Pammon, a happy old monk with childlike eyes, sat in silence and prayed. Theodore was his usual self. He wanted to talk.

"Did you hear, Piety" he asked "that Julian has given public monies to the Jews to rebuild the Temple of Jerusalem so that they can resume their bloody sacrifices?"

I had not heard that.

"Our Lord foretold the destruction of the Temple. He said that not one stone would be left upon another—that it would be left desolate."

I scanned river for sight of the police. They were bound to have discovered by now that we were on the Nile headed south.

"Exactly," replied Theodore intently. "Julian wants to prove Christ's prophecy to be false. He provided timber, stones, brick, clay—all the Jews need to rebuild the Temple. Just after they cleared the land and were ready to lay the foundation, an earthquake struck and devastated the area, killing many of the workmen. When the work resumed, fire burst up from the earth and consumed the workmen's tools and killed a number of the workmen themselves. Most mysteriously of all, the sign of the cross appeared on their garments! It was uncanny! The work has been abandoned."

I made no comment. Squinting, I shielded my eyes with my hand and once more scanned the river. No one was in sight. I settled down to try to pray as the monk Pammon and Mark were doing. Half an hour passed in silence. When the wind began to ripple the water, making it even harder to move against the current, the monks and Mark got out of the boat and began to tow it by ropes from the shore. In my soul, I cried out to the Father, the Son, and to the Holy

Spirit to strength me in the hour of danger. Remembering how the human flesh of our Lord had shrunk from suffering when he prayed, "Father, if it be possible let this chalice pass from me," I begged for grace to suffer courageously whatever Providence had in store for me. Such were my thoughts when Pammon tried to cheer me up.

"Everything is going to be all right, Your Piety."

My interior struggle must have shown on my face for him to speak to me in this way.

"I am not afraid Pammon, I have been persecuted many times. I have never felt greater peace than during those times. I find great consolation in suffering. If it is Christ's will that I die a martyr's death for him—may his holy will be praised and accomplished in me! I am confident that he will give me the grace to be martyred for him, if that is what he wishes of me. If I am slain, I am certain that I shall find mercy with the Savior."

Pammon glanced at Theodore and laughed softly. Theodore wanted to laugh also but repressed it.

"Why are you laughing? You think I am a coward?"

Theodore laughed out loud. Before I could say another word, he remarked, "Pammon, you tell His Piety."

"No! No, you, Father Abbot, you tell him."

"Tell me what?" I insisted. The two monks sat grinning at each other.

Theodore cleared his throat. "At this very hour Julian has been killed in Persia. In the words of the prophet, 'the haughty man, the despiser and the braggart shall finish naught.'"

I stared at Theodore in astonishment. Pammon nodded his head vigorously with his soulful eyes peering at me intently.

"Pammon had a vision. "The new emperor will be Christian. Your Piety must go at once to meet him as he returns from the war."

"This is true, Pammon?"

"Yes, Piety. The new emperor will help you. Go to him at once!"

I returned to Alexandria secretly with Mark. It was true. It happened just as Pammon had seen it in his vision. Julian was dead!

I learned the details of Julian's death from Serapion. Upon approaching Ctesiphon, Julian found a blocked canal that in former times connected the Tigris and the Euphrates. He cleared and opened it. With his ships floating besides his troops, Julian marched toward the city. When the Persians suddenly appeared along the banks of the Tigris in frightful array, Julian realized that his army was in danger of destruction for he was besieged between the two rivers. Because Julian so devastated the villages through which he led his armies, no supplies would be available in them. Retreating was out of the question. To make his men fight more bravely Julian ordered his officers to throw the army's provisions and baggage into the river, thinking that if he made them desperate they would fight all the harder.

At dawn the battle began with both sides suffering heavy casualties. The Roman army set up camp near Ctesiphon. After commanding his ships to be burned, Julian began to retreat along the Tigris.

The Persian Shapur II outwitted Julian. Selecting two of his Persian nobles and cutting off their noses, he then sent them to Julian disguised as men who had deserted the Persian army. Because of the cruelty of Shapur in cutting off their noses, they were able to convince Julian of their eagerness to guide the Roman armies the shortest way to the Roman frontier. For twenty miles, Julian trustingly followed his Persian guides into desolate wasteland, as they kept assuring him that they were leading him the shortest way to safety. After three days of wandering in the wastelands, Julian became suspicious. When he put the Persian guides under torture, they confessed that they were betraying him into the hands of his enemy.

Exhausted by the long desolate march and without provisions, the Roman army was suddenly attacked by the Persians. The wind blew violently, whipping up the desert sands. Dark clouds hid the sun. Wearing absolutely no armor, Julian rode into the fray of the battle.

An unknown assailant galloped up to him and thrust a javelin into his side. When he was thrown from his horse, Julian defiantly dipped his fingers in his blood and tossed it heavenward.

Carried into a tent by his men, Julian heard a physician tell him he had only a short time to live. Before he died calmly, he spent his last hours discussing philosophy with his pagan friends Maximus and Priscus. Interestingly, it is said that it was not a Persian who felled the emperor, because no Persian went forth to claim the reward that Shapur offered to the man who killed Julian. The pagans insisted that a Christian murdered Julian.

In conclusion, Serapion told me the following: "Julian boasted that after he conquered the Persians, he planned to treat the Christians with severity, saying that the Son of the Carpenter would be unable to help us." Serapion sighed deeply and added, "It was strange. One of our priests here in Alexandria, who had a premonition of Julian's death, upon hearing this boast remarked that the Son of the Carpenter, as Julian called Christ, was even at that time making a wooden coffin for Julian.

"And who is the new emperor?" It was good to be once more at my desk in the archiepiscopal residence. We had returned secretly in the night unbeknownst to any one in Alexandria.

"Jovian. He is a good Christian. He refused to deny the faith when Julian threatened to discharge all Christians from his army. Because Julian needed Jovian too much to discard him, he retained him even though the latter continued the practice of his faith."

Serapion walked to the windows and stood gazing out to sea. The moon was just rising over the Mediterranean.

"The army proclaimed Jovian emperor?"

"Yes, and immediately he refused. He said that he was a Christian and did not wish to be emperor for a pagan people. At once, the army proclaimed its faith in Christ." Serapion, leaning heavily on his cane, made his way to the chair across from my desk.

"What do you plan to do, Piety?"

"I must get to Jovian at once before the Arians do!"

It was imperative that I reached Jovian before he marched his armies into Antioch. Already, I later learned, Eudoxius, the Bishop of Constantinople, who believed that Christ was a mere man, had selected Lucius, an Arian priest of Alexandria, ordained by George, to go to petition Jovian to install him in the see of Alexandria in my stead. Selecting a number of bishops to accompany us, Mark and I took passage on a new, sea-worthy vessel that would make the trip in record time. With southerly winds prevailing, we raced across the Mediterranean. Only twelve days after we left Alexandria, we reached the Euphrates. Crossing it, we soon arrived at the site where Jovian was encamped with his army.

From the soldier who led us to the emperor's tent, I learned that the new Augustus had signed a thirty years truce with the Persians and had relinquished to them four of the five satrapies that Diocletian had wrestled from them some seventy years before.

When I entered Jovian's tent, he was busily studying a map of the terrain he would cover on his march to Antioch. Glancing up and observing my episcopal robes, he rose reverently and welcomed me as a most honored bishop of the Church of God. At once, he asked me to bestow my blessing on his reign as emperor.

He was short of stature and had a crisp military way of enunciating his words. Being accustomed as I am to granting audiences to a large number of people in the course of a day's work, I always appreciate it when a man states his business immediately and comes right to the point straightforwardly. I extended this courtesy to Jovian.

"I have come to request the permission of Your August Person to return from the banishment inflicted upon me by the former pagan emperor." I began to plead my case.

"I am familiar with all you have endured for Christ and the Catholic faith." Jovian extended his hand to me and clasped mine in friendship. "You have not flinched from any labor, or from the fear of persecution. You have regarded danger and the threats of the sword as so much dung," continued the former captain of the guards made emperor. "Even under the most adverse circumstances, you have upheld and still uphold the orthodox faith, fighting constantly for the truth." Sincerity was in his eyes. "Your Piety, you are a example of all virtues to the people of my realm. Our Imperial Majesty recalls Your Piety to your see and desires that you return to your holy churches at once and pray for us."

With my mind at ease as to the question of my recall to Alexandria, I went to Antioch, where I hoped I could achieve harmony in the Church, although both Lucifer of Sardinia and Eusebius of Vercellae had failed in their attempts to heal the breach among the Antiochan Christians. The troubles that were harassing the Antioch Church were of long standing. In 344, his fellow Arians deposed the Arian Stephanus for permitting his clergy to introduce a harlot into the bedchamber of the Catholic Bishop Euphrates in an attempt to destroy him. Leontius who had castrated himself so that he could sleep with the so-called virgin Eustolium succeeded Stephanus in the bishopric of Antioch. Leontius ordained Aetius to the deaconate and gave him permission to preach. Aetius took the ideas of Arius and drove them to their furthest extreme, preaching the blasphemy of Paul of Samasota that Christ is a mere man. Aetius was to become a scandal to the bishops who were political Arians, but who choked at swallowing the blasphemies of Paul of Samasota that Aetius and the ultra Arians were trying to force on them.

When Leontius died in the summer of 357, a certain Eudoxius of Germanica in Syria, who held the views of Aetius, rushed to Antioch, fraudulently installing himself in the see of Antioch. There was much about Eudoxius that reminded me of my old enemy Eusebius of Nicomedia, for Eudoxius was not content with grasping the see of Antioch. When the opportunity presented itself he seized the bishopric of Constantinople and transferred himself there in 360.

Finding themselves without a bishop, the people of Antioch called Meletius, the Arian usurper, to be their bishop. Much to the surprise of everyone, he proclaimed and preached for all to hear the Nicene faith in the Trinity. Because of this, Constantius immediately banished him and made Euzoius bishop of Antioch.

I knew Euzoius. I had a personal interest in the Church in Antioch, because he was one of the original Arians. Having been a priest in Alexandria, we deposed him together with Arius.

Lucifer of Calaris, who came to Antioch as he hurried from his banishment in Egypt after the death of Constantius, tried to reduce the chaos, but only made matters worse. Because Arians ordained Meletius, the Catholic party in Antioch refused to acknowledge him as their legitimate Catholic bishop. Instead of instating Meletius, not yet returned from banishment, as the legitimate Catholic bishop of Antioch, Lucifer in his impetuosity ordained a third bishop for the sec—a holy man named Paulinus.

I decided to winter at Antioch where Jovian was also in residence until December 21. The emperor, as soon as he arrived at his court in Antioch, made it known that he favored Meletius and wanted unanimity in both church and state.

The political Arians, those who had been in the Arian ranks because Constantius was an Arian, began to reaffirm the Catholic faith as defined at Nicaea. At the same time, Eudoxius, in his powerful see in the imperial city, was doing everything he could to prevent them from so doing, because he was especially interested in placing his nominee, Lucius, on the episcopal throne of Alexandria. When Jovian refused to grant an audience to the Arians from Alexandria, they importunately stopped him at the Roman Gate one day when he was departing for camp.

"Give us a bishop!" they insisted, pushing Lucius toward him, because they did not want me to return.

"I recalled your former bishop," replied Jovian.

One of the emperor's soldiers stepped forward and said to Jovian, "Your Majesty, these are the remnants of the unholy George whom the pagans killed in Alexandria."

Without another word, Jovian spurred his horse and rode away. On three other occasions, the party of Eudoxius tried to gain the ear of the Augustus and make accusations against me.

"Please send anyone, except Athanasius, to Alexandria as bishop," they begged in desperation. Furiously, Jovian told them that the matter was settled. I was to return to my see.

Early February, with a letter from Jovian reinstating me, I set sail for Egypt, wanting to be home for Lent. Four days after my arrival in Alexandria, February 14, 364, something totally unexpected happened. Mark was the one to break the news to me.

We had just become comfortably settled in Alexandria, when Mark came rushing into my office to tell me what he had heard.

"Jovian is dead!"

I was stunned and waited for the details.

"He was on his way to Constantinople. He stopped at a wayside inn at a place called Dadastana that is located on the frontiers of Galatia and Bithynia. The emperor ate a hearty supper, retired for the night in a room that was very damp having recently been plastered with unslaked lime. They were burning coal in the room to dry it out. The cause of Jovian's death was listed as being due to inhalation of charcoal fumes. He was only thirty-three years of age."

"Is there a new emperor?"

"Yes. The army proclaimed Valentinian emperor. I know absolutely nothing about the new Augustus.

"Get all the information you can on the new emperor" I called to Mark who had settled down to writing letters. "The correspondence can wait. I must know about the emperor at once."

It did not take Mark long to supply me with the facts I needed. Bowing his head ever so slightly, he informed me what I needed to know. "I already have the information, Piety. I was certain you would want it so I took the liberty of learning all I could about him."

"So, what did you find out?"

"He was banished by Julian because of his Christian faith, the same as Your Piety." Mark paused.

"A soldier? Banished by the emperor for his faith!" This was something novel.

"Oh, Julian gave the reason for his banishment as misconduct of military affairs, but everyone knew the real reason was because of an incident that happened when Valentinian accompanied Julian, as the law requires, to a pagan temple. It happened in Gaul. Wanting to sacrifice to a pagan god, Julian demanded that Valentinian accompany him, as his bodyguard. When they were about to enter the temple, the pagan priest sprinkled them with water, as is the custom. A drop of water fell on Valentinian's clothing, causing him great distress and anguish. Loudly rebuking the pagan priest while Julian looked on, Valentinian ripped off the portion of his garment on which the drop of water had fallen and flung it away. Soon after that, Julian banished him to Melitine in Armenia. Jovian recalled him."

Mark handed me a report on the new emperor.

"I have written down all I could gather about him."

Reading the report carefully, I rejoiced to learn that Valentinian professed the Nicene faith. Finally, I thought, all the dark clouds had vanished from the horizons of the future and all the tempestuous seas of the present were calmed. I had not reckoned on Valens, the brother of the Emperor! Deciding to share the rule of the empire with his brother Valens, a weak and parsimonious man, he gave him the eastern territories. To further complicate matters, Valens chose the strong-willed Eudoxius as bishop of his imperial capital. In the autumn of 364, the same year in which the two new emperors assumed the purple, a council of eastern bishops, who were horrified by the bold blasphemy of Eudoxius and the ultra Arians, met at Lampsacus where they insisted upon enforcing the more moderate Arian views, stating the essential likeness of the Son to the Father. Condemning ultra Arianism, they sent delegates to Emperor Valens and informed him of their decisions.

Being the first to reach Valens, Eudoxius, by virtue of his control over the powerful see of Constantinople, convinced the weak emperor to support the ultra Arians. Thereupon Valens, insisting that everyone must agree with Eudoxius, proceeded to banish the delegates that were sent to him.

"It looks bad," Serapion remarked as he came tapping into my study with his cane. "Valens has gone to Antioch, I hear, and has banished Meletius. He is harassing everyone there who will not accept Eudoxius. I am afraid we are going to see more persecution. Unless I miss my guess, Valens will be another Constantius."

"We have weathered many storms together, Serapion. We will survive this one."

I knew something my suffragen bishop did not know. I spoke confidently. "Actually, Valens is doing the Church a big favor in supporting Eudoxius."

"A favor?" Serapion narrowed his eyes and pondered my meaning. "I am afraid I don't share Your Piety's optimism because…"

Joyfully I broke the news to Serapion. "Valens and Eudoxius have driven the conservative Arians to Rome. They have decided that they would rather go to His Holiness Liberius and accept the Nicene faith than to have Eudoxius and his blasphemies forced on them by the emperor."

A seraphic smile illuminated the face of the little monk-bishop who had shared so much hardship with me in upholding the true faith in the Trinity, when even Pope Liberius had faltered and signed his name to false creeds. With great satisfaction, I told Serapion of how Eustathius, Bishop of Sebastia, Theophilis, Bishop of Castabalis, and Silvanus, Bishop of Tarsus in Cilicia had been sent by the eastern bishops as delegates to His Holiness, bearing a letter beseeching the pope to receive them in order to confer on the state of the Church. They had received oral instructions to submit to the doctrines of Nicaea.

When the three bishops arrived at the Lateran, Pope Liberius refused to see them saying that they were Arians and as such could not be received into communion with the Catholic Church, since they had rejected the Nicene Creed. The bishops, charged by the almost seventy bishops that they represented to agree whole-heartedly with Liberius, told him that they accepted the Nicene Creed. Explaining to His Holiness that their dispute had been only one of words, they confirmed their belief in the Nicene Creed.

In conclusion, I told Serapion, "All things work for the best for those who love God and are called according to his purpose. Valens, in championing the blasphemies of Eudoxius, has served the cause of Christ without intending to!"

"I never thought I would live to see this day! However I fear, Your Piety, that Valens will persecute us, as Constantius did!"

"There will more battles before we can claim victory, my son. The Church will be besieged by enemies until Christ returns."

I picked up my cloak from the chair and put it on.

"No matter how dismal the state of the Church might be, the Holy Spirit will never allow the gates of hell, the jaws of heretics, to prevail against her. Christ has overcome the world, the flesh and the devil, and all other adversaries of truth. And right now, we are having a bit of peace and quiet."

I took Serapion by the hand. "Come, old fellow! I have something I want to show you. I have bought a house…a charming place in the country. I think I might be retiring there soon. It has a lovely little garden. Just the place for an old man like me to pray and get his soul ready for the final victory over death! It won't be long now before I shall leave this world." I felt death approaching and I did not anticipate that I would be a martyr. Such were my thoughts, as we strolled from the archiepiscopal residence out into the gentle spring rain that was refreshing to the spirit.

With councils being held in Sicily and Tyana, an ever-increasing number of bishops were eager to reunite with Pope Liberius and the

Catholic Church. In May, a council was to be held at Tarsus in Cilicia where I felt certain that still more bishops would return to the faith of Nicaea.

Still undaunted and up to the old Arian tricks, Eudoxius and Valens were furious that the bishops of the East were rallying around His Holiness Pope Liberius. Under severe penalties, the bishops were forbidden to assemble at Tarsus. On May 5, 365, an imperial Edict was delivered to Alexandria to the effect that all the bishops that Constantius banished and who returned to their sees after the death of Julian should be cast out again!

I was almost seventy years old. Once more I was faced with exile. I have almost lost count of the number of times that I have been forced to leave my rightful see.

"There are riots all over the city protesting your banishment, Piety!" Mark reported. "The people are maintaining that Your Piety does not come under this order for it was Jovian who recalled you, not Julian."

"If it is God's will that I go into exile again, I am ready." I felt great peace of soul.

The Prefect referred the matter of my banishment to the emperor. As we waited to hear what Valens would do with me, I spent the autumn preparing my little house that I purchased on New River that divides Alexandria from its western suburbs. I determined to stay at the official residence as long as I safely could. Finally on October 5, I packed a few belongings and gathered together the church records. Secretly, I made my way to the lovely little house and garden that were awaiting me.

That very night, Prefect Flavian and Duke Victorinus, thinking that I was hiding at Dionysius Church, broke in the back door of the church and searched it from top to bottom, looking for me even on the roof! Momentarily I expected a bloody persecution to be inaugurated by Valens and Eudoxius against God's people. Undoubtably it would have occurred had not something else arisen to distract Valens.

An usurper, Precopius gathered a large army at Constantinople and began to march on Valens, throwing the whole Eastern empire into a panic. Valens, afraid of popular discontent, spent the entire winter confronted with the problem of putting down the revolution Procopius started.

On February the first, I was puttering around my garden on the riverbank when I heard a loud commotion in front of my house. Going inside and peering out at the mob from a window, I saw the notary Bresidas and a number of soldiers, accompanied by a multitude of civilians, approaching my door.

"Mark!" He was working on some correspondence in a room at the rear of the house.

"Mark!" I called again.

He came running.

"They have discovered my whereabouts! Even now they are at the door waiting to arrest me!"

Mark signed himself with the cross in the name of the Trinity and cried, "Hurry! The boat is waiting. We can slip out the back door and be away before they even know that we are gone."

Walking to the back door and looking out, I saw that soldiers and civilians surrounded the house. Wistfully, I eyed the boat that was hidden in the shrubbery that lines the riverbank behind the house.

"It won't work, Mark. This time they have got us! There are a dozen men between the back door and the river. They have caught me at last!"

I was resigned and ready to face martyrdom.

Mark raced feverishly around the room searching for a hiding place for me.

"Quick, Piety, get in this chest. It is big enough to hide you."

"No, Mark," I protested. "If Christ wishes me to shed my blood for him, I shall do it willingly—eagerly!"

Loudly the soldiers pounded on the door.

"Open the door, Mark," I insisted softly, "I am ready. I am too old to run anymore."

Great peace descended upon my soul. Confidently I stepped toward the door where the notary was waiting for me. With a trembling hand, Mark threw open the latch and the door was violently pushed opened. Pompously the Notary surveyed me.

"Whom do you seek?" I asked employing the words of Jesus to the mob that came to take him prisoner in Gethsemane.

"Archbishop Athanasius!"

"I am he."

I held out my hands for him to chain them.

The notary, shouting for all the multitude that was pressing around the door to hear, said, "By order of the emperor, I command you to come with me! You are to return at once and take up your duties in your official archiepiscopal residence as Archbishop of Egypt, Pentapolis, Thebes and the Libyas!" Turning to the people he yelled, "Here is your Bishop Athanasius that you demanded Valens to return to you."

A roar of cheers broke out. In utter amazement I watched as the notary summoned a chair, borne by soldiers, and asked me to honor them by letting them bear me back to the city. I shot a glance at Mark who was too stunned to speak. I winked at him and sat in the chair. When I was lifted up, I began blessing the crowds of people who lined both sides of the streets the entire way we traveled to the Dionysius Church. For thirty-eight years, I had been Archbishop of Alexandria. From the demonstration of the people that day, I knew that they had come to love me. My old heart was very happy. All the years of suffering and trial vanished into insignificance at the sight of God's faithful people, welcoming the return of their pastor.

Now my candle is burning low. My weary soul cries out for rest. The night is far spent. Seven years have passed since Notary Bresidas came to escort me from my house on New River back to the city. Little has happened to disturb our peace during these years,

Although Valens has been persecuting the Church far and wide, since he captured Procopius and had him torn in half, so emphatically did the Alexandrians demand my return as their archbishop that the emperor has feared to trouble us further. Lucius, who was ordained as Bishop of Alexandria by the Arians, did try, a few years back, to enter the city. Two days after his arrival, he was escorted out of Egypt, because the military had to rescue him from the violence of the people who resented his intrusion.

One of the most gratifying things we have done was to build a church in the Mendidium quarter of the city. I suppose every priest—every bishop—cherishes the dream of building a church. Mine was fulfilled. We dedicated the new church August 7, 370. The people insisted on calling it the Athanasius Church.

We were also very much gratified to hear Damasus was made Pope upon the death of Liberius. We received from him a letter telling of the synod he held in Italy.

The harmony among the bishops of Egypt has become so great that in recent times they sign each other's names when one chances to be absent from our deliberations. Truly we are of one mind—the mind of Christ. God is raising up great men in the episcopate all over the empire. Eudoxius has died. We have chosen an orthodox Catholic as Bishop of Constantinople.

In Cappadocia, two great men of God–Gregory of Nazianzus and Basil of Caesarea–have appeared. With such bishops as these to uphold the faith, a worn out old bishop like I am can go to his reward in peace. I have taken to corresponding with Basil. I can see from his letters that he is such a bishop that any church should be happy to call him its own. Into his hands, I commit the torch of faith that I have held aloft the past forty-six years of my episcopate. In the years to come, the Bark of Peter might be tossed on some tempestuous seas, but I know with a certainty that it will never sink.

For seventy-five years, I have watched people come and go. Now my vision is turned more toward heaven than toward earth. The other day a lovely young woman came to call here at the residence. Her name is Melania. She is the granddaughter of a woman named Melania who sold her lands and went to Jerusalem to start a monastery upon the death of her husband.

"Your piety." my young visitor began as she perched on the edge of her chair, "I wanted to talk to someone about my life…about my soul. You see…I want to do as my grandmother did."

"That is a very laudable intention."

She was a trifle nervous in my presence so I did my best to put her at ease.

"Your grandmother was a wonderful woman. Her husband died—I believe when she was only twenty-three."

"Yes, Your Piety. My husband Pinian is still alive, but I have I persuaded him to sell our extensive estates in Spain, Gaul and in Italy and to free our eight thousand slaves." She passed quickly over the mention of her wealth and continued. "We went to Carthage. We have been living the ascetical life there. Now I want to do as grandmother did. I want to belong completely to God." Her face was afire with religious zeal.

"What is it that makes a beautiful and wealthy wife want to leave her husband and fortune to go live in a monastery?"

I already knew the answer; I merely wanted to hear her tell me. She thought a minute and with shining eyes she whispered: "Love!" She smiled sublimely and sighing added, "I have fallen in love with God. I am leaving a lesser love for a greater love. I have found the pearl of great price!"

"The Pearl of great price has found you, Melania. Thank Him for it every day of your life. I am convinced that the life you wish to embrace is of inestimable value to the Church. One such soul as yours, living a life of prayer and sacrifice…hidden away in the desert…is of more value to the Church than anyone can conceive.

Wonderful benefits will accrue throughout the whole Church from your prayers. By all means, give yourself up to the silent and hidden apostolate of prayer…for in so doing you will contribute much more to the increase of the Church and the welfare of humanity than those who labor in tilling the vineyards of Christ."

Heaving a big sigh, the lovely and gracious Melania leveled her deep violet eyes at me and exclaimed, "I knew you would understand. You knew the great hermit Anthony, didn't you?"

"Yes. He was my spiritual father. I have relied on the prayers of the holy monks and women of the desert all the years of my episcopate. I know personally from experience the value of contemplative souls to the Church."

"I am so happy to find someone who understands. You see there are many people–good people–in the Church today who do not understand the life of prayer. They tell me that I shall be wasting my time–that I could pray while doing works of mercy, living with my husband, in my own home. They say that it was all right to go and live in the desert and pray when the pagans persecuted the church in the days of Diocletian, but that the hidden life of prayer is an anachronism more in keeping with the Church's past than with its present or future."

I reached across my desk and patted her affectionately on the hand.

"The contemplative life will never go out of date! Monasteries will no doubt change in years to come in many ways, but the Church will always have need of those souls who retire from the world and the active works of mercy to pursue with all their strength the spiritual life—the life of prayer and sacrifice. Perhaps the day will come when contemplatives will no longer wear hair shirts like Anthony or sleep sitting up like Pachomius, but the essence of the contemplative vocation shall never pass away. There must always be men and women in the Church whose sole concern is seeking God. Go to your monastery and with my blessing!"

She knelt for me bless her. When she rose to her feet, I handed her the sheepskin that had belonged to my Father Anthony.

"My holy Father Anthony gave me this sheepskin when he died. He used it as an instrument of penance. I have treasured it for a long time. I am certain he will be pleased for you to have it."

She took the relic of the saint and pressed it to her heart, remaining silent waiting for me to explain.

"I won't be needing a keepsake of our holy father any longer. You see, I expect to be reunited with him soon. Pray for me, Melania. Pray for an old bishop who longs to dissolve and be with Christ."

More and more of late the thought of heaven fills my mind. "The time of my liberation is approaching. I have fought the noble fight, I have finished the race—I have kept the faith. As for the rest, there is waiting for me a crown of justice which the Lord, the good Judge, will present to me in that hour." The thirst for the vision of God consumes me. I partake of the Food of Life, the Body of Christ, and constantly I thirst, delighting my soul always in His precious Blood, but yet—I long for the eternal banquet of heaven!

God, You are my God whom I seek—for you my flesh pines and my soul thirsts like the land—parched, lifeless and without water. As the doe longs for the running waters, so my soul longs for you, O God! Athirst is my soul for God…the living God! When shall I go and behold the Face of God?

About the Author

Dr. Allienne R. Becker received her B. A. degree from Duke University, and two M. A. degrees from West Virginia University, and a Ph.D. from the Pennsylvania State University. She is the author of several books published by Greenwood Press, including *The Lost Worlds Romance*, 1992 and *Visions of the Fantastic*, 1996, among others. She is also the author of *I, Paul...: The Life of the Apostle to the Gentiles*, iUniverse, 2002.

0-595-21393-6

Printed in the United States
732000003B

A Nobel prize in spam?

No, there isn't really a Nobel prize for spam. But a famous economist named Ronald Coase won a Nobel prize for writing, among other things, about why sometimes governments must step in when the marketplace is broken. Specifically, Coase discussed the dangers to the free market when an inefficient business — one that cannot bear the costs of its own activities — distributes its costs across a large population of victims.

The classic example is pollution: It's much cheaper for a chemical manufacturer to dump toxic waste into the local river than to treat it and dispose of it in a more environmentally sensitive manner. By creating such externalities, as economists call them, a polluter can maximize its own profit, even if it comes at another's — or everyone's — expense. Certainly those who are harmed by poisons in a river may be able to sue, but for the vast majority of victims, the cost of hiring a lawyer, assembling evidence, hiring experts, and bearing all the other costs and complexities means that most victims can never hold the polluter accountable for the harm it has done.

Much is the same when it comes to spam. Although some companies have successfully sued junk e-mailers for the damage they have caused, few ISPs can afford to fight these kinds of cutting-edge cyberlaw battles. As a result, the economics favor the abusers and disfavor the spam victims. Indeed, spammers are counting on the incremental cost of each spam, foisted on each individual member of the public at large, being ignored.

As Coase pointed out, this situation is a prescription for economic disaster. When inefficiencies are allowed to continue, the free market no longer functions properly. The "invisible hands" that would normally balance the market and keep it efficient cannot function when the market is carrying the dead weight of spammers. Unchecked, businesses that depend on stealing time, money, and resources from unwilling recipients must be stopped, or else they will continue to leech the life out of our economic system.

The price of speed: Accuracy

SMTP is fast and simple — so simple that it has no mechanism for verifying the validity of either the identity of the sending server or the accuracy of the From address. The SMTP server has no way to verify assertions such as "This message is from your bank and concerns your account" or "This message contains the tracking number for your online order" or "Here is that newsletter about investment tips that you paid $29 per month to receive."

So why not replace SMTP with something better?

Well, Winston Churchill once said that democracy is the worst way of doing government, except for all the others. SMTP is, as Churchill may have said, the worst way of "doing" e-mail, except for all the others that have been tried. The reality is that SMTP works reliably and has been pretty much universally implemented.

To swap out SMTP for something "better" would be much like telling American automobile drivers that, starting next Thursday, we all have to start driving on the left side of the road. Not only would lots of people be completely confused, but lots of the fundamental infrastructure would need to be redesigned. And lots of people simply wouldn't be able to get stuff done for a very long time.

In short, the need for speed creates a system that has virtually no technical consequences for being a liar. That is precisely why spammers have been, and continue to be, incredibly effective in delivering unwanted e-mail. So, until somebody thinks up a better way of doing e-mail, as well as a way to implement it without bringing everything to a screeching halt, we're stuck with this simple way of doing e-mail that is also quite vulnerable to abuse.

Whitelists, blacklists, filters

Some ISPs do try to take steps to deal with spam during the e-mail delivery process. Three popular approaches are shown in this list:

- ✔ **Whitelists** are lists of servers known to be sending good, legitimate, nonspam e-mails. During the SMTP conversation, the address of the sending server can be compared to a whitelist and, if it's on the list, the mail gets delivered.

- ✔ **Blacklists,** also called *blocklists*, work just the opposite of whitelists. Blacklists are lists of servers that are known to be operated by spammers or that have been used to send

spam in the past. When a sending server attempts to con-
nect to the receiving server, the sender's address is compared to the blacklist, and if it's there, the mail is rejected.

✔ *Filters* allow programs to look at e-mail messages and
guess whether they are spam. After an e-mail message
has been delivered, the filter compares it against a list of
words, phrases, or other kinds of identifiers that can be
used to determine whether the message is legitimate or
spam. New filtering techniques, including something
called Bayesian filtering technology, make filtering much
more accurate than it used to be. (Look on a nearby page
for the sidebar "Bayesian what?" for more information on
this new filtering approach.)

Unfortunately, although whitelists, blacklists, and filters can
catch lots of spam, they are not without their downsides. The
kinds of powerful e-mail servers that ISPs run can send and
receive hundreds or thousands of e-mails per second. But when
the server has to stop and compare each message to a list, or
run the message contents through a filter, that processing
speed can slow to a crawl.

The maintenance of whitelists and blacklists can also be quite
time consuming, and can often produce errors. For example, it
may be necessary to call up somebody on a telephone to verify
the identity of a sender before an ISP will add a server's address
to a whitelist. Similarly, a server that may send legitimate e-mail
may also send spam occasionally, and may require additional
investigation before it can reliably be added to a blacklist. Even
then, no guarantee exists that a whitelisted server won't start
spamming tomorrow and that blacklisting a server won't result
in losing legitimate e-mail.

Can You Really Fight Back Against Spam? Yes!

Before we go any further, we should apologize if this chapter
is depressing. Spam is a difficult problem that causes tremendous frustration for many people, including you — otherwise,
we suspect that you would be reading another, more exciting,
title in the fine *For Dummies* book series.

Bayesian what?

The current cutting edge in spam-filtering technology is a category of e-mail filters built around something called *Bayesian analysis*. Named after the British-born church minister and part-time mathematician Thomas Bayes (1702-1761), the Bayesian approach is based on a theory of statistical analysis described in an essay that Bayes wrote, but that wasn't published until 1764, three years after his death.

Bayes' idea was that you could determine the probability of an event by looking at lots of similar circumstances and working out the frequency with which previous judgments about the occurrence had been accurate or inaccurate. In other words, Bayes said that a mathematical equation can be created that would not only tell you how probable a particular event is, but also automatically fine-tune the equation so that the next prediction would be a little more accurate.

If you think that this idea sounds like a mathematical theory that would allow, for example, a computer to learn by itself automatically, you have grasped the awesome power of Bayesian analysis!

When applied to spam, *Bayesian filters* start by looking at a whole bunch of e-mails, which it asks the user to identify as good mail or bad. It then figures out on its own which characteristics are common to the good mail and which characteristics are common to the bad mail. Each new e-mail message that passes through your system is then compared against that base of knowledge, and a probability rating is assigned to it. It then reworks its calculations after looking at all the good and bad e-mail it has processed and continues over time to learn and refine its analysis methods.

As a concept, Bayesian analysis has been proving effective at identifying spam, and therefore is a frequent feature in many new antispam technologies, some of which we describe in greater detail in Part III of this book.

The purpose of this chapter isn't to make you run away screaming from all Internet technology. Rather, its purpose is to make sure that you understand that fighting spam is an ongoing and sometimes complicated project.

If somebody out there could invent a magic wand to wave over an Internet e-mail server and make spam go away, somebody would have done it long ago. No, spam has no quick solutions.